As he came closer to her bed, ready to take her home, Zach wondered if he had ever wanted anyone as badly as he wanted Delany Sheridan.

Without any makeup on her face, her hair pulled back in a ponytail, and wearing sweats, she still made his stomach tighten with desire.

The waiting had made him want her all the more. But in the process of waiting, he had come to love her. It was loving her that was going to make making love to her so special.

"Are you hungry?"

Delany's question startled Zach out of his reverie. "Yes. Very." It was the simple truth.

"Well, maybe we should get something from the hospital cafeteria before we leave."

His answer was low and heated. "I think it will take a little more than that to satisfy *my* hunger...."

Dear Reader,

Welcome back to another month of great reading here at Silhouette Intimate Moments. Favorite author Marie Ferrarella gets things off to a rousing start with *The Amnesiac Bride*. Imagine waking up in a beautiful bridal suite, a ring on your finger and a gorgeous guy by your side—and no memory at all of who he is or how you got there! That's Whitney Bradshaw's dilemma in a nutshell, and wait 'til you see where things go from there.

Maggie Shayne brings you the next installment in her exciting miniseries, THE TEXAS BRAND, with *The Baddest Virgin in Texas*. If ever a title said it all, that's the one. I guarantee you're going to love this book. Nikki Benjamin's *Daddy by Default* is a lesson in what can happen when you hang on to a secret from your past. Luckily, what happens in this case ends up being very, very good. Beverly Bird begins a new miniseries, THE WEDDING RING, with *Loving Mariah*. It takes a missing child to bring Adam Wallace and Mariah Fisher together, but nothing will tear them apart. Kate Hathaway's back with *Bad For Each Other*, a secret-baby story that's chock-full of emotion. And finally, welcome new author Stephanie Doyle, whose *Undiscovered Hero* will have you eagerly turning the pages.

This month and every month, if you're looking for romantic reading at its best, come to Silhouette Intimate Moments.

Enjoy!

Leslie Wainger
Senior Editor and Editorial Coordinator

Please address questions and book requests to:
Silhouette Reader Service
U.S.: 3010 Walden Ave., P.O. Box 1325, Buffalo, NY 14269
Canadian: P.O. Box 609, Fort Erie, Ont. L2A 5X3

UNDISCOVERED HERO

STEPHANIE DOYLE

Published by Silhouette Books
America's Publisher of Contemporary Romance

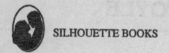

SILHOUETTE BOOKS

ISBN 0-373-07792-0

UNDISCOVERED HERO

Printed in U.S.A.

STEPHANIE DOYLE

began her writing career in eighth grade when she was given an assignment to write in a journal every day. Her own life being routine, she used the opportunity to write her own sequel to the *Star Wars* movies. One hundred and six handwritten pages later, she discovered her life-long dream—to be a writer.

Currently, Stephanie resides in South Jersey with her cat, Alexandria Hamilton Doyle. Single, she still waits for Mr. Right to sweep her off her feet. She vows that whoever he is, he'll decorate the cover of at least one of her books.

For Mom and Dad:
who've made everything possible.
Some day we'll share spirits on deck at LBI
and wave to all the people.

Prologue

Dressed in black and armed with Mace, Delany Sheridan, high school history teacher and regular citizen, patrolled the streets of Tacoma, Washington, in her compact car. She was terrified and felt like a fool for attempting the impossible.

The streets were empty except for the occasional bum and the lights had all been smashed, so only the moon provided any illumination. It couldn't even be called light. It was more an eerie glow. Suddenly, Delany felt like a teenager in a slasher movie. Any minute, Jason would spring up in front of her car with a chain saw in hand.

It didn't help that she was driving around one of the tougher areas of Tacoma. But in Tacoma there were only a few neighborhoods that weren't tough. What had begun as a booming frontier settlement turned into a virtual ghost town as nearby Seattle began to prosper. The local economy became stagnant, industry left, and poverty took over. It wasn't an original story. Now the only thing that blossomed in Tacoma was the gang population. Crips and Bloods killed each other at rates so fast that neither the police nor the hospitals could keep up with them. Delany was thankful that she had already grown up. Unhappily, the same couldn't be said for her students. And that was why she was out in the middle of the night, looking for a group of killers.

Get a grip, she ordered herself sternly. As F.D.R. had put it, "The only thing to fear...blah, blah, blah." He was an overrated president anyway. Block by block, Delany kept the car to a maximum speed of ten miles per hour. Fortunately for her, in the Hilltop, which was Crip territory, traffic after dark was not a problem.

Shouts. She definitely heard shouts. Delany craned her neck as the car rolled slowly through an intersection and saw a group of teens wearing what appeared to be bandannas on their heads. They stood in the middle of the road as if the idea of a car's attempting to drive past them was ludicrous. Low-level apartment complexes lined the street with some run-down row houses mixed in between. A garbage dump had been rolled out into the middle of the street, acting as a barricade against cars. Delany decided the only way she would be able to see if Cici was in the middle of that group was to get out of her car and walk down the street.

Don't get out of the car.

It was good sense talking, and Delany was very tempted to listen. It was suicide to think that she would be able to help Cici in the midst of her gang. No. It wasn't her gang yet. Cici Delores was a good student, a great athlete and an even better kid. She attended St. Joe's Prep on an honors scholarship program that Delany herself had set up. She bagged groceries for Mr.

Gonzales at a nearby supermarket. Her sponsor family, the people who paid for her tuition as long as she maintained her grades, took her to dinner every week. They loved her. Everyone loved her. Except, of course, her brother. He was a Crip, and he was making her do this. He wanted to force her to quit school and give up all hope of a future…for the gang.

Not Cici. It was all Delany could think about since the moment Cici had said she was leaving school. She owed her brother, Cici had said. He fed her and gave her a bed. If she didn't join the gang, then she didn't eat and she didn't sleep. So Cici was going to do what she was told to do. Only Delany couldn't let that happen. She had to do something.

Yeah, so what are you going to do about it? the logical side of her brain asked.

I know karate and I've got Mace, the naive part of her brain replied.

And they've got guns. The logical side of her brain won that particular argument.

She was about to put the car into reverse when she saw a girl walking toward her. Because the car was still in the middle of the intersection, she couldn't possibly duck and hope that whoever it was would think the car was empty. She could reverse and get the hell out of there, but that act smacked of cowardice. The approaching figure was a girl, a young girl at that.

No, Delany would deal with whoever was out there. Cower in her car? Drive off? These were her options. Delany decided to go on the offensive. With Mace in hand, she opened the car door and stood, keeping the door between her and any potential bullets the girl might decide to fire.

As the girl came closer, Delany thought she looked

familiar. With no streetlights, it was difficult to see the girl's face, but something in her carriage revealed her identity.

"Cici," Delany sighed in relief and dropped the Mace back into the car.

"What the hell are you doing here, Ms. Sheridan? You know better than to drive through this area at night." Her tone of voice was almost parental.

"Hey," Delany reminded her, "I'm the teacher, remember? You're the one in trouble. Now get in the car and let's get out of here before your friends realize you're here."

Cici shook her head, amazed at the woman's stupidity, but at the same time awed by her courage. "Nothing's changed."

"Everything is changed. I won't let you do this. And if that means I have to face your brother, I'll do it." If Delany could only talk to Cici's brother, perhaps she could convince him how important it was for Cici to stay in school, and how important it was for him to leave the gang. It was a long shot, but Delany was feeling lucky tonight.

"Ms. Sheridan..." Cici said, exasperated. She didn't believe anyone could be so smart and still be so naive.

"Hey, Cici! Tell us who your friend is."

Delany and Cici turned their heads simultaneously and discovered that they were no longer alone. A group of about ten slowly surrounded them. Delany felt actual pain from the force of her heart beating against her rib cage. Not one was older than twenty. And Delany was petrified of them.

She started counting. There were six boys. Four girls stood behind the boys, making comments to Cici that Delany didn't catch.

It was as if they spoke a foreign language. And in many ways, they did. Gangs created their own language. They wore certain colors, listened to certain songs and lived in certain places, forming a culture all their own. They had a power hierarchy and ran a profitable business. If they had a constitution, they could be called their own country. They did call themselves a nation.

"I'm taking Cici home." Delany's voice was firmer than she thought possible. She knew that to show fear would not accomplish anything. So with that in mind, she stepped away from the car door and closed it. Seconds later, she cursed her foolishness. She had left the Mace in the car.

"Enrico, let us leave." Cici looked at her brother, who led the gang.

How could she have been so stupid as to leave the Mace in the car? Calm down, Delany told herself. You had one can of Mace. These teens are armed with guns. None of the guns was visible, but Delany wasn't fooled into thinking that they weren't there.

"Oh, you come to take Ci home, did ya? Well, didn't ya know that Ci was home?" Enrico was the tallest of the group; his skin was darker than Cici's, and his scalp looked to be shaved under the rag he wore on his head. A Raiders jacket, with nothing underneath, was worn over a pair of jeans that started low on his hips, exposing his boxer shorts to one and all. Condescension oozed from every pore. He was the man who had all the power in this situation and he knew it.

"Look, I don't want any problems. I'm just going to take Cici, get in my car and drive away. She's your sister," Delany said as if that was supposed to make a difference. She turned and looked at Cici, who stared

back at her. There was fear in the young girl's eyes,
and a look of resignation.

"Maybe you got a hearin' problem. Cici ain't goin'
nowhere. Cici is gonna initiate to show that she can
hang with us." Enrico stepped forward as if to grab his
sister's arm, but Delany stepped between him and his
target.

Summoning more courage than she thought she had,
Delany looked into his soulless eyes. "What am I going
to have to do to get her out of here?"

For a moment, Delany thought he would ignore her
and her question. Then a smile appeared on his face,
his white teeth glowing in the dark.

"You wanna save Ci? Maybe you can take her beating. You show us how tough you are, and maybe we'll
let you go." He thought the words would send her running.

They didn't. Delany turned to Cici, and her eyes
glowed with determination. "Get in the car," she whispered. Casually, Delany took off her small hoop ear-
rings.

"You can't do this, Ms. Sheridan," Cici cried. "Enrico, please." Cici tried to push her out of the way.

Delany took hold of the girl's arms and held tight,
unwilling to be moved. "Listen to me," she commanded in a harsh whisper. "As soon as this thing
starts, get in the car, lock the door and drive away. The
keys are in the ignition."

"Come on, lady. We ain't got all night," Enrico
taunted.

"What's the matter? Am I making you late for your
next murder?" Delany sneered. She turned around,
ready not only to take the pain, but to inflict a little of
her own.

Enrico actually laughed. Then in a slow, methodical voice, so she could be sure to understand every word, he said, "You are one stupid lady, lady."

"You think so? Maybe that's because you've never loved anyone enough to want to protect them. Now, Cici!" Delany backed away, hoping to somehow create enough distance to make a break for it. When she saw them start toward her, she knew escape was impossible.

A fist slammed into her cheek. She threw a side kick into someone's stomach. The night went black. The clouds rose over head, shading the moon. And it looked as if the sun was never going to rise.

Chapter 1

Ow! It was her one and only prevailing thought. She hurt, and she hurt bad. Part of her didn't want to know what had caused such pain. Perhaps she'd been in a car accident, or maybe something had fallen on her. Whatever had happened to her, she didn't want to remember.

Unfortunately, Delany was not graced with selective amnesia. As if a curtain was raised at the beginning of a play, the actors began to move and images flashed behind her eyes. Delany pictured with vivid detail the blackness of the night. She saw the gang members surround her. She saw the color blue close in on her. She saw heavy fists swing at her. She remembered the pain those fists had caused. Explosions of pain still echoed in her memory. It made her hurt all over again. Had they killed her?

No. The afterlife couldn't hurt this much unless she was in hell. Not cheered by that particular thought, she decided that she was alive. Once that decision had been made, she decided it was time to investigate her surroundings. Her first task was to open her eyes.

Even that was painful. A crust had formed over her eyes, and she struggled to open the tightly woven lashes. She brought her right hand up to help rub away the sand. She was about to bring the other hand up when she realized that her left arm wasn't cooperating. With her right hand she rubbed both eyes until they opened, then gingerly lifted her head to look down at her body.

What she saw frightened her. Her left arm was in a cast. Both her legs were in casts and raised higher than her head. Automatically, she tried to wiggle her toes, but found she couldn't. She couldn't even feel them. But she didn't know if that was from the casts or from something else.

Reluctantly, she lowered her head. She tried to focus on where the pain was coming from. If the pain came from her legs, at least she would know she could still feel them. But the pain came from her arm and, oddly enough, from her face. Delany had no feeling in her legs. Please, she thought, don't let me be paralyzed.

"No," she sighed, not actually knowing if she'd made a noise or not. She heard the door open and watched as a nurse came in with a hypodermic in hand. "Wait," Delany ordered. She was awake now. They couldn't just do things to her body without her being aware of it.

The nurse looked down and smiled. "You're awake. We thought the painkillers would keep you out for a little while longer. Do you hurt anywhere?"

"Everywhere," Delany groaned. Her face throbbed with pain, and she knew it was because she had spoken. "Can I see a mirror?" she asked, moving her mouth as little as possible.

The nurse hesitated. "Why don't you wait until the doctor comes in and explains everything to you. I promise you there was no permanent damage."

Delany didn't take much comfort from that statement, but accepted the fact that she wasn't going to get a mirror. "Am I paralyzed?"

Again the nurse hedged. "I really think you should wait for the doctor. I'm going to inject this painkiller into your IV now. It will help you to rest."

"No," Delany commanded. "I don't want to fall asleep again. I want to know what's wrong with me."

Despite her weakened state, Delany's stubborn streak was as powerful as ever. The nurse dropped her needle and was about to leave to fetch the doctor when Delany reached out to grab her arm.

"Who's that man in the chair?" Delany had just noticed him. He was a stranger to her and was sound asleep, if his slight snores were any indication. Perhaps he was visiting another patient in the room, but when Delany turned her head she saw that the bed next to hers was empty.

"He rode with you in the ambulance. Don't you know him?"

"No." Delany stared hard at the man, unaware that the nurse had left the room. He was tall, over six foot if the way his legs slumped off the chair was any indication. He wore the remains of a suit, the tie and jacket now discarded. His jet black hair fell in clumps around his face as if he had styled it, but the effects of the hair spray had worn off. Whoever he was, he had a very intense face, which included sharp, angled cheekbones, an aquiline nose and a square jaw. His smooth skin was evenly tanned. Either he spent a great deal of time in the sun or his parents had gifted him with a compelling complexion. Hard lines were etched into his face around the eyes and mouth, but somehow Delany didn't think those lines were a true indication of his age. He was mid-thirties, max.

She was suddenly incredibly curious about his eyes. Maybe it was unusual to be so fascinated with a stranger, but for now it took her mind off the pain.

"Hello." Her voice was hoarse, probably from screaming. He didn't hear it above his snores. Delany tried again, this time with a little more oomph. "Hey, you in the chair. Wake up."

The man stirred. His head jerked up sharply as if he'd been struck.

"Sorry to wake you," Delany said. She was sorry that she had disturbed him, now that she realized how soundly he had been sleeping. Then she recanted. "Wait a minute. I'm not sorry. Who are you, and why are you in my room?"

The man's response had to wait in deference to a fierce yawn that overcame his whole body. After standing to stretch his cramped limbs, he walked to the bed and stood over the now-alert patient. "You look horrible."

Delany was stunned. "Who are you?" An imbecile, for one thing. Who walked up to a woman in a hospital bed and commented on her looks? And a stranger at that! Then she began to worry. How bad *did* she look? "Do you have a mirror?"

He disappeared into what Delany figured was the bathroom connected to the room. He returned with a small shaving mirror.

Her gasp filled the room. "Oh, I do look horrible."

He nodded. "Broken nose and a cracked cheekbone. It'll heal."

Delany's eyes lit up. This man knew something about her condition. Was he a doctor? "Am I paralyzed?"

"They don't know."

"They?"

"The doctors."

Delany was confused, and she didn't think it had anything to do with her pain. "If you're not a doctor, then who are you?"

Zachary wasn't quite sure how to answer the question. Now that she was awake and obviously concerned about her condition, he didn't feel it was the right time to spring the news that he was the DEA operative who'd let her get beaten up. No, he wasn't ready for the outrage, the hurt, the sense of betrayal this woman would feel when he told her the whole sordid story. Then again, there was no reason why she had to know right now. He was an undercover agent in the unending war against drugs. He could assume an identity and give her some time before she learned the truth. She needed time to recover from the shock she'd already suffered. He needed time, too. For what, he didn't know. But he needed it. Desperately.

"My name's Zach Montgomery." At least the name was for real. "I was driving by when I saw a group of kids run off. I stopped my car to take a look and found you." It was feeble at best, but she had no reason to distrust him. Much easier to pull off one of these stories when the person you were trying to scam wasn't sniffing for bacon, or whatever they called cops these days.

"So you don't know if I'm ever going to walk again." Delany didn't care as much about who he was as about what he knew.

Shaking his head, he moved even closer and patted her arm in an awkward gesture of comfort. "You've got a cracked vertebra and a lot of swelling. When the swelling goes down, your back may heal, and you'll be fine with some therapy. Or…"

"Or when the swelling goes down, I might be paralyzed."

"That's not the attitude to have. You've got to believe you're going to walk again, or not only are you fighting your body, but you're fighting your mind, too." Zach didn't know where the words came from. He wasn't used to speaking so profoundly. He only knew that it was true—from experience.

"You sound like you've been there." Delany was becoming intrigued by the man named Zach Montgomery.

"Car accident," Zach lied easily. Again she believed him without question. But then, why shouldn't she? He was an excellent liar.

"I will walk again. Will I run?" Delany pushed. She wanted not only to recover, but to recover fully. She ran every day after school. It had become the school challenge to see who could run longer than she could. Every year she held a marathon to raise money for her scholarship program for needy students. Every year the student body would attempt to run more laps than their "old" teacher could. Every year they failed.

Zach laughed. "Now that's what I mean about having the right attitude. Anyway, your doctor can answer these questions better than I can. I met him last night when they brought you in. Dr. Man…Man something."

"Dr. Manuela?" Delany provided.

Stunned, Zach nodded. "You know him?"

Delany tried to nod, but she found she lacked the strength. "I'm a teacher. I raise money for a scholarship program at the school by holding a yearly race. Since doctors have the dough and they typically keep themselves in shape, I ask them to participate. Dr. Manuela's a regular.'' She was babbling. She just didn't want the conversation to end.

Zach, too, sensed they were running out of things to say to one another. They were strangers. It was hard to remember that, after everything she had put him through last night. Quickly, he shook off the memory. He wasn't ready to deal with that yet. Later. Still, he didn't want to leave her. So he found a way to prolong the conversation.

''You probably aren't up to talking much more, but you said something about a scholarship fund...'' Zach left the sentence unfinished, not wanting to force her to answer.

''The money is to help needy students offset the cost of the private school where I work. Families that can contribute adopt a student. It gives students who normally wouldn't have the opportunity to attend a college prep high school a chance.''

Delany thought about all the students who had benefited. *Cici.* Since she had gained consciousness, she hadn't thought of Cici at all. Cici could be hurt, and Delany had wasted energy talking about a race.

''Oh, my God. Cici?'' She looked up at Zach and hoped he would know the answer to her question. Then she realized it would be unlikely. Cici might have been gone before this man ever arrived on the scene.

''Was she there?'' Zach remembered only one girl. The one who cried for her teacher.

''Yes. Tall, thin, with skin a little darker than yours.''

''Yeah, that's her. I put her in your car and told her to get the hell out of there. She's all right. You saved her.'' The words sounded corny, but they were a fact.

Saved her. It sounded strange to her ears. It's not as if she were Superman, or Superwoman for that matter. She wasn't a doctor or a paramedic. She hadn't done anything to warrant such illustrious words. All she had done was stay still while the young thugs worked out their inner frustrations on her face.

"Well, if I saved her, then you saved me."

It was so preposterous, he wanted to laugh. But he was too disgusted with himself to do that. "I didn't save you."

"You found me. The nurse said you rode in the ambulance. Why did you?" What Delany should have said was "Thank you. I'm fine now, so you can leave." She didn't know this man. He was nothing more than a person who stopped to satisfy his curiosity and unfortunately got caught in something that he couldn't get out of.

But she did like talking with him. And she appreciated that he had told her the truth about her appearance instead of hedging or feeding her a line. He was a decent human being. Not an almighty doctor, or a compassionate nurse, or an intimidating cop. He was a regular guy who had stopped to lend a hand. But that didn't explain why he'd ridden with her or why he'd stayed.

Good question, Zach thought. It was something he'd ask, too. Some people might just say thanks and then goodbye. Not Zach. He'd want to know why the person did it and what was in it for themselves. In this case, he was trying to ease a guilty conscience. Unfortunately, he couldn't tell her that. "I...was worried. You tried to help a kid and got beat up for your troubles. I guess I felt badly for you."

"I don't need your pity." Delany was proud as well as stubborn. Besides, she was hoping that there had been another reason. It was comical considering the way she looked, but she felt an attachment to this man that she hadn't felt in...ever.

This time he did laugh. "You're a feisty little thing, aren't you?"

"I'm not that little, and you would see just how feisty I am if I wasn't flat on my back. What is this thing around my waist anyway?" She'd been so busy worrying about her casts that she had just noticed how constrained she actually felt. It was almost claustrophobic.

Zach sat down on the edge of bed, watching to see that he didn't jostle her unnecessarily. Perhaps it was too intimate for two people who had just met, but he wanted to sit down and didn't want to be as far away as the chair. "It's a back brace for the injured vertebra. You're definitely going to be out of school for a while."

Delany supposed she should feel bothered by that news, but she couldn't get past her feelings of relief. It was like a snow day. Unexpected, but as soon as the school was officially closed, you realized how much you needed the break.

"Are you going to be all right? I mean financially. I know schoolteachers don't make that much."

The feistiness was back. "What do you want to do? Give me some money because you're concerned about me? Maybe you should take up a collection. Better yet, a tin cup and some dark glasses, and you can just roll me out onto the streets. I'd clean up."

"I think people would be too turned off by your face to actually get close enough to give you money." Zach's face was expressionless. Only someone who knew him well would know that it was his idea of a joke.

Despite the pain it caused, Delany couldn't suppress

her laughter. Her answer had been so self-righteous, and all he'd done was ask a simple question. "Don't make me laugh. It hurts."

"Sorry."

"I'll be fine. My medical insurance will cover the bills. Plus, I've got plenty of sick days coming to me, probably two months worth. Besides that, I've got some savings. But thank you for your concern," she said in her most polite voice.

Silence ensued. All questions seemed to have been answered, aside from the reason why he had stayed so long. It was probably time for her to let him off the hook.

"Thank you for staying with me. It probably sounds strange, but it was easier to take the news from you than from a doctor, even Dr. Manuela. You didn't hedge or try to mince words. You just said it like it was. That's how I needed to hear it. You're free from all responsibility now." She felt a catch in her throat and was aghast to realize that she was on the verge of tears.

She had let him off the hook. Only she didn't know how big a hook he was on. But it wasn't just the guilt factor. There was something else that still tugged at Zach, goading him into staying. "You know, there's a proverb about having to look out for the person you save. It says *you're my responsibility.*" He had meant it to sound lighthearted. A way to break the tension and to garner him an invitation to visit sometime. Somehow, in the quiet room, it sounded more like a solemn oath.

Brown, Delany realized. His eyes were dark chocolate brown, and they burned right through her own blue eyes into her soul. She was about to tell him something, but was interrupted by the arrival of a friendly face.

"Doc Manny. I hear you put my legs in these casts on purpose to eliminate me from the upcoming race."

The good-natured doctor laughed at her friendly teasing. "I see you stuck around, Mr. Montgomery," he said, turning to see Zach.

Zach didn't want to make a big deal out of it. "I fell asleep in the chair."

Somehow, Zach sensed Doc Manny knew there was more to it than that, but Delany broke into their conversation, diverting his attention.

"Hey, remember me? I'm the one in white plaster. Tell me what's wrong, Doc Manny. Will I ever beat your butt in a race again?" She tried to smile, but it hurt, and it wasn't really that funny.

The doctor grabbed her chart. Delany could imagine the thoughts running through his head: *These things need to be said delicately so the patient doesn't panic.* "You see—"

"I know about the legs and the arm, obviously," Delany stated, shooting an evil look at Zach. "I've also been told about my face. And I know about my cracked vertebra and the swelling. All I want to hear from you is your gut reaction. When the swelling goes down, will I walk?"

"My gut instinct is that you'll walk," Dr. Manuela said easily. "Only one vertebra was cracked, and not in too bad a spot, either. You'll be on your back for a good long while, though. And when you get out of those casts, you'll need some physical therapy to strengthen the weakened muscles in your arm and legs. I can't promise anything, but with some good care and a little luck, I think you should make a full recovery."

Delany sighed deeply, and again tears threatened. She was going to walk. It wasn't wishful thinking; it was something she knew. Her body was broken, but it would heal. Now all she had to do was battle the images that hadn't been far from her mind.

Zach saw it. Something disturbed Delany, and it wasn't her injury. A cloud drifted over her and carried her to someplace dark and evil. He missed her. "Hey, what's the problem?"

"Blue," Delany responded. But no one would understand what it meant to her.

"You'll never be able to look at the color again without remembering."

Zach's perceptiveness amazed her. Again, his blunt words weren't meant to comfort, so much as they were to plainly state a fact. Delany nodded. It was as if they were speaking about things no one else could comprehend. But more than that, they seemed to be able to communicate without words. It was as if she had bonded with this stranger immediately, and the stranger with her.

"I've prescribed some more painkillers." The doctor interrupted her thoughts. "Let the nurse give them to you. They'll help you sleep more comfortably, which is something your body needs right now." Turning toward Zach, Doc Manny said, "I hope to see you around, Mr. Montgomery. Thank you for...falling asleep." He left the room. It was quite obvious that Zach was in no hurry to follow him.

"You should find one of those self-help groups," Zach suggested lamely, not knowing what else to say to allay her fears.

Delany arched her brows, almost amused at how sensitive he was trying to be. She didn't know how she knew, but he wasn't the sensitive type. No one could tell her how horrible her face looked, and then be accused of being sensitive. "You mean a victims' group? There's something about the word 'victim' that just doesn't sit well with me. Besides, most people in those groups are random blameless victims. Me, I asked for what happened to me." It didn't help to alleviate her pain any, but it did seem to give her a sense of control over the situation. No one had done this to her. She had done this to herself. Stupid, but in control.

"That's true. You want to tell me what you were doing there? Or rather, what you thought you were going to do there?"

"No. I don't want to talk about it right now. It's still really raw." She felt guilty about not confiding in him. Which was ridiculous, because she didn't owe him any explanation. At the same time, she knew one day she would want to talk about it, and he would be a good person to listen.

Zach nodded in understanding. "Well, if you ever want to talk, here's the number where I'm staying." Zach opened the drawer of the nightstand next to the bed and found a pen and pad. He jotted down the number and handed her the pad.

"Room 215?" Delany questioned. "Are you staying in a hotel?"

"Motel, actually," Zach clarified.

"You don't live in Tacoma?"

"No, I move around a lot. Right now, I'm staying here. I'll be around for a while." It was all very vague, but it bought him some time. Next, she was going to ask what he was doing here, and the stall gave him some time to work on his cover story. He thought about coming clean with the truth, but he wanted to keep the tenuous friendship he had struck with her. If he told her who he was now, she would throw him out of the room and never give him a second chance. He didn't exactly know what was going on between them. It could be explained simply as two people who had hit it off. If they had met in a bar, they might be sharing more than just a hospital bed right now. *A bar...*

"So what are you doing in Tacoma? It really isn't known for being a hotbed of tourism. The gangs prevent that and it's a shame. Tacoma really does have a lot to offer."

"Actually, I'm thinking of going into business for myself. I've heard about some of the renovations going on down in the south end of town. I thought I might open a bar and grill." It was a legitimate story. He had read an article about such occurrences in the paper that morning.

"Oh, you're going to try to capitalize on the University of Washington campus's coming to town. Everyone here is excited. They're hoping the young blood will bring new life to the place. Where you're looking is a prime spot. Lots of room for growth." Delany's eyes grew animated, as if she, too, were looking forward to the growth of the city.

It made him curious. "If you wanted some excitement, why not move to Seattle? It's only about a forty-minute drive, depending on traffic."

It was hard to explain, but Delany tried. "My parents raised me in Tacoma. I've been through a lot here. I feel like I owe this city. It would be traitorous to leave when so many others have left. I've always been a sucker for the underdog, and Tacoma is the underdog."

"You're as loyal as a dog," Zach remarked cynically.

"And I look like one, too, right?" Again Delany tried to smile. Then she remembered she couldn't.

"Only when you smile." Zach laughed as her attempt at a smile quickly faded into a fierce scowl. "I'm teasing. You really don't look that bad. I figured if you were worried about your face, it would take your mind off your legs. The threat of paralysis is scary. You've been scared enough."

He was a good guy. "Thanks."

Just then the door was pushed open, and the nurse was back with a hypodermic in hand. Delany wanted to protest, but Zach stopped her with a gentle hand on her wrist. "Take it. The doc was right. You need to sleep."

But I don't want to go to sleep. I want to talk about you. I want to know where you came from and who you are. I don't want to go to sleep only to wake up and find you gone. She didn't say it, but she thought it. She also thought of one last question that she wanted to ask him, but she hesitated. It wasn't in her nature to ask for things. But she wanted this badly. All he could do was say no.

"Will you visit?" Her voice was reduced to a whisper. So soft he could barely hear her.

Zach dropped his head down and saw his hand on hers. This was right. His gut told him so. It was interesting to him that in the past twenty-four hours, his coolly planned, completely methodical and well-thought-out life had just undergone a serious transformation. He was thinking with his gut and going with his instincts. Frightening, yet liberating in a way.

"Do you want me to visit?" It was a useless question, but he wanted to hear the words.

"I want you to visit. You've been helpful."

"You've got to have friends. Surely there's someone you would rather have here. What about your parents?"

"My parents are gone," she stated brusquely. "And

yes, I do have friends. Lots of friends. I just thought that if you wanted to come by and say hello, I wouldn't kick you out of the room," she finished indignantly.

She was feeling woozy. The drugs were starting to kick in, but she fought them because she needed to know how this conversation would end. The nurse saw her eyelids droop and left as anonymously as she'd entered.

Zach saw her eyes begin to close, too, and was glad to know that she would sleep. "As long as I know you won't kick me out, I guess I'll stop by."

She didn't answer him. She had already fallen under the effects of the medication.

Zach stayed to watch her for a while longer. He began to notice the details. She had ice blond hair tied on top of her head in a ponytail. He remembered her eyes were pale blue. With the bruises and the swelling, he couldn't say if she was attractive or not. To him, it didn't matter what her face looked like. What she did. What she risked. Zach already knew she was beautiful because of her courage.

Her breathing was deep and even, and she looked peaceful although he knew that her dreams would probably haunt her. Zach found himself wishing her sweet dreams. He touched his fingers to his lips, then touched them to her forehead.

"Don't let the bedbugs bite," Zach whispered. He left the room without glancing back.

Opening the door to his motel room, Zach was disappointed, but not surprised, to see that the room was exactly how he left it. It wasn't a ritzy place. Tacoma wasn't a ritzy city. But it wasn't a slum, either. Zach demanded clean sheets and a television. These were his only requirements, though. Now, of course, looking at the mess, he wished he had spent the money and gotten one of those places with a maid.

His suitcase was open, and clothes spilled from its mouth. Some clothes had been belched up onto a chair. Others had simply limped down onto the floor. A half-empty soda was on the table next to a crumpled hamburger wrapper. He could still smell the stale meat and the special sauce. Hell, he used to tell himself that his life was orderly.

Apparently, not this part of his life.

Who was he kidding? Zach shucked off his clothes, let them drop where they fell and headed for the shower. The hair gel was beginning to clump and fall from his head in pieces. Originally, the mention of styling his hair had made him laugh. Mort thought doing it would lend itself to his cover. Greasy hair and scumball drug dealers went together. But then Mort always did like his operatives to play their roles to the hilt.

Troublesome thoughts plagued Zach, as images from the previous night began to flash through his mind. It was time to face up to what he did and deal with it. It was going to be even harder now that he knew her. It was going to be impossible now that he liked her....

"Look, I'm only going to explain this to you one more time. Right now you're dealing with a middleman. You buy your drugs from me and you're dealing direct." Zach talked slowly and used small words so the man had a chance of understanding. Hell, the guy in front of him was an overgrown kid. He still had zits on his face.

"But if I deal with you, ain't I dealin' with a middleman?" O.G. asked, his voice laced with sarcasm.

Zach could tell that he was annoying the kid, but he was damned if he was about to kowtow to the Original Gangster. The only reason the kid had the title was because he was good at ducking when the bullets flew. Of course, Zach did have to acknowledge that with the title came a certain amount of power. O.G. was in charge of all the drug distribution in Crip territory. The gang's organization was not unlike that of the Mafia's, with a hierarchy all of its own. O.G. was king. The rest were pawns.

O.G. initiated young blood into the gang to sell drugs. More accurately, these kids jumped at the chance to hang with O.G. He was their father, and they were his willing children. When their territory was threatened by rival gangs, the children would kill for their family. They would die for it.

Zach closed his eyes in irritation and started from the beginning. "Listen, you buy from a man in Seattle, who deals with a group in Los Angeles. The L.A. group buys from the Colombians. That means that the Colombians have got to take their cut, the L.A. group has got to take their cut, and your contact in Seattle has got to take his cut. I buy directly from the Colombians and I'm willing to sell to you. More profit for you. More profit for me. No Seattle man. No L.A. group. Simple." Like you, you idiot, Zach finished silently.

O.G. shook his head. "The Seattle man ain't gonna like it. You're cuttin' him out, and he might decide to take it out on me."

This was it. Play it cool, then ease in for the kill. "You're right. No man is going to let me in on his action. So I'm going to have to deal with him before he deals with us. Termination. Give me the name and where you meet, and consider it done."

Zach watched while O.G. attempted to think about this. Zach knew that to give up the contact was the quickest way to the grave. He hoped O.G. considered the money he was going to make if this deal went through. "No way, man."

Damn. Apparently, life outweighed money. But Zach needed that name. These drug contacts were the most wanted men in America. Local police wanted them, state police wanted them, the FBI wanted them, and most certainly the Drug Enforcement Agency wanted them. Zach wasn't greedy. He wanted this contact. The FBI could have the next one. Zach decided to take a new approach.

"The Bloods are moving into your hood. You know you're going to have to go to war. Not only can I make you some quick cash, but I can put you in touch with some friends who deal in serious weapons."

"How serious?"

"Well, they're a hell of a lot more advanced than the pop guns you're playing with." Zach could see the gang leader's eyes start to twinkle.

"I can't rat out the man." O.G. played it cool, but the truth was he needed the money and the guns. "That don't mean we can't start dealin'. Maybe start slow."

Zach shook his head. "No good. You want a wife and a girlfriend, too? If your man knows I'm sniffing around, he'll be all over me. All I need is his name and where you meet him. This guy will be stiff before he ever realizes you gave him up."

Tempted. O.G. was definitely tempted. "You good at what you do?"

He meant the killing part. Yeah, Zach was very good at what he did. He didn't particularly like it, but he wasn't about to share that information with O.G.

"Yeah, I'm real good," Zach said with enthusiasm. He moved to the window, feeling a sudden need for air. When he glanced down at the street, he saw a group of kids in blue circled around...something. Initiation. It must be. Now he really needed air. "What's going on down there?" he asked. From his vantage point three floors up in a condemned apartment building, he had a hard time making out what the figures below were doing.

O.G. walked to the window and looked down. "I don't know. Initiation maybe."

"Shouldn't you be there? You are the O.G."

"Man, I'm like the damn president. I don't deal directly with the masses. I leave that to my men. Now let's get back to business."

Business. The word echoed in Zach's mind. O.G. was right for once. He needed to focus. What did Zach care if some stupid kid wanted to join a gang? The kid should've been smarter. It wasn't Zach's job to save every stupid kid from himself. The problem couldn't be fixed one kid at a time. His job was to stop the influx of drugs into this area. If he did that, then the gang couldn't make a profit on children's addictions. No profit, no weapons. No weapons, no war. No war, no death. Then everyone would be safe. If one kid had to be sacrificed so that all kids could be safer in the future, then that was the nature of the game that he played.

"You were giving me the name of your contact," Zach reminded O.G., as he tried to keep his gaze from the window. He couldn't help the kid, but he didn't want to see him get beaten up. Unfortunately, his neck wasn't listening to his mind. It kept craning back to the window, to the street. Then someone moved, and Zach saw something, or rather someone, lying on the ground.

It was a woman if the long blond hair was any indication. She was attempting to crawl away from them. This
wasn't an initiation, Zach realized. They were attacking
her!

Save her.

It was his conscience talking, but he couldn't listen.
One word of concern would brand him a cop. People
of O.G.'s ilk didn't care about a woman being beaten
to death. Zach didn't know what the woman was doing
down there, and it wasn't his problem. He was here for
the name of the contact. One name, and an entire drug
ring could be shut down. Hundreds of kids wouldn't
become addicts. Hundreds of lives would be saved. He
couldn't give all that up for one woman.

"The name," Zach demanded, his voice harsh with
unleashed rage. He was pushing O.G. too hard. He
knew it. But damn it, he was sacrificing that woman's
life for this name. He twisted his neck again. She had
fallen to the ground and was either dead or unconscious.
The teens didn't back off. He saw one draw a gun.
"Your boys down there are about to kill a woman. The
cops will crawl all over this place if that happens. I
don't like cops. I don't want them around." Zach
prayed he'd convinced him.

Apparently, he had. O.G. opened the window and
called down, "Hey! What the hell are you doin'?"

Enrico looked up toward the window and shouted
back, "Just showin' the lady a good time."

"Leave her alone. I'm conductin' business up here.
I don't need no pigs sniffin' around." The group backed
off reluctantly.

Zach's stomach rolled in disgust. As they moved
away from the body, he could tell that both her legs
were broken by the way they stuck out at odd angles

from her body. She was probably suffering from shock. If she didn't get to a hospital soon, shock alone was enough to kill her. If she wasn't dead already. And Zach had let it happen.

"The name. Give me the name." Zach's voice allowed for no argument.

"Maxwell. Tony 'Iceman' Maxwell. He meets me at the hotel across from the Dome on Mondays at 3:00 a.m. Same time every week. Like a damn TV show. Next Monday you meet him, and the show is canceled." O.G. laughed at his own humor and walked away.

Zach couldn't take his eyes off the woman. He needed to get down there and at least try to help her. Of course, it was all her fault if she died. What in heaven's name was she doing in this neighborhood at night anyway? Didn't she know that only scum like him and O.G. populated this area? She'd asked for trouble and she got it. But did she deserve to die?

"I've got to leave," Zach informed the gangster. The other Crips still circled the woman. It would be impossible to get to her without their attacking him. He couldn't think of a single legitimate reason why he should be concerned about a strange woman. It smacked of a man who cared. Caring wasn't part of the role he played. Caring wasn't part of him anymore, period. No, if he so much as looked at her twice, his cover would be questioned. He'd blown his last cover because he cared. He simply couldn't do it again. His decision had been made. He was going to have to let her die.

No! Save her.

Zach left the room instantly. He took the rotted steps that led down to the lobby two at a time. He'd seen a car. It wasn't far from the body, so it must be hers. If he could get to her, throw her over his shoulder, then get to the car before anyone realized what he was doing, he might have a chance. If the car was still there. If he didn't kill her when he picked her up. If he could get to the car, open the door and start the engine before they started shooting. Too many ifs. The truth was, he and the lady were going to die.

The sad part was that death didn't bother him as much as blowing his cover did. They would know he was a cop, and that really upset him because he'd worked so hard and so long, and he'd fooled them all. Zach was panting from his rush downstairs as he reached the first floor. He stopped for a moment in the lobby and gazed out the door. The group was still there, completely oblivious to the life that was fading away at their feet.

With a deep breath and determination, he opened the door and started walking toward the body of the woman. Fate beat him to her. The sirens were loud and close. Someone must have alerted the police to what was happening. When he looked up, Zach saw the group disperse quickly. From behind him, he heard O.G. run out onto the street.

"Pigs!" he called as he ran past Zach. Evidently, O.G. wasn't too concerned with Zach's welfare. It was just as well. Now, nobody would witness his show of concern. Zach ran toward the unconscious woman. Then he noticed a younger girl leaning over the woman.

"Who the hell are you?" Zach asked. "Didn't you hear the sirens?" He wanted to scare the girl away.

She wasn't budging. "You don't understand," she sobbed. "She did it for me. She wanted to keep me out of the gang."

Zach barely understood her words, but he got the gist. "Who is she?"

"She's my teacher," the girl told him. It looked as if the girl was about to move her when Zach pushed her away.

"No! Don't move her. Go to the intersection and wave the police down. Tell them we need an ambulance," Zach instructed.

The girl obeyed without blinking. Zach was good at giving orders. As he stared down at the body, he sighed and felt himself fill with self-loathing. He pushed his fingers against her neck and found a pulse. For that, and that alone, he was grateful.

"I'm sorry, lady. So sorry." She never heard him.

The ambulance came, and Zach impulsively followed the stretcher into the back. But not before he told the sobbing girl that if he ever saw her in the colors, he would shoot her himself. The ride to the hospital was the longest trip of his life.

Zach couldn't say why he had gone with the woman. Impulsiveness was not in his nature. He was, or at least imagined he was, a methodical and logical sort. Logic had nothing to do with him that night. He held on to the hand of the unknown woman, the teacher, and willed life back into her failing body. He thought of men he believed to be brave. Not one compared with her. She *was* bravery. And he wanted her to live.

At the hospital, Zach placed a phone call to Mort and gave him the name of the contact and the time of the meeting. In the next breath, he told his boss that he was due for a vacation. Another impulsive move. Mort didn't question the suddenness of the request. He just granted it.

* * *

Thinking about it now, as he stood under the steaming shower, Zach realized that if he had told Delany the truth about what happened last night she probably wouldn't have yelled or screamed curses at him. After he turned off the shower and reached for the towel, he began to imagine how the entire scene would play out.

He would have explained that he was working a bust and that he had accomplished his mission. Drug trafficking in the area would now be cut in half. She probably would've patted him on the shoulder and said that he'd done what he had to do. She would've told him that she was the one at fault for putting herself in such a dangerous situation and that there was nothing else he could have done.

If he told the truth, his conscience would be guilt free, and she wouldn't be that angry with him. If anything, she would be more upset for having been deceived by him. So perhaps the truth wouldn't be so bad. Then he could actually be forgiven. She was the forgiving type.

Perhaps too forgiving. It was an evil thought, but an accurate one. It crept into Zach's mind. Throwing the towel aside, he threw himself onto the bed and began to sink into the pillows. He'd slept little the night before in the hospital chair, and although it was early, he wanted to go to sleep immediately. But he knew he wouldn't. His mind churned with hundreds of thoughts and questions all regarding one woman. Delany: the forgiving one.

He was curious to know what made her so altruistic. Sure, Zach had met people who donated to charity. He had grown up with those people. He also knew people who donated their time to soup kitchens and to other noble causes. But never had any of those people risked their lives in the name of charity.

It would be interesting to know what motivated her, but at the same time he found himself not wanting her forgiveness. Whether she knew it or not, that kind of self-sacrifice was incredibly intimidating to those who were its recipients. How humiliated he would feel to be forgiven for being such a cad. Much better that he should continue lying to her, yet maintain his equality with her on some warped level. If he got close enough, maybe he would discover a flaw in the diamond. The more flaws the better as far as he was concerned, if he wanted to consider himself at all equal with her. Flaw finding was going to take time, though. That was a bad idea.

The logical decision was not to return to the hospital. It was a dismal thought, but one that had begun to take root in his mind as soon as he'd left Delany. Right now, he had a lot of things he needed to sort out in his mind. He needed to learn what kind of man he really was.... He had almost let Delany die and he couldn't say that didn't sound like something he would do, because he didn't *know* what kind of things he would do when he wasn't under cover. When you spent all your time as someone else, it was easy to forget who the someone was.

But Zach couldn't blame his lost identity on the job.

It would just be one more lie. Zach Montgomery had ceased to exist years ago, long before he was a full-time undercover operative. He had suppressed himself. Other people had suppressed him. His job suppressed him. He was a garbage bag that had been stuffed with too much garbage. Now the garbage was poking holes through the bag.

Spontaneous words spewed from his mouth. Spontaneous deeds were carried out by his body. The hidden personality that had lain dormant for so long now searched for weak spots where it could poke through. Delany Sheridan might prove to be such a weakness.

That was why he shouldn't return to the hospital. The only consequence would be a few moments of disappointment on Delany's part when she finally realized he wouldn't be returning. She would regret that they hadn't met under better circumstances, and her friends would tell her that any guy jerky enough to default on a promise to a woman in a hospital was not the type of person you wanted beside you in the hospital in the first place. She would share a pint of chocolate ice cream with the girls and then she would cease to think about him.

As for Zach, it was time to put Tacoma behind him. The job was done. Now, he had a few months and a great deal of hard-earned savings to spend. Thoughts of tropical islands and rum drinks floated through his mind. He could let his impulsive streak run amuck. Perhaps a passionate island affair and a homemade hut on the beach were just what he needed to take his mind off his troubles. After a few months of such an idyllic existence, he would crave to get back into action again. The need to do his duty would urge him on, and he would return to make the world a safer place to live.

Of course, he'd regret passing up the opportunity to get to know Delany a little better. And guilt would more than likely dog his steps no matter where he went. Images of her in those casts would rise like the tide, and his passion would fall just as quickly. Women would laugh at his impotence, and piña coladas would rule his life. Death would come quickly as soon as the liver failed, and his last thought would be of the one person who had caused it all: Delany.

So, he was creative as well as impulsive. Another

surprise for Zach. There were so many interesting facets to his personality that Zach simply didn't know what was going to pop out next.

Where did that leave him?

Delany. Somehow he knew that she would play a major role in his future. Simply dismissing her wouldn't work because her voice and her eyes and her humor would prey on his mind. The best thing to do would be to binge on her. He needed to get his fill of her, spend all his time with her, obsess about her until he lost interest. She would play the role of villain, and he would play the psychologist who discovered what made her tick. As soon as he learned that she wasn't the angel he imagined her to be, he would be able to leave without a backward glance.

Nobody was that good. Everybody was human. So that meant Delany was as imperfect as any other human being. It was an encouraging thought.

Sleep finally started to overcome his turbulent thoughts. Zach was grateful. Tomorrow, he would wake up and start on his journey of self-discovery. He could never repeat those words aloud, of course. He didn't want people to think he was an overage hippie. Still, it was a truthful reflection of his future. As in any mystery, the clues would lead to the truth. And the first and most important clue was Delany Sheridan.

He couldn't wait to see her again. And then, from out of nowhere, he wondered what she would look like without the broken nose and the busted cheek. Pretty, he bet. All angels were pretty.

Chapter 2

The only thing Delany Sheridan had in common with an angel was the white hospital gown she wore. Zach stared at her for a minute before he let her know he'd arrived. He still didn't know if he should be there. But his impulsive nature was back in full force.

"Take your damn needle and stick it in *your* butt, and then tell me how it doesn't hurt that much!" Delany's face was red with indignation, although it was difficult to tell with the black-and-blue marks that decorated her face. They seemed even more pronounced in the midafternoon light than they had yesterday morning. The clearest indication of her rage was the fiery red scalp beneath her ice blond locks.

With a smile that said, "I've dealt with tempers like yours in the past, and you don't frighten me," the nurse replied, "Roll over."

It was a futile command, of course. With her legs extended in the air, and her back in a stiff brace, Delany wasn't rolling anywhere. The nurse simply reached under Delany's gown and stabbed. Delany howled with rage and spat out a word that Zach simply refused to believe came from his alleged angel. The nurse only smiled.

"At least I'm off that rotten IV," Delany muttered, rubbing her now-sore bottom with her good arm. "I swear I'm going to have a hole in my hand the size of a penny for the rest of my life because of that thick needle."

"How's the patient today?" Zach asked the very cliché question as he entered the room, but the truth was he didn't need an answer.

"Fine," Delany replied.

"Cranky," the nurse said simultaneously.

Delany shot the nurse a look that would have killed had she been gifted with the laser eye of Superman. Dismally, she realized that the nurse's succinct summation was far more accurate than her own. It was just that she hated hospitals. She hated the medicinal smell—Eau de Rubbing Alcohol. Her nerve endings were rankled by the sound of the slight squeak the nurses' rubber-soled shoes made on the vinyl floor as they marched up and down the corridor. All the doctors, with their artificial smiles and their superior attitudes, made her want to snarl. Okay, so Doc Manny wasn't that bad.

Neither were the nurses. As long as she was being honest, Delany realized that what she hated most about hospitals was being in one. The thought of people moving around her, doing things to her and caring for her made her feel helpless and vulnerable. More than that, she hated the memories that a hospital invariably brought to the surface. Her brother, Michael, had died in this very hospital, and even after all these years, it still hurt to think about it.

In an attempt to push that thought away, Delany forced herself to smile, despite the pain in her cheek. "So I'm not the best patient in the world. I realize that. That's why I very rarely get sick."

The nurse chuckled, then left them alone. Delany tried not to stare as Zach walked toward the bed. The suit was gone. In its place, was a snug-fitting pair of faded blue jeans and a flannel shirt. His slightly long hair, now free of gel, fell softly and naturally along his neck and over his forehead. His heavy boots signaled with each thud on the floor that he was getting closer.

He wasn't exactly handsome—his face was too rigid and sharply angled for that. However, there was a certain virility about him that made Delany tingle with energy. If she had to choose one word in all the English language to describe him, it would be the one her female students used most frequently: hot! She wanted to curse the fact that he'd entered her life at the very moment she looked and felt her worst.

"I just came to check on you. I'm sure you've had a ton of visitors by now, so just let me know if you're too exhausted to talk."

Zach looked around the room, expecting to find some reminders of the visits. There were no brightly decorated cards or cheerful bouquets. There was only one flower arrangement sitting in the corner of the room. Casually, as if he was studying the work of the florist, Zach hovered over the flowers. It wasn't difficult to spot the white card stuck in the middle of the blooms.

"'Get well soon. From the gang at St. Joe's,'" Zach read aloud. He turned and found Delany staring at him with an uncertain expression. "It's not the most inspiring note I've ever read." Hell, even the guys at his office had done more for him after he'd been shot, and they were used to agents going down in the line of fire.

"It was nice of them," Delany defended. Then she added in explanation, "I told them it wasn't too serious. Just a small accident."

"Then I imagine it will be hard to explain the three casts and the back brace when they come to visit," Zach returned.

She tried again. "I didn't want everybody to make a big fuss. I also didn't want to answer a lot of questions. My principal will come out later this afternoon. I'll explain the whole story to him. It's easier that way." Delany loved the school secretary to pieces, but had she mentioned how seriously she was injured, she would've been described as near death before Kristine got through retelling the tale.

Zach nodded, but he still didn't understand. Where were Delany's friends? Why weren't they holding her hand and telling her everything was going to be all right? It was something he wanted to ask but didn't because they were still in the "practically strangers" category. Zach pulled up a chair close to the bed and decided to make small talk.

"So how do you feel?" Dumb question. "I mean how are you?"

Delany smiled at his attempt to make idle chatter, but she didn't mind the obvious questions. She was thrilled that he had visited at all. She hadn't been sure that he would. It made her feel special, yet Delany was certain it was an illogical feeling to have. "I ache a little, but it's not too bad."

"Your back?"

Shaking her head, Delany found herself at a loss for

words, an ailment that had never afflicted any teacher she had ever known before.

Zach saw that she didn't know what to say, so he leaned toward her to give her some of his strength. He reached out to take her right hand and again felt something more than just flesh touching flesh. He would have described it as electric. He was glad he didn't have to.

Tears threatened Delany, and she chided herself for being so weepy. She never cried, never. As a child, she had spent too much time crying and not enough time doing. As an adult, she had corrected that imbalance. But now, she was flat on her back and crying again.

"You're afraid." It was a statement that would hopefully compel her to talk.

"Yes. I don't want be paralyzed. I know that's selfish of me. Nobody asks to be paralyzed. Bad things just happen. But I don't know if I could take it." Delany wanted to believe that she would walk again. She felt that she would, but at the same time she couldn't be sure. It was the uncertainty and the waiting that were threatening her resolve to be positive.

She'd been nearly beaten to death because she had tried to save the life of a student, and she'd just called herself selfish. Zach frowned. There had to be such a thing as too good. "Listen, you aren't selfish. It's natural to feel that way. I felt that way."

Delany looked up at him. She remembered he'd said something about a car accident. "What happened? Did you have a similar condition?"

Not technically. What Zach had was a .38 caliber bullet pass through a vertebra because he was stupid. But she didn't have to know that. "My accident left me paralyzed for almost four weeks before the fracture healed and the swelling went down. It was a long recovery. But I did recover, and Doc Manny believes you will, too.''

Zach's words helped, but they didn't completely extinguish all of her fears. There were too many uncertainties. Delany wanted to change the subject to avoid dwelling on her worries, but she couldn't think of anything to say. She looked down at their joined hands, and a question popped into her mind and out of her mouth before she had a chance to stop it.

"Are you married?" Yow! How did she let that slip? It sounded as if she didn't want him to be married. From that, he might construe that she cared about him. But that was ridiculous. He was a stranger. Not only was he a stranger, but he was an appealing stranger. She currently looked like something the dog ate and threw back up. He would think her pathetic. She should retract the question immediately and save her pride a lashing, but if she did that, she would never know the answer.

"No, I'm not married. Are you?" Zach hadn't seen a ring, but it could've been stolen, or removed by one of the nurses. He had tried to pump Doc Manny for information, but either the doctor didn't know much or he was respecting his patient's privacy. Damn it. Zach wanted—no, he needed—to know more about Delany. She was fast becoming an obsession.

"No. Don't you think my husband would be here if I were married?"

Zach was taken aback. "I don't know. Maybe he's a jerk."

Delany was affronted. "Do I look like the sort of person who would marry a jerk?"

Zach knew he was treading on some tricky ground. Cautiously, he defended himself. "No, I just wanted to be sure."

"Why?" It was a bold move on her part, but she was still stinging from the jerky-husband comment.

What the hell was he supposed to say now? Then it struck him that two could play this game. "Why did you ask if I was married?"

A furious blush formed beneath her bruises, but she wasn't licked yet. "I asked you first."

Zach couldn't remember being so exasperated so quickly and by such a childish exchange. "I guess I didn't want some guy to walk in here and see me holding your hand. He might get the wrong idea."

"Well, I didn't want your wife to call the hospital wondering where you were, only to learn that you were holding some stranger's hand. She might get the wrong idea." It was a bold-faced lie and it didn't make much sense, but it seemed to put an end to the conversation. Delaney felt at a loss as to what should happen next. Self-consciously, she tugged her hand away from his.

Irrationally, Zach was angered. "I don't even know what I'm doing here. Your friends should be here to take care of you. Where the hell are they?"

Ruffled by his tone and the question, Delany attempted to avoid answering by retorting, "I told you, I don't need anyone to take care of me."

Zach was angry, but not angry enough to overlook the fact that she was evading his question. "Where are your friends? Why aren't they here? For that matter, where's your family?"

"That's none of your—"

"It is my damn business," Zach claimed. He knew what she had been about to say and ignored the fact that she was right. Then he reconsidered. He had no right to intrude on this woman's life, despite the compulsion he had to get to know her intimately. "You're right. It's not my business. I'll go."

Delany watched him stand and walk out of the room. As soon as the door closed behind him, the tears that had been threatening for two days burst from her eyes. Deep sobs were wrenched from her chest. Her ribs, her face and her whole body ached, but she couldn't stop. Delany didn't care about the future or what it would bring. All she knew was that she was tired...so tired.

"Before I leave—" Zach said, as he pushed the door back open. He was prepared to inform Ms. Sheridan of a few more things that he had thought of on his way out, when he was stopped short by her tears. She was sobbing so hard that she didn't notice his return. Had he done that to her? Or was she in pain? Spurred by that thought, he rushed to her side. "What is it? Are you hurt?"

Delany shook her head, unable to speak past the sobs in her throat. She didn't want him to see her like this, but she couldn't make herself stop. Why had he come back?

Zach waited patiently and stroked her blond locks to soothe her. He murmured what he hoped were comforting words. "Shh. I'm sorry. Shh. It's okay."

Finally recovering her voice, Delany felt compelled to tell him everything, "My family's gone. My parents and my brother are dead." Delany took a deep breath, holding back the tears, "I miss them. I miss them very much. I know people. I know lots of people. But I don't really...I mean, I don't have..." Delany couldn't finish the sentence.

It seemed so horrible that at her age she had no real friends. But it had dawned on her as she lay in the hospital bed that she was lonely. Minutes had ticked by, and the only faces she saw were those of the nurses. Delany felt angry and betrayed that none of her friends had come to see her, despite the lie she had told them about being in a car accident. Someone should have come.

When Delany tried to think of who that might be, no one came to mind. She was friendly with all of the teachers at her school, but she had always been too busy to socialize with them outside of work. Dan, her principal, was a great boss and a great ear to bend, but that was as far as their relationship extended. She didn't know the people in her apartment building. And all her activities outside of school focused on the children. In truth, they were the people she was closest to, but they were the last people she wanted to see. Not like this.

Her breathing under control, Delany turned to face Zach. "I don't have any friends. Isn't that the most pathetic thing you've ever heard?"

It was the most ridiculous thing he'd ever heard. "I don't understand. I haven't known you that long, but I know you're selfless. I know you're stubborn. I also know you're amusing. And aside from a few harsh words that you said to the nurse, you seem to be a genuinely friendly person." Zach smiled as he remembered how shocked he'd been that such a delicate-looking thing could say what she did.

Delany smiled, too, only slightly ashamed that she had used such vulgarity. As for an explanation, she was still working on it. "I guess I don't have much time for friends. I do a great deal of charity work. I spend most of my free time organizing fund-raisers and speaking with sponsors. I hadn't realized how much I'd isolated myself until this morning."

"What happened to your parents and your brother?"

"My brother—" Delany started hesitantly "—my brother died of a...drug overdose. It affected my parents badly. They were older when they had us. My mother was forty when I was born, and forty-two when Michael arrived. After Michael's death, Mom aged a hundred years. She was crushed. A year later, she had a stroke and died. The next year, my dad suffered a heart attack and followed her. I think he died of a broken heart."

Zach was stunned. To lose all of her family in two years was expecting too much of one person. He marveled at how strong she was. Brave. Selfless. Strong. Intimidating. "I'm sorry about your parents and your brother."

Delany nodded in response to his sympathy and let the sorrow wash over her. It had been two years since she lost her father and the pain had lessened. There were moments, though, when she realized that she was alone in the world and that she always would be alone. Those moments haunted her. Reaching out, she again clasped Zach's hand in her own. She didn't feel so alone anymore.

"Is that why you do it?" Zach wasn't sure he should have asked the question, but he felt that if nothing else, he had gained her trust. He sensed that she hadn't mentioned her brother's death in a long time, judging by the hesitant quality of her voice.

"Do what?" Delany asked.

"Play the crusader. You're here because you tried to save some girl. You have no friends because you spend all your time raising money to help people. Hell, you felt guilty because you prayed that you wouldn't be paralyzed. Do you do it because of your brother? Are you still trying to save him?" Zach was no psychologist, but it seemed clear to him that Delany's parents weren't the only ones affected by her brother's death.

A flash of indignation rose in her eyes, but then she resigned herself to the fact that he had realized something about her that no other person ever had. "He was my younger brother. I loved him. It was my job to watch out for him. I was a college senior, and I was worried about graduating and getting a job. I didn't know about his friends. I didn't realize his grades had dropped."

"It wasn't your fault that your brother decided to take drugs. Blame him for making such a stupid choice. Blame the dealers who sell it and the people who supply it. Don't blame yourself." Zach didn't tell her to blame the agents who hadn't been able to stop the sellers and suppliers. He knew there would have been too much guilt laced in his voice. She might have suspected he hadn't been up-front about what he did for a living.

Delany was not about to let herself off that easily. "I should've done more. My parents realized he was addicted long before I did. He seemed distant, aloof, even abrupt at times, but I never thought... He was my little brother. My parents sent him to a detox center. But he ran away. A week later, an officer showed up at our door. Michael had overdosed and was in a coma at this hospital. Two days later, he died."

"What do you think you're accomplishing by devoting your life to his memory, your whole life to other people? It won't bring Michael back, but it will burn you out before your time. You deserve to have your own life, your own family."

His words made sense, and they were things that her subconscious had whispered to her before, usually late at night when she wished desperately for a husband and

children of her own. She had always felt guilty afterward. She wanted a life that Michael would never have.
Her warped logic reasoned that if Michael had been
deprived of a life, then she should be, as well. It was
only fair, especially since she hadn't done enough to
save him.

But after listening to Zach, she thought her logic
sounded awfully like that of a would-be martyr. Delany
didn't want to be a martyr; she just wanted to get over
the pain and the self-recriminations. "How do you stop
the guilt?"

It was a good question. One that Zach himself hadn't
answered in his own life. He was here now because he
felt guilty. No, that wasn't true. Initially, he had stayed
with her out of guilt. Now he was here because he was
her friend. "I don't know how you stop it. But I do
know this. Right now you've got to concentrate on
yourself. You've got to work hard to get healthy, and
when the casts come off you've got to work hard to
walk again. You're going to need a friend."

"Are you my friend?" Delany asked, knowing what
he implied by his words.

"Yeah, I'm your friend." Zach squeezed her hand in
recognition of the bond they had just made. He didn't
want to be only her friend—there was too much between them too quickly for that—but it was a good start.

"As your friend, can I ask you a favor?" Delany's
voice was sweet, full of warmth and humor, the tears
and the bad memories now left behind.

"Sheesh. Give me, give me, give me. Is that all you
think about?"

She laughed at his teasing. He was going to be a good
friend to have. "I want a diet Pepsi, and these stubborn

hospital people refuse to cooperate. Would you get one for me?''

With a deep sigh, Zach stood. "I suppose so. Next thing I know, you'll be demanding chocolate."

"Now that you mention it...a chocolate bar would go a long way toward curing me of my loathing of hospitals."

"I'll be back with the goods. Don't go anywhere, okay?" Zach warned in all seriousness.

Her legs had been hoisted three feet in the air. Her whole body was immobilized, and he was telling her to stay put. "You're funny. You're very funny."

With a smirk, Zach left the room.

For one sinful moment, Delany took that opportunity to admire his tight buttocks encased in soft denim. His shoulders were wide. So wide they looked like they could carry the weight of the world on them. Yes, he would be a good friend to have.

Gosh, what she wouldn't give for a little foundation right now, and perhaps a lipstick. Delany didn't have many moments of vanity, but this was one of them. She wanted to be attractive to this man. She wanted this man.

It was a stunning thought, especially in her present condition, but a liberating one. For years, Delany had tried to deny her sensuality, her femininity. It wasn't something she allowed herself to think about because it wasn't necessary to her cause. Fighting as she did for the underprivileged children of Tacoma, the last thing she needed to be was sensual. Concentrating all her efforts toward helping those in need, Delany had denied her femininity.

Now she wanted it back. Zach was right. She'd spent the past few years dedicating herself to others in an attempt to eradicate her guilt. It wasn't that she didn't believe in what she did, and she doubted that she would ever give up trying to do the best for her students, but she wanted a life of her own. She deserved a life. It felt good to admit that. And sometime, between yesterday morning and this afternoon, she had realized that she wanted Zach to be a part of that life.

Never before had she connected with someone so quickly. Delany didn't believe in love at first sight, but she did believe that some people clicked right off the bat. She and Zach clicked. It was amazing really, since she had been such a shrew both to the nurse and to him at times. Not only had she behaved badly, but then she had burst into tears and wept all over him. It was a wonder that he stayed.

Which brought up the question, why did he stay? Delany hated to think that there was any reason for his presence other than his sincere desire to be her friend. But nowadays, people often were hesitant to go around making friends. Originally, of course, he had stayed to check up on her. That was understandable. But why did he return? Although she had wanted him to, her skeptical self said something wasn't right.

The door opened, and Delany assumed Zach was returning with her treats. She was quick to cover her disappointment when her principal walked through the door.

"Oh, my God!" Dan cried, stunned. "Kristine said you were in a small car accident. I would hate to see what a big accident was like," he finished sympathetically.

"Sit down, Dan, and I'll tell you the gruesome tale."

Her shocked visitor nodded and took the seat recently vacated by Zach. Delany began to relay the details of the attack with great detachment. She had begun to focus on getting well, and to do that she had to let go of the fear and the pain of the assault. It was over.

"There is one thing I need you to do, Dan. I want you to find Cici. I need to know that she made it out safely and that she's back in school." Delany was selfish enough not to want her efforts to have been in vain.

Dan shook his head. "I can't believe the lengths you went to on behalf of a student. I'll find her. But the other students will want to know what happened. How should I schedule their visits?"

"I don't want them to visit," Delany stated firmly, prepared to answer this question.

"How can you say that? Those kids think the world of you. How am I to explain your absence, for what appears to be the rest of the year, without some sort of explanation? And if I do explain, they'll insist on coming to see you."

Delany sighed. She understood Dan's dilemma, but she was going to have to be insistent. "I don't want them to see me like this, Dan. I've worked very hard to gain their respect and to prove that I wasn't some kind of young, dumb blonde. If they see me like this, like a defenseless victim, it will affect the way they treat me when I'm better. It's hard for kids to see any authority figure in a position of weakness. I don't want to put them through that. I don't want to put myself through that. The last thing I need is pity."

The principal nodded, reluctantly respecting her position. "What should I tell them?"

"Tell them I was in a car accident. I'm fine, but the doctor recommended some rest, so I'm taking a long vacation. Or tell them I ran off with some handsome rogue, got pregnant, and now I'm having my child in secret to protect the good name of St. Joe's.'' Delany chuckled at her own dramatic fabrication and the look of horror that crossed Dan's face.

"I'll tell them you took a long vacation at the doctor's request. There isn't anyone who wouldn't believe that you work too hard." Dan stood and smiled down at Delany. He reached out, took her hand and gave it a squeeze to let her know that she had his support.

At that moment, Zach walked back into Delany's room with a diet Pepsi and a chocolate bar, only to find some man standing over her. A surge of jealousy rushed through him, almost causing him to gasp. She was his. He found her first, so he got dibs. Zach didn't know the joker who was holding her hand, but he was going to have to leave. If he had wanted Delany, then he should have acted sooner.

After those first childlike emotions ran through him, Zach waited for his sanity to return. He'd just met the woman and now he was behaving like a jealous fool. He had typically mocked friends who would allow a woman to affect them that radically. They would return his laughter now. After allowing his initial reaction to subside, he could now calmly and rationally deal with the situation before him.

"Who the hell are you, and what are you doing to Delany?" Okay, not so rational, but damn it, he couldn't seem to control himself.

Dan looked at him, but instead of answering the question, he asked Delany, "The handsome rogue?"

Delany had to laugh. Dan's question had hit the proverbial nail. Perhaps she had been subconsciously thinking about Zach when she told Dan the story. Or more accurately, she hadn't stopped thinking about Zach since the moment she woke up and found him asleep in the chair next to her bed.

Zach knew he was being excluded from a private joke, and if the hand-holding hadn't sent him over the edge, this did. "I asked you a question and I want an answer. Who are you? You're not her husband. And if you were any kind of friend, you would've been here yesterday at her side doing everything you could to comfort her."

The impact of Zach's words wasn't lost on Dan, if his look of guilt was any indication.

"He's right, Delany. I haven't been much of a friend," Dan apologized as he looked down at her, seeing in her bruised face a testament to her courage. "As for who I am, I'm Dan Banks, her principal at St. Joe's. She works with me."

"Nice to know you're so concerned about your staff. Must be a hell of a place to go to school, what with such caring colleagues." Zach's voice was controlled, but his sarcasm wasn't missed by Delany.

"Zach, stop it," Delany scolded. Secretly, it felt good to have someone stand up for her. However, it wasn't good policy to insult the boss. "St. Joe's is a wonderful place. If anyone has been distant, it's been me. Dan, this is Zachary Montgomery. He found me after the attack and made sure I got to the hospital."

Rather than offer his hand, Zach crossed his arms over his chest, the cola and the candy bar acting like the Egyptian symbols of authority for a pharaoh. It was a clear message, one that the principal couldn't miss. "I guess I'll be leaving. I'll check in on you later, Delany. Mr. Montgomery." Dan hesitated. "Thank you for being here."

"Somebody had to. You don't need to check in, either. I'll be here to watch over her." It wasn't a command or an order. It was a warning to keep his hands off. For a second, it looked as if the principal might consider challenging Zach's words. But only for a second.

"Take good care of her," Dan warned, then left the room before Zach could reply.

Delany was stunned. She didn't know whether to be furious or flattered. Zach was calmly opening her treats as if he didn't care about the harsh words he had uttered to her principal.

"He's my boss," she said, stating the obvious.

"He's a jerk. And he should have been here yesterday. He knows it, too." Zach was not perturbed by her outrage as he unwrapped the candy from its package.

"You had no right."

"I have every right. You're my responsibility now. Mine to take care of and watch over. I can't do that with people like him in the way." Zach broke off a piece of the chocolate bar.

Delany tried to make sense of what he said. "I've always been my own keeper. Even as a child, I was fiercely independent. I'm responsible for me. No one else."

Sitting on the edge of the bed with candy in hand, Zach tried to put into words what he felt. He accepted the fact that he was responsible for her being here. He acknowledged that part of him had connected with her as soon as he'd looked out that window and seen a lone woman trying to fight off a group of attackers to save a child. She was fierce, this lady. Fierce, proud, and stubborn. She was also very afraid and very weak. Whether she realized it or not, she needed someone else's strength right now. She needed someone else to shoulder her burdens. She needed to rest. He would see that she did.

"You need to be taken care of now. I know you hate it. I hated it, too. People like us aren't used to the pampering. We're not used to saying the words, 'I can't.' But you know you need help. Once you accept that, you'll save yourself a great deal of frustration. Now open up."

Obediently, Delany opened her mouth, responding automatically to the words used so often in the past two days. Only the people who had said those words before were women in plain white uniforms with cold thermometers in their hands. This time, Zach used his fingers to gently push the soft, tasty chocolate into her mouth. Her cheek was still sore so she quickly closed her lips, and in the process trapped his fingers inside her mouth. Stunned at the warmth that seemed to seep into her belly, Delany looked up into his eyes.

If she had to describe them, she would say they smoldered. His lips were turned up in a smile as if he was pleased with the predicament he was in. With gentle care, he extracted his two fingers from her mouth, but not before he ran them along the length of her bottom lip and used the gentle pad of his thumb to brush the remaining chocolate from her lips.

With a gulp, Delany swallowed the chocolate. "Good," she muttered inanely as she felt the heat rush to her cheeks. Thank goodness for the bruises. She hadn't blushed since…she never blushed. "The chocolate, I mean," she corrected belatedly, realizing what he might interpret from that one word.

"Yes, it was," Zach replied, mysteriously. He was delighted with this new technique he'd discovered to devour a Butterfinger candy bar. Perhaps he should write the company a letter, although he doubted such steamy stuff would make it in a television commercial.

It took a moment to regain her composure, and when Zach broke off another piece of chocolate, she quickly held up her hand to ward him off. Her body was in no condition to be aroused twice in one day. Frankly, her mind wasn't, either.

She returned to the topic that had been forgotten in the midst of such tasty fingers. Uh, chocolate, she revised furiously. "So my job is to let you care for me?" she asked. "I thought that's what the doctors and nurses were for," she stated a little flippantly, not content to let him get away with such high-handedness.

Zach thought about that for a moment, then accepted her challenge. "The doctors and nurses can help to heal you. But only I can feed you a Butterfinger. I can also fetch you an unlimited supply of diet Pepsi on command." He smiled at his own gallantry.

"How handy. What else can you do?"

Zach arched his brow in shock. "Diet Pepsi isn't enough for you?"

"Diet Pepsi can only take you so far, then you have to go to the bathroom."

Zach laughed at her offbeat humor. "What else would milady wish?" he asked, striving to be even more gallant.

Delany decided to play along with his game and, in response, raised her chin several inches. "Well, occasionally I like to be read to." That wasn't quite true. Delany could vaguely remember her father reading to her as a little girl, but that had ended when Michael came along. She was just old enough to look at picture books on her own by then.

"Let me guess," Zach said, imagining the type of books a teacher would read. "Faulkner?"

Delany shook her head.

"Shakespeare?"

Again, she shook her head.

"I got it. Sir Arthur Conan Doyle. You're a classical mystery fan, right?"

Delany shook her head again, this time allowing a small smile to break free from her pretended snobbery.

"I give up," Zach relented, a little wary of her answer.

"Romance novels," Delany stated, without a hint of hesitation. She burst out laughing at the groan Zach emitted. His face was a picture at agony.

"Not those sappy books with that Fabulous guy on the cover," Zach moaned.

"It's Fabio," Delany corrected. "And yes, you can bet that anything with his face on the cover is bound to be perfect."

"Romance it is," Zach sighed, his shoulders slumping. The motion made him look down at his watch, and he realized that visiting hours were over. Had he been here that long?

Delany saw him look at his watch. "Time's up?"

He nodded reluctantly and eased his weight off the bed so as not to shake her body. The back brace kept her immobile, but he didn't want to do anything that might jar her and cause her pain.

"Zach?" Delany questioned as he stood, something suddenly occurring to her. "When you were in the hospital, who took care of you?"

"I had doctors and nurses like you do. A few buddies from the office would stop by off and on." Zach's family hadn't been able to deal with his situation. In retrospect, Zach had been lonely. Maybe that's why he stayed now. He didn't want Delany to feel for one minute the emptiness he'd felt. It was too consuming at times.

"If I'd been there, I would've taken good care of you." Her words were strong; her tone adamant.

Zach looked down at Delany's pale blond hair, her face a mass of bruises. She seemed to be the frailest human being in the world. If a feather landed on her head, she would break into pieces. Yet, he believed her. Had she been there, she would've taken good care of him. The best care.

"You get your rest. I'll see you tomorrow." Zach turned and started to leave.

"Oh, and Zach," Delany called right before he opened the door.

He turned in response and saw a twinkle in her blue eyes. Those eyes made him forget all the bruises. "What?"

"Fabio has got nothing on you," she confessed in an attempt to tease him. Unfortunately, it sounded all too true.

"Damn straight," he replied, his tone firm. And then he left the room.

Chapter 3

Delany must be dreaming. Actually, it seemed more like a nightmare to Zach's eyes. For the second day in a row, he stood in the doorway of the hospital room, and hesitated before he stepped inside. He was carrying one of the books she had requested, lurid cover and all, and a six-pack of diet Pepsi. The medical staff wouldn't be too thrilled with him, but what the hell? It was all Delany wanted, and it was the least he could give her.

Delany was stretched out on the bed, her arm, legs and torso immobile. Only her head moved. She thrashed it back and forth against the pillow as if she were being slapped. Whimpered sounds of pain and fear burst past her lips. Zach knew that she was in the middle of a very intense nightmare. He didn't have to guess what it was about. Delany didn't have very far to search for her nightmares. All she had to do was remember.

There was a rule. You weren't supposed to wake people if they walked in their sleep. It startled them and caused irreparable damage. Zach couldn't recall whether or not that rule applied to someone in the grip of a nightmare. He didn't care. At the moment, all he knew was that he couldn't stand to watch her suffer for one more minute.

Quietly, he made his way toward the bed. He didn't want any sudden noises in the room to add to her fear. He dropped his gifts on the table by her bed, then very deliberately moved his hand over her forehead, brushing the bangs away from her damp cheeks as he did so, in an attempt to still her thrashing head. As if there'd been a laying on of hands in a revival meeting, a miracle occurred. Delany instantly quieted at the gentle touch, only the small whimpers emanating from her throat giving any indication that she was still afraid.

"Delany," Zach said, his voice firm but soft.

Now the whimpers stopped. However, Delany's eyes remained closed. Zach realized that she didn't want to wake up. Maybe she didn't realize she was dreaming. Maybe she thought if she woke up, it wouldn't be just a nightmare—it would be real. Or perhaps her subconscious knew what was waiting for her in the real world. Better to stay in a fearful dream where you were whole and walking than to wake up and realize you were broken and paralyzed.

Hiding from reality wasn't going to make it go away. Zach knew that from years of experience. It was part of the reason, he believed, that he went into undercover work in the first place. Being no one, with no identity, no home, and no close connections made it easy to think that there was nothing real in this world. Zach had spent his youth in a world as fake as a glass ring. He had spent his manhood in a lie, as well. He couldn't say what reality was. But as he gazed upon Delany's face, he was beginning to think that he was getting closer. He wanted Delany to join him there.

"It's time to face the music, blue eyes. You'll see it's not so bad. I'm here, and I'll stay with you." Zach couldn't say what compelled him, but he bent over her stiff body and placed a gentle kiss atop her forehead, between the eyes that had so captivated him when he first saw them. He was Prince Charming and she was Sleeping Beauty, or was it Snow White? Zach didn't know which. What he did know was that ever since he'd met Delany, he'd felt as if he'd walked into the middle of a fairy tale. Everything was coming into focus for him, but at the same time he refused to believe that the real world could be so wonderful, so dreamlike.

"Wake up, Snow White."

Eyes popped open to reveal a sea of blue. There was terror in those eyes, but that soon receded and what replaced it Zach couldn't say.

"You're back," Delany whispered as if she were still dreaming.

"Of course I'm back," Zach replied, slightly offended that she doubted him.

"I wasn't sure. I'd hoped, but I wasn't sure." Delany had struggled valiantly through the night not to get her hopes up. He's not coming, she'd told herself a thousand times. Each time she said it, her heart whispered back, Yes, he is. She then countered, No, he's definitely not coming. The war raged on between common sense and wishful thinking all night long until the wee hours of the morning when Delany had drifted into a restless slumber.

Restless. Delany wondered why she knew that. Then in a rush it all came back to her.

"Ahh, hurt," she cried, unmindful of what she said.

Zach knew what she meant. Instantly, he reached out to clutch her hand in his. He bent low so that his face met hers with only inches to spare. "You were dreaming when I walked in," he explained.

"No, I wasn't dreaming. I was remembering. Why do I have to remember it, Zach? I don't want to remember it. I don't want to think about it ever."

"You'll have to think about it when you talk to the police," Zach stated.

"The police were already here. I told them I couldn't remember anything." Delany's voice was firm.

"Why? You must have gotten a good look at these monsters. Your testimony could put them in jail." Zach was incensed. He believed in the justice system. He knew that it was up to people to make it work.

"I don't want to spend the next year of my life trying to put these kids in jail only to have them walk free a few years later. Most of them were under eighteen. They wouldn't even be tried as adults." No, that wasn't the truth. Delany owed Zach the truth. She just hoped she could make him understand. "It was personal, Zach. I put myself in that situation. I did it for Cici. It has nothing to do with the police; it has nothing to do with the legal system. It was me against them, and I lost. Now I have to deal with consequences on my own."

Zach shook his head. He didn't agree with her, but he accepted her decisions. He also knew what it meant to deal with the demons. The demons from his own shooting still chased him. When he first woke up, he didn't want to recall the details, either. Nothing about that night was worth reliving. On the other hand, he hadn't been able to push the thoughts from his mind. All the times he'd tried, the obnoxious demons had pushed their way into his head and stayed there, refusing to relinquish their hold on him.

Zach finally came to terms with the idea that if the memories weren't going to go away, he was going to have to deal with them head-on. He was still dealing with them. All he could say about the experience was that it didn't get any harder.

"You may not want to relive the experience in court. I don't agree with you, but I understand. But Delany, you have no choice other than to remember. The gang didn't leave you with amnesia. They left you with broken bones." Zach moved away from the bed and brought the chair close so that he could sit with her. He felt silly for being here so early in the morning as if he had nothing better to do, but then, he didn't have anything better to do. Change that. He didn't have anything that he wanted to do more than he wanted to be with her.

"Will the fear always stay with me? I feel as if I'm being watched right now. If I walked out that hospital door, if I could walk, I know some of them would be there waiting for me. It's like they're not done with me yet." Paranoid, people would call her, but Delany couldn't stop feeling that way.

Zach pondered on her fears. "You said you didn't want to go to a victims' group because you didn't feel like a victim. It was a good mind-set to have. I think you need to go back to that. They're the cowards. They're the ones who sit in their cars and fire bullets at anything that moves. They're the ones who beat women and make twelve-year-old children sell their drugs. You don't need to fear them. You need to pity them."

"Can I hate them?" She didn't want permission, only his opinion.

"Don't worry. I'm not some shrink who's going to tell you that hate will only fuel the anger inside you, or anything like that. I'm all for hate." It was what the shrink had said to him. In all fairness to the doctor, he had helped Zach work through some stuff. If Zach had been more inclined to open up to him, maybe he could've helped some more. Zach wouldn't let himself be that vulnerable to anyone. The issues in his life that he needed to deal with, he would deal with on his own.

"I don't think hate will take over my life. But it's not going away. I have every right to hate them. Maybe it's wrong, but I can't let go of it yet. I don't think I'll be able to until I know I can walk."

With a shrug and a nod of his head, Zach agreed. "Sounds like a good plan to me."

Having talked about it, Delany felt better. The fear wasn't gone, but Zach had pushed it aside for the moment. It was a welcome relief. "Thank you for listening. It helps."

"Talking about it is a way of confronting the demons. It makes them seem smaller in your mind somehow. I'll be here to listen any time you want to pull those demons back out of the closet." Zach smiled, his impish grin suddenly making his face seem boyish.

"You're not very old, are you?" Delany reached out to touch him with her good hand, briefly tracing the harsh lines around his face. It wasn't until she'd made contact with his skin and the power of that touch had made its impact on her that she realized how intimate she was being with a near stranger. No, not a stranger anymore. A friend. "I'm sorry," she apologized hastily. She lowered her eyes and toyed with the cast on her arm. "I didn't mean to be so forward."

It was Zach's opinion that she could be as forward

as she liked as often as she liked. For some reason, her touch had jolted him like an electric shock. He wasn't even sure if he liked it. Touching someone shouldn't be so intense. Zach felt intimidated, yet powerful at the same time, as if he was a part of something that was larger than himself.

"I'm not old. Not yet anyway. The lines," Zach commented, as he pointed to the marks in his face Delany had previously investigated, "were hard earned. They're not really an accurate representation."

"It's only going to get worse when you open up your restaurant," Delany informed him. "Speaking of which, shouldn't you be out speaking with real-estate agents? I don't want to pull you away from your work. Although I am glad you came." Delany didn't want to sound ungrateful. She couldn't be more grateful if she tried. Zach had pulled her out of a nightmare that seemed to consume her.

The lie. Zach almost forgot. He was a liar. It was what he did for a living. It was what he did for a life. "I've spoken to some people. Don't worry, I've got plenty of time."

"What are you going to call the place?"

It had been hard enough to come up with the restaurant idea. Now she wanted a name. "I don't know. What do you think?"

Delany seized the challenge. It was something she could put her mind to while her body lay inert. "It would have to be something catchy, but cool. It's vital that it be only one word. Or it has to be a name that can be shortened to one word. If you're trying to appeal to the college crowd, you don't want them to have to tax their brains enough to remember more than one word. They've got enough information crammed in there already."

Zach was surprised by her zeal, but intrigued, as well. "Do you put all this thought into your lessons?"

"Absolutely. You can't just feed a bunch of high school kids lectures on wars that happened eons ago, and stories about presidents who are long dead, without some sort of presentation. It's all in the packaging." Delany was proud of her skill as a teacher. Since it was the only thing of value she had in her life, she felt she ought to be very good at it.

"And how do you package it?" Zach surprised himself by being fascinated with what Delany was telling him. In his line of work, Zach didn't have many chances to meet normal people. He dealt with other agents and scum. He never went to regular places or talked with regular people, like teachers or doctors or businesspeople. His previous romantic relationships were usually with female agents looking for the same kind of commitment he was—none. Delany was like a creature from another planet to him.

"I stand on top of desks and recite famous speeches. I reenact battles. I dress up in costumes. I do cartwheels if I have to. Whatever it takes to get the job done."

Those were ominous words. Words that Zach had always lived by. He did whatever it took to get the job done, too. At least cartwheels weren't part of what was required of him. He was hell at gymnastics.

"I would like to see you teach someday. I bet I'd learn a lot more the second time around." Actually, Zach couldn't imagine being able to concentrate on history with a teacher who had eyes like Delany's. Yes, his high school experience the second time around would be something special if she were his teacher.

"What I love about history is that there are so many new things to know. People assume it's a dead subject, but it's not. We learn new things about the past every day. It keeps unfolding and changing, just like nature." With an embarrassed smile, Delany put her hand over her mouth. "I get carried away sometimes."

"It's important to love your work." Zach didn't anymore. "So tell me about some of the changes. I haven't heard of any significant breaks with the history I learned."

"Well, take the Kennedy assassination," Delany offered, thinking back to the reports she had piled high on her desk at school. It made her anxious to think of all that work being left undone. There was no way for a substitute to correct them, at least not to Delany's specifications. Perhaps she could have Kristine deliver the work. It would give her something constructive to do.

"Oh, no! You're not one of those fanatics who believe it was some kind of government conspiracy, are you? Why can't you just accept the fact that Oswald killed him?" Zach didn't dwell on imaginary theories. Until something could be proven to him, he wanted no part of it.

"Because Oswald didn't kill Kennedy. Evidence bears that out. In the seventies, sound research was done on the Zapruder film that proved conclusively that shots had been fired from at least two different directions. The government has it on file, but has kept it so quiet that people don't even believe it exists. You can't tell me that's not a conspiracy." Delany's face was infused with color, and her eyes sparkled to life. The thrill of a historical debate was in her reach. She lived for these moments. That thought made her pause. If she'd been living for historical debates, how much more of her life had she missed?

"Whose conspiracy? Are you saying all the government agencies got together and planned the assassination of their president? All the government agencies can't get together over what brand of toilet paper to buy. You can't tell me that they were able to pull off a conspiracy so large. The press would have been all over it." Zach knew from experience the impracticality of coordinating operations between the various agencies.

"The press was in on it," Delany whispered as if members of the conspiracy were outside her door, waiting to pounce. Wow, maybe she really was paranoid.

Zach burst out laughing, not so much because of what she said, but at how she said it. "You are a true romantic. Let me tell you, the government and its agents aren't as exciting as you give them credit for being. They're really pretty ordinary."

"And how would you know this?"

Caught in his lies once again. It was becoming increasingly difficult to avoid the traps he set for himself. "A good friend of mine worked for the FBI." That was true. Mort had worked for the FBI for years before he moved over to the DEA.

Delany sighed with resignation. She didn't know anyone who worked for the government. Still, just because he did, didn't mean he was right. "Believe what you will. Personally, I think the people have a right to know what actually happened. And so do my students. One of them even wrote a paper on it for his research project."

"Research projects, huh? I hated those when I was in school," Zach confessed.

"Of course you did. They take hard work, patience

and diligence. Few high school students are gifted with those qualities at that age.'' That's why Delany assigned the reports, so that she could encourage those qualities as well as teach some history. ''Speaking of those reports, I left a pile of them on my desk. I hate to think how long it's going to be before the kids have a chance to know how they did. It's really important to give them instant feedback. If you wait too long, they'll forget what all the work was about.''

''You're not in any condition to be grading papers.'' Zach didn't want to state the obvious, but she was flat on her back and she was going to remain there for a long time.

''All it takes is a strong pair of eyes and all the patience that my students don't possess. I know I've already burdened you by asking for favors,'' Delany began, her eyes pointing in the direction of the soda and the reading material. She hoped that Zach would get the hint.

''Fabio isn't going to be enough, I take it.'' His tone was sardonic, but Zach truly admired her dedication to her work. Especially when he felt himself lacking the same dedication.

Impishly, Delany grinned. ''If I asked the secretary to bring the papers by, she would be spreading rumors of my near demise all over the school. I don't want the students to realize the extent of my injuries. I'd ask Dan, but he's too busy.''

''Can I ask why you don't want the kids to know?'' Many people in Delany's place might feel that those injuries were a testament to her courage. They should be worn with pride, if such a thing made sense.

''I know my students would want to come and visit, but they wouldn't know how to treat me. I don't want to put them through that sort of awkwardness.'' She didn't want to put herself through it, either.

The angel was back. He couldn't help but respect her and admire her. He also couldn't help feeling like a rodent around her. Where did her goodness come from? Where did someone learn to be so giving? Zach considered the idea that he had witnessed too much evil in the world. His life spent among the dishonorable and depraved must have left him tainted. It wasn't that he wanted to paint everyone he knew with the same brush, but it had been his experience that badness was more a part of human nature than goodness.

Delany was the exception. Or his first assumption was correct, and she was an angel.

''So you want me to go to the school and bring you back these papers. I assume your...boss—'' Zach tripped over the word ''—will know how to get into your classroom.''

''Yes,'' a slightly bemused Delany replied. Zach's distaste for Dan was evident. The reason for it was still vague. ''You'll find a stack of about ten papers piled on top of one another on my desk.''

''Ten? That's a small class.''

''It's only half the class. The rest I put in my book bag,'' Delany clarified.

''Where's your book bag?''

''At home.''

Her tone verged on the hesitant. What was left unspoken was the question of whether or not Zach would be willing to go to her home for the remaining papers. Home implied an intimacy that maybe Delany wasn't prepared to share. Zach didn't know if he wanted her to share, either. He asked anyway.

''Do you want me to go to your apartment? Get the

rest of the reports?'' As soon as the words were out of his mouth, Zach knew how much he wanted her to say yes. How she lived would teach him so much. Her angel wings would become tarnished if he saw socks scattered on the floor, dishes piled in the sink, and dust accumulated on the shelves.

No, her mind answered readily. Her mouth, however, wasn't cooperating. It wasn't that she wanted the reports that badly; she just didn't want to refuse Zach entrance. Allowing him inside her apartment was tantamount to allowing him into her life. The private part of her wanted to refuse him, to push him away with everything inside her. She wasn't used to sharing her life with people. Her family was all she had had for a long time, and she never called herself close even to them. Delany was too independent by nature. With her family gone, she accepted the idea that it was going to be only her. Alone. No one else. Now, if she let Zach into her apartment, he'd be a part of her life. Now, there'd be someone else.

More casually than she felt, she answered, "Sure. If you don't mind?''

"I don't mind at all. The keys?''

"You can get a spare from the apartment manager. I called to let him know where I was. He's collecting my mail. Tell him that I sent you. He's the cautious type, so I'll let him know you're coming. Don't be insulted if he gives you the third degree.''

An awkward silence descended.

This was a mistake, Delany thought.

How long do I have to stay here before I can start snooping? Zach wondered.

"If you'll give me the address, then I'll be going. That way I'll have time to get your stuff back to you before visiting hours are over." Zach stood then, careful to keep his tone neutral and relaxed. He didn't want to spook Delany at this point. Not when he was so close to her inner sanctum.

"It's the Waterfront Gardens, on Stadium Way." Delany rattled off the rest of the directions and her apartment number, knowing that it was too late to change her mind. Besides, it wasn't as if she had something to hide. "St. Joe's is on Union Avenue. You can't miss it. There's a sign at the bottom of the driveway. Turn after you see the sign."

"I'll be back soon. Get your rest."

"My rest didn't get me anywhere last time," Delany reminded him, not anticipating another nap.

Ripping one of the cans from its plastic holder, Zach placed the soda in her hand. "Drink this and read a few pages of the book I brought. That should be enough to hold back the demons until I return. Then we'll deal with them together." With those words, Zach left the room, his pace something less than a trot.

Together. It was a foreign concept to Delany. She couldn't deny that she liked the sound of it. She especially appreciated the idea that she wasn't going to have to face her fears alone. Zach called them demons, and he wasn't wrong. They were beasts with claws, and they caused her as much pain as the actual blows the gang members had inflicted upon her.

Thank goodness Zach was here to help her through this. Delany didn't know if she'd be able to handle everything by herself. For the first time in her life, she needed someone. For the first time in her life, someone was there for her. What if she was relying on him too much? What if he left? It happened. People changed their minds. Zach was nothing more than a Good Samaritan. Once he decided that he'd done enough, he would leave, wouldn't he?

Delany couldn't answer any of the questions that plagued her. All she could do was hold on to Zach with both hands, and pray that he wouldn't let go quite yet. Her only other option was to let go completely and discover for herself if she was going to drown in her fears and pain. Surviving tragedy wasn't new to Delany. It was a question of whether she had already survived too much. Her reserve of strength was dangerously low. One more tragedy, and the fragile threads holding her together might snap. No, Delany thought, I need Zach. I need him. Just for a little while, please let me keep him.

Zach drove his rented car out to Union Avenue in search of the illustrious St. Joe's Prep. He wanted to pick up Delany's papers and leave as quickly as possible to avoid any contact with students or staff who might be curious about Delany's condition. She'd made it perfectly clear that she didn't want the kids to realize the kind of shape she was in, and Zach had no problems keeping her wishes.

The scenery drifted by as he drove. Tacoma was different during the day. Different from the Tacoma Zach knew at night. The Hilltop was a frightening place, but it was only a section of the whole city. Zach saw that neatly kept houses lined the streets. He saw kids riding their bikes and playing tag on their front lawns. Shops and restaurants dotted the landscape like any other town. It was a city with a small-town feeling. Zach began to understand why Delany chose to remain. Tacoma needed loyal and caring citizens. Citizens who would help to clean up the rough spots and make it a safer, more attractive place to live in. Tacoma needed legitimate businesses that would employ people, and it needed to eradicate the gangs, the drugs and the accompanying violence.

Tacoma needed Zach. It was his inflated ego talking, but Zach couldn't argue with it. His idea of a restaurant had been a lie, but the more he thought about it, the more he liked the sound of it. A classy bar and grill, with the right atmosphere, could attract people from the surrounding suburbs of Tacoma. He could organize a baseball league with the other bars. Kids would have other alternatives to gang life. Not a bad idea.

Zach shook the meandering thoughts out of his head. He might be disgruntled with his job, but he had no plans to leave it forever. He was a DEA agent. Being one was in his blood. Of course, Zach wasn't quite sure how it had gotten there. It certainly wasn't genetic. Nevertheless, it was what he had chosen to dedicate his life to. He couldn't help the world by pulling a few potential gang members off the street. Zach needed to work on a larger scale, a more encompassing scale. Drugs, for him, were the cornerstone of juvenile crime in America. Stop drugs, and you stop gang profit. Stop the profits and you stop their gun-buying potential. Stop the guns and you save the world.

Sure, Zach might be burned out right now because that reasoning, although sound, hadn't lived up to his expectations. To halt the influx and distribution of drugs in the country was to stop the earth from spinning. It seemed inexorable. It was also slowly driving Zach insane to know that he was helpless in the face of peoples' addictions.

But as burned out as he was, he couldn't walk away from it all. A few months of rest and he would be ready for the next round. He was sure of it. For now, his time was well spent helping Delany get back on her feet. He owed her that much. When she was well, his guilt would be relieved. More than that, he might feel capable once again. He could do things for Delany and watch her smile. The gratification would be instantaneous. Delany had said instant feedback was important. She was right.

St. Joe's Prep. The sign appeared on his right, seemingly out of nowhere. He turned immediately after the sign as per Delany's instructions and drove up the steep hill to the high school. It was a small building, much smaller than he expected, considering the size of its reputation. The grounds surrounding it were well kept and lush with flowers. No graffiti defaced its walls, no smokers hung out in dark corners and no food wrappers littered the lawn.

Zach parked in the first available space, got out of his car and asked a student to tell him where to find the main office. Once inside the building, Zach realized it wouldn't have been hard to find it on his own. The office was the first room on the right as he entered the building. To enter the office, he had to maneuver his way around a bunch of students complaining about their schedules. The principal's door was open.

"I'm sorry, sir. You can't go in there without an appointment." The school secretary seemed to protect her boss like a mother bear guarding its cub. Zach could imagine that parents were always on the rampage about something, and the woman probably tried her best to give Dan warning before he was compelled to listen to their venting.

"I'm looking for the key to Ms. Sheridan's room. I

told her I would pick up some work for her. The principal knows me.''

Immediately, the students in the office stopped their bickering and turned toward Zach like heat-seeking missiles. One girl stepped forward to speak for the whole group.

"You know Ms. Sheridan? Do you know if she's all right? Is she coming back?'' Her tone was urgent, conveying to Zach how much Delany was missed around this place.

"Patti, Mr. Banks told you that Ms. Sheridan was in a small accident and that she was going to be taking a leave of absence,'' the secretary interceded. "There's no need to bother this man.''

"I'm sorry, Ms. Collitin, but I don't believe it. Ms. Sheridan wouldn't leave in the middle of the year unless something was really wrong. The runathon is coming up, then the senior class trip. No way she'd bail out on us.''

The kid was right. It was silly of the adults to all conspire to keep the truth from them when they knew what the truth was anyway. Ms. Sheridan wouldn't bail out on anyone. These kids had a right to know that.

"Listen, Patti?'' When the girl nodded, Zach continued, "Ms. Sheridan was in a bad situation. She's really hurt. But she's going to be fine. She didn't want anyone to worry, so she came up with the leave-of-absence idea.''

"Can we see her?'' The other students behind Patti pushed forward, eager now to find out more.

"No. Ms. Sheridan doesn't want you to see her right now. You can understand that, can't you? It would be like your boyfriend catching you without your makeup on." Zach hoped the analogy hit home. He didn't want to blow Delany's trust in him.

"For your information, sir," Patti declared, "that was a very sexist comment to make. However, I do understand that Ms. Sheridan might not want a troop of students in and out of her room while she's trying to recover. Knowing Ms. Sheridan, she probably wants to spare us the awkwardness of seeing her all banged up."

High school students were a lot smarter than Zach remembered. He felt sheepish for having underestimated the girl. "You're right. Ms. Sheridan doesn't want to put you through that. Just know that she's going to be all right and that she'll be back as soon as she can."

Patti took the measure of the man standing in front of her. Her judgment was that he told the truth. "Are you looking out for Ms. Sheridan? Are you her boyfriend?"

Boyfriend. It was an old-fashioned word that never seemed to go out of style. "Yeah, I'm her boyfriend. Zach Montgomery." Zach held out his hand to the girl and was surprised again by her firm grip and her direct eye contact.

Patti didn't miss the look he gave her. "Ms. Sheridan taught us that a handshake makes a very firm first impression. It's important to make the right one."

"Ms. Sheridan is a very smart lady," Zach agreed.

"Ms. Collitin, why don't you give me the key. I'll walk Mr. Montgomery down to Ms. Sheridan's room."

Kristine handed over the key and watched him follow Patti down the hall.

"Here it is," Patti said as she threw open the door she had unlocked.

It was like any other schoolroom that Zach had sat

in throughout his educational career. Small tables were connected to the chairs. In even rows, the chairs faced a desk and a large chalkboard. Posters lined the room, adding spots of color to the beige walls. Zach read a few of the captions and grinned. Delany's warped sense of humor in action.

"Ms. Sheridan says the posters are there for us to read when we decide to zone out of her lectures," Patti explained, noticing where the man's eyes were looking. "She says we're allowed one zone-out per month. Any more than that and we would never survive the test. She's right, too."

Zach moved around to the desk. "What are all these mugs for?"

"They're gifts that students have given Ms. Sheridan over the years. This is only a sample of the collection. She says she's got a whole shelf at home dedicated to her mugs."

"You really like her?" Zach asked.

Patti sat on the corner of the desk, examining one of the mugs. "All of us love and respect Ms. Sheridan. She's the kind of teacher you hope you get at least once in your life. She doesn't just teach us history. She teaches us about life." Patti raised her eyes to Zach. "Are you telling me the truth? Is she really going to recover?"

"I promise she's going to be fine." It was Zach's solemn oath. The stack of reports was exactly where Delany said it would be. He lifted the stack, surprised at its weight. "How long do these reports have to be anyway?" he asked the girl, who was now heading out the door.

"Ten pages at least, with a minimum of ten sources.

I said we liked Ms. Sheridan. I didn't say she was easy." Patti chuckled as she left the room.

With the reports in hand, Zach left the building and headed toward his car.

"Mr. Montgomery," someone called from behind him. Zach put the reports down on the passenger seat and turned to face Dan Banks.

"What can I do for you?" Zach forced himself to be polite. The man was Delany's boss after all.

Dan was slightly out of breath by the time he caught up to Zach. Pausing a moment to catch his breath, he asked, or rather accused, "I thought Delany made it plain that she didn't want the students to know about her condition. I assume she told you the same thing she told me."

"Yeah. I wasn't specific. The kid knew what the situation was anyway. I just confirmed what she had already guessed." Zach wasn't about to explain himself further. He moved to the driver's side of the car and put his key in the lock.

"It was clearly presumptuous of you. It was also presumptuous of you to call yourself her boyfriend." Dan's face was red with anger.

"Does your wife know that you're in love with one of your teachers?" Zach asked, a threatening hint in his tone.

"I respect Ms. Sheridan as a professional. I like Ms. Sheridan as a friend. I resent your coming here and countermanding her request. Not to mention you assumed a relationship you have no right to. You only met her a few days ago, for Pete's sake!"

"If you can call yourself her friend, then I can damn well call myself her boyfriend. Good day, Mr. Banks."

Zach got in the car and slammed the door shut, making it clear the conversation was over.

He sped away from the school, refusing to allow the principal's words to mean anything to him. So it had only been a few days. He was connected to Delany in ways that her boss would never understand. Maybe he wasn't her boyfriend. But they were close. She needed him, and he needed her. What was wrong with that?

"Thanks, I appreciate this," Zach commented to the apartment manager, who opened Delany's door.

"Delany called me a little while ago. She said to expect you. She didn't want me to worry about letting a stranger into her apartment. She's real considerate that way."

Yet another fan of Delany Sheridan. For a woman who claimed to not have any close friends, she certainly was admired by a great many people.

"Yeah, she's real considerate," Zach repeated, although his tone suggested this quality was a negative trait. Please, let there be something out of place in there. Just one pair of dirty socks.

"The door locks automatically when you shut it, so I'll take the keys with me and leave you on your own." The manager, an older man in his sixties with a kind face, walked off, leaving Zach to his own devices. Apparently, Delany's word was enough to quiet any suspicions the manager might harbor.

Zach stepped into the tiny studio apartment. Aha! The bed was unmade! Sheets were tangled at the bottom of the daybed, and a comforter was rumpled into a large blob. She left for work without making the bed. Tsk, tsk. Zach felt instantly better.

The rest of the apartment was in decent enough

shape. It needed to be vacuumed and dusted, but there weren't any open pizza boxes on the floor or anything of that nature. Next to the daybed was a huge bookshelf that nearly covered the wall. On the top three shelves she displayed her accumulation of coffee mugs with various teacher sayings. *Love a Teacher Today. Help Make the Future: Be a Teacher.* Patti was right; the mugs on her desk were only the beginning. This woman would never want for coffee cups.

On the shelves below the mugs, she had what appeared to be over a hundred paperback books, many of them sporting Fabio on the cover. She not only read them, she collected them. Surely that had to be marked down as a fault. After all, as a teacher she should be reading the latest literature on teaching techniques, as well as the latest history periodicals to keep her apprised of changes in her field. Instead, here she was, sacked away with a bunch of sappy novels. Romantic fool.

Zach grabbed a few, thinking she might want some of her favorites to keep her company in the hospital. On the opposite wall across from the shelves was a desk with a computer sitting on top of it. These days, it was a necessary piece of equipment, like a telephone or a calculator. Over the desk were shelves that contained a mishmash of framed pictures. Zach spotted one photo of an attractive older couple. They were smiling at each other instead of the camera. Zach guessed from the facial features that they were Delany's parents. Next to that picture was one of a boy about sixteen or so. He wore a football uniform with the number three on it and he looked as proud as a peacock in it. Her brother.

Zach took both pictures and placed them near the books he planned to take with him back to the hospital. The kitchen was a small room adjacent to the main living area. No luck there—the dishes were all washed. It was functional and decorated with pictures of flowers and sunsets.

Moving back into the living room, Zach noticed that Delany's decorating was sparse. It seemed evident that she didn't spend a great deal of time in the tiny apartment. As it was, she only had a daybed, a desk, a futon couch in the corner and a small entertainment unit near the bed.

Some snoop he was. He still hadn't found her book bag. There was another room across from the small bathroom that Zach had spotted when he entered the apartment. He retraced his steps and entered what he assumed was a changing room. It contained a dresser and an open closet. A few belts were piled over a chair that sat in the corner. On top of the dresser were cosmetics and other toiletries that only a woman would know how to use. Not exactly the most orderly dressing room, Zach thought smugly.

Near his feet, at the entrance to the room, was the book bag. He was about to pick it up and leave when an idea came to him. As long as he was taking some pictures and books to make Delany feel more comfortable, he might as well take some clothes, as well.

When he looked inside the closest, the first thing he spotted was a blue terry-cloth robe. It screamed comfort. Zach removed it from the hook and placed it over his arm. Then he searched her drawers for some sweats that would be easy to pull on and off when the casts were finally removed. Jackpot. Zach found a drawer filled with nothing but sweats of various colors.

Back in the living room, he took another glance at her bed. The comforter might be warm, but its color was a dull white. Delany would do better with some-

thing cheerier than that. He committed himself to stop
at a mall and pick her up a colorful afghan that would
add some cheer to the drab hospital room. His task finished, Zach picked up all the items he had collected.
He took one glance around the apartment and tried to
imagine Delany bustling about in the kitchen or snuggled in her bed. It wasn't hard, and it caused his chest
to tighten. He hated the idea that he was going to have
to return to the hospital and see her as she really was,
broken and battered.

Then he realized if it wasn't for that battering, he
might never have seen her at all. It was a sobering
thought.

Chapter 4

"A little more blush, I think," the nurse said, more to herself than to her patient.

Delany viewed herself in the small hand mirror. "I don't know, Debbie. I want to cover the bruise, not join the circus."

"I don't see why you need any makeup at all. The bruise is almost gone. Your cheek is healed. Your nose is healed. Your face looks fine. In fact, I wish I looked as good as you. You think maybe I ought to smash my face into a wall? It might help." Debbie laughed self-mockingly.

The older woman had become a good friend to Delany in the two months she'd been recovering. She stood average height and was thick around the middle. Her gray hair was peppered with black, and her face bore the marks of her stressful profession. Despite the nurse's somewhat mild-mannered appearance, Delany soon came to learn that she was harder to deter than a

bulldozer. After a few heated moments staring at each
other over the sharp end of a needle, Delany quickly
discovered that it was perhaps wiser to make friends
with the woman than to antagonize her. Once an understanding was reached, and Debbie had made it clear
who would win in an all-out struggle, the woman had
become like an older sister to Delany.

"You're beautiful the way you are, and you know it,
or else why would Ralph still be married to you after
all these years?" Delany questioned logically. She
knew all about Ralph and the couple's sometimes tumultuous relationship. She also knew all about Debbie
and Ralph's five children and their tumultuous relationships. It was quite a family.

Debbie raised her eyebrows. "Are you kiddin' me?
He stays with me because I do his laundry, cook his
meals and massage his back after a long day at work.
He stays with me for the same reason every other man
stays with a woman for thirty-five years."

Despite her cynical words, Delany knew that wasn't
the whole picture. Debbie loved Ralph. It was in her
eyes when she spoke about him, and in her laughter
when she joked about him. And Delany had no doubt
that Ralph loved his wife equally.

"That's not true. I haven't done any laundry or
cooked any meals or rubbed any backs, but Zach shows
up every day nonetheless. It hasn't been thirty-five
years, but clearly men must have other reasons for wanting to be with a woman. And we both know it couldn't
be because of my stunning appearance." Delany cocked
her shoulders as if to pose in the comfortable, but somewhat sexless, blue terry-cloth robe that Zach had gar-
nered from her apartment.

The robe wasn't the only item Zach had pilfered from

her apartment. Other odds and ends decorated the sterile hospital room in an effort to make her feel more at home. Pictures of her parents and her brother decorated the end table, along with a stack of mystery and romance novels. He'd bought her a brightly colored afghan to hide the white casts, along with some violet and rose pillows to match. All in an effort to make her feel better.

Of course, Zach was a decent and honorable man. That was one reason why he came. As for the other reasons Delany mentioned, the truth was she didn't really want an answer. He came every day without fail and would often spend the better part of it with her. It was more than she could possibly ask for.

He told her that he'd rented a small apartment in the Stadium District of Tacoma. It was within walking distance of the hospital. They were practically neighbors now, as Zach had put it. He claimed to be searching for the perfect location for this bar and grill of his, but Delany knew that he didn't spend much time in that pursuit. One, it didn't take a month to rent a location. Two, real-estate people often worked from eight to five like most people, and those were the hours he spent with her.

Why? It was a question that haunted her every waking hour. More often, it crept into the recesses of her mind at night, when she would relive every moment she'd been in his company. In her heart, she wanted to believe that he cared for her as much as she cared for him.

No, that wasn't true. She wanted to believe that he loved her as much as she loved him. Because she did love him. Desperately. Sometimes she wished she could pinpoint the moment when it happened. Other times she believed that there wasn't one moment, that it was more a culmination of every minute they'd spent together. The rather frightening aspect was that it continued. Delany had always thought that once you fell in love, that was it. Like falling out of a boat. Once you were wet, you couldn't get any wetter.

But love wasn't like that at all. Her heart was a glass, and each day Zach filled her up some more. When she heard his familiar tread outside her room, her heart would speed up. When he came into the room, her heart would stop. When he leaned down to give her a peck on the lips, her heart would explode. And each day the feelings grew more intense instead of less. She should have been used to him by now.

It never happened. She never got over the feeling that he had been put on this earth especially for her. It was the most exhilarating feeling in the world. Despite her injuries and the confinement of hospital life, she felt as if she'd been blessed.

To be blessed, surely, was enough for her. She couldn't ask for more. And she couldn't bring herself to ask *Why?* Zach must have his reasons, and she was content to let him keep them to himself. In turn, Delany chose not to burden Zach with the knowledge that she loved him. To say the words aloud would demand a response. Instinctively, Delany knew that Zach wasn't ready to give her the response she desired. And she knew she wasn't ready to hear anything else.

Every day he came. It was enough. For now.

"Do you want to hear why I think he comes?" Debbie asked, jarring Delany from her worrisome thoughts.

Delany hesitated for a second. "No. I know why he comes. He comes because he's my friend." Delany put the blush down on her lap table and picked up the lipstick, applying it carefully with one hand while she held the mirror in the other one.

Debbie's eyebrows arched with doubt. "Friends, huh? Is that why you're putting on all this makeup and doing up your hair? Is that why you blush every time he walks into the room and frown every time he leaves? That sure is some friend."

Delany didn't dignify her friend's teasing with a response. She knew what Debbie was getting at, but she wasn't about to fall into that trap. "Today is a special day. I wanted to look nice for…the doctor," Delany fibbed. "My legs will be beyond horrible when the casts come off. I need to have something to balance them out. Remember my arm?"

Giving it a quick glance, Delany saw that the limb was still pale and weak. It had, however, shown some improvement. Every day for the past two weeks, she had worked with hand weights to regain her strength and build muscle tone. She had also used that time to increase her upper-body strength in preparation for the grueling rehabilitation program to come. She was nine months old again and she had to learn to walk. Fortunately for her, this time around she had a coach. A great coach. Zach often lifted weights with her, pushing her when she wanted to quit. As he had explained it, getting the arm back in shape was the easy part. If she was going to have a chance at a full recovery, she would need to learn to go beyond her point of endurance from time to time. If Zach led the way, it wouldn't be a problem.

One last swipe of lipstick and Delany was ready. The familiar thump-thump of Zach's boots sounded on the hospital floor. "Debbie, that's him. Help me put this makeup away. I don't want him to think that I put it on for—''

"The doctor?" Debbie asked sweetly, laughing at Delany's sudden blush. Finally, she relented and swept the cosmetics back into a bag and placed it in the drawer of the nightstand. Delany blew away the remains of face powder, straightened her robe and checked to see that the curlers she had rolled into her hair that morning were all out and the curls still held.

Zach entered the room, but stopped when he saw the two women staring at him, both silent and unmoving. "Did I interrupt something?"

"All I know is that it's a good thing you don't wear sneakers," Debbie replied as she made her way around the bed. "I'll leave you two alone, but the doctor will be in soon with the buzz saw."

The door closed behind her. Mentally, Delany winced. The great part about today was that the casts were finally coming off. Unfortunately, she just remembered how a cast came off. The sound of the saw was still ringing in her ears from the last time. One false move and she was footage for the next *Texas Chainsaw Massacre* movie.

"Sneakers?" Zach asked, still trying to understand Debbie's first statement.

"Inside joke," Delany replied weakly. Then she tilted up her head as Zach walked toward her, ready to receive her first kiss of the day. She got two per day. A peck in the morning and another when he left in the afternoon. Both were quick and basically sexless on his part. Not so for Delany. She felt a rush of heat run through her body every time Zach's lips touched hers. She wasn't wise about sex. Perhaps that's why his kisses seemed to rock her world a bit. And lately, although it could have been her imagination, it seemed as if their lips were touching for more than just an instant. She held her head up to him longer, and as a result his lips clung to hers longer. Both of them were reluctant to end the gesture.

Head tilt. That was his cue. Zach bent down to offer her a restrained kiss. It had been hell to keep to this ritual twice a day. He wanted to take her in his arms and crush her mouth against his. Let his tongue plummet to the very depths of her mouth, let his mouth learn her taste.

Cool it, Montgomery, his conscience warned his raging hormones. And you cool it, too, down there, he told the lower part of his anatomy, which hardened at the mere thought of kissing Delany as he truly wanted to. But she wasn't well enough yet. Her back needed to heal. Her legs were still in casts. She wasn't ready for sex. Her body wasn't ready for it anyway. She needed his companionship and his comfort. He was here to be her friend. Her buddy. What a disgusting word.

No, Zach was noble. Zach would sacrifice his needs for Delany. Zach did the right thing.

Liar.

Okay, so it wasn't only for Delany that Zach restrained himself. He did it for himself. He couldn't have a little taste of Delany and not want the whole meal. To spare himself the pain that hungering for her caused, he kept himself as distant from her as he could.

Zach considered himself to be a very sexual man. He enjoyed sex and he enjoyed it often. He wasn't stupid enough to be promiscuous in this day and age, so all his relationships were long lasting, monogamous and solely sexual. When he looked back over his romantic history, he was surprised to realize that there wasn't much of a story to tell. He could remember little more than the names of the women he'd been with. It was shallow of him, he knew, but then he'd never met anybody he'd talked with more than he'd slept with.

Until Delany. Talking was like sex with her. It was when they communicated that they were the most intimate, the most probing. Only it wasn't enough anymore. He desired her mind, but he needed her body. He ached for her. Every night he dreamed about her, and every morning he woke up hard and wanting. When the bruises were fresh and her legs were suspended in the air, it was easy to see her as someone who needed him as a friend. But as the bruises faded and her face began to reveal its beauty, it was easier to see her lying on her back while he hovered over her, then pushed into her heat, watching as her eyes grew stormy blue with desire.

Zach remembered that color. He remembered what it did to him....

"'Slowly his hand moved down her back, making its journey to her firm buttocks,'" Zach had read, his voice overly exaggerated as he tried to make light of the romantic scene about to take place between the hero and the heroine in the book he was reading to Delany.

"I don't want you to read it, if you're going to do it like that, " Delany complained, although at the time she was trying to stifle her giggles. She didn't know what it was about romance novels. When she read them herself, they seemed wonderfully romantic and very erotic. But when Zach read one, it sounded silly.

"I thought you liked my dramatic interpretation," Zach reminded her. His impression of Romana had put her into stitches the first time he read aloud her dialogue. Just the idea of Zach trying to be feminine was laughable.

"I do, but this is a serious scene."

Zach humphed. The truth was he had overdramatized the book to make it seem silly so she wouldn't realize how much he actually liked it. Sheesh, what would the guys from his office say if they knew he read romance novels and enjoyed them. They'd send him tickets to the ballet and give him pink silk shirts for Christmas, that's what.

Grouching and mumbling the whole time about how stupid it was, Zach had shifted in his chair and started over again. With a quick look at her sympathetic face, he was assured that she believed he dreaded every moment of this. His macho image was safe!

But as he began to read, his voice serious now, he felt the impact of the words. "'Thrusting again and again, he plunged into her hot depths. The heat all but burned him alive,'" Zach read, his voice husky. Suddenly, it wasn't Romana and Brent. It was him and Delany. Zach thrusted and Delany held him in her heat, arching her hips to meet him. He stopped and glanced up at her. Her eyes were at half-mast and she struggled to hide her tiny gasps of breath. When her eyes met his gaze, he saw their color.

They were the color of the ocean, but not quite. They were the color of the sky before a storm, but not quite. He couldn't name the color, but he did recognize it. It was the color of desire. A desire that he couldn't satisfy while she was wounded and weak. With a frustrated growl, he had slammed the book down and exclaimed, "Drivel!"

After that day, he started to read her mystery novels. Only under penalty of death would he ever admit that he went to the bookstore that night after leaving her side, bought the book and finished it, visualizing Delany as Romana the whole time.

She wore cosmetics. It was a first. Foundation to hide the imperfections only she was ashamed of. Eyeliner to exaggerate the blue of her eyes as if he would ever forget it. Lipstick to color her lips red, a color that made Zach think of cherries. All of it was unnecessary. Zach saw through it all to the woman behind the mask. Pretty. She was that now. Elegant. She would grow to become that when she was fifty.

The thought of cherries tempted Zach to lower his lips until he touched the softness of hers. Unable to stop himself, he quickly put out his tongue to sample just a taste. Definitely cherries. Then abruptly he backed off. One kiss. That's all it could be.

"You look nice," he said, brushing a finger across her lips where her lipstick had smeared.

Delany released her breath on a sigh. The anticipation of what could be made her react strongly to his brief kiss. But she needed more. She needed his hot breath, his warm, soft lips, his sensual tongue. Stop it, she commanded herself. The kiss was over.

"So, any luck yet?" Delany asked once she had regained her breath. It was the habitual first question of the day. Delany asked it mainly out of a lingering sense of guilt. She didn't know what Zach did for money, but she was beginning to worry about him. She didn't want him falling on hard times because of his devotion to her.

He hated this part. The lying part. Several times over the past few weeks, he had wanted to tell her the truth about himself. When Mort called with the news that the sting had gone down, Zach longed to tell Delany that her sacrifice hadn't been in vain. There was purpose to her agony.

The DEA had been ready for O.G.'s contact from Seattle. The man had been busted with over half a million dollars' worth of cocaine. He would be spending the next several years in jail after he revealed the names of his contacts in Los Angeles. The flow of drugs into Tacoma had been cut in half. It wasn't perfection, but it was a start.

Not only had the DEA done its job, but once the drug kingpins found out who'd leaked the name of their contact, O.G. would suffer a far worse fate than that of the man he'd given up. News of the gang leader's demise would have made Delany very happy. And it would have made her feel safe.

Instead, he kept it to himself. He told himself he lied for her benefit. She was in a fragile state. She didn't need to deal with his deception right now. But he knew that was only half the truth. Zach didn't want to lose her. The time that he had spent with her had brought contentment to his life. It was an emotion he'd never experienced before, not even as a child. He was reluctant to give it up.

"No luck," Zach said, answering her question. "Maybe I'm too picky, but a restaurant is made or broken on its location, so I have to be careful." Zach pulled up a chair and sat down. He frowned and wondered how long this story would hold out for him.

"Zach, I know I'm prying, but...what do you do for...rent?" Money was a touchy issue to bring up despite the fact that they were no longer strangers. But Delany needed to know that she wasn't sending him to the poorhouse. "I assume you had a job before you came here. You never seem to talk about your past or your family. I don't even know if you have a family.'' It all came out in a rush, and it wasn't until Delany asked the questions that she realized how many she had.

Zach leaned over and brushed her hair away from her flushed cheek, anxious for any excuse to touch her. He thought about what he should tell her. There wasn't much he could say, but he knew that he could no longer remain mute on the subject. Certainly talking about his family couldn't hurt. "I wasn't hatched, you know."

"Ha-ha," she muttered, decidedly unamused. This was the man she loved, and she knew next to nothing about him.

"My family..." he began, not knowing where to start. "I have a mother and a father. I have a brother, and he has a wife and two children. They all live in Beverly Hills and are quite happy."

"Beverly Hills? No wonder they're happy."

"Yes. And your assumption is correct. They are very wealthy. My father is quite a successful movie executive. My brother is an equally successful plastic surgeon. So you can put your mind at rest about where my next rent check is going to come from." Zach finished his tale with another lie, but at least the part about his family was true.

"You're lying," Delany accused.

Zach was startled. He made his living lying, and he'd never blown it before. How had she known?

"You wouldn't take money from your parents or your brother."

"How do you know that? They're rich. I have a huge trust fund, given to me on my eighteenth birthday. What makes you think I'm not using it?"

It was true. He had been given a trust fund, but he

had never touched a penny of it. He lived now on the savings he had put away over the years. As an undercover agent, he hadn't needed much in the way of possessions. He didn't need to drive a fancy car because the agency provided him with wheels. His apartments had always been sparsely furnished because he never spent much time in any one place. As a result, the bulk of his paycheck, month after month, had been put into a savings account. Ten years later, that account was pretty hefty, despite the fact that he hadn't invested in bonds or played the stock market as his father had insisted. Money wasn't Zach's concern. It never had been.

Delany answered his question bluntly. "I know you. Or at least I think I do. You're not the kind of man to take money from anybody. You're also not the type to let somebody else's labor support you." With a smug look on her face, Delany waited for him to confirm her belief.

Zach just smiled. "You think you're pretty smart, don't you?"

His smile was returned. "I'm smart about you," she said, hoping she hadn't revealed too much. "So tell me where you really get the money from."

"I was a cop." That was true, too. He had started his career with the L.A.P.D. "I've never been materialistic so I was able to sock away a lot of money. That's the money I'm using to open the restaurant. Satisfied?"

"Yes." No. A police officer? Had he been shot at, had he been hurt? Fear left her mouth dry. "Now tell me about your parents. Do you see them much?" She wanted to know more, to know everything.

Zach hesitated. He wasn't comfortable talking about his parents. On the other hand, he knew she hadn't been comfortable talking about her brother. She had shared herself with him, and he supposed it was only fair that he do the same.

"My parents and I don't really have much in common. And I have less in common with my brother. They enjoy being rich. They enjoy the luxuries. Don't get me wrong. They've worked hard to get those luxuries, I was just never into that kind of life," Zach admitted, talking about this for the first time in his life. It didn't surprise him that Delany was a wonderful listener.

"Tell me what that life was like," Delany asked. She wanted to know the sort of life he spurned, so she would better know the one he would welcome.

"It was fast cars, glamorous clothes, parties, parties, and more parties. My mother is a social whirlwind. She lives to host the most successful party in Hollywood," he said, chuckling in remembrance.

Although Zach didn't have much in common with his family, Delany saw that he wasn't bitter about it.

"I grew up with beautiful actresses on my arm. Like father, like son, everyone assumed, although I had no plans to go into the family business. My brother, William, had the same problem, but he never seemed to mind the clinging women. In fact, he married one of them. Shallowness doesn't bother him, either. He wallowed in the money when we were young, and became a plastic surgeon to the rich and famous so he could continue to wallow in it."

"And you became a cop because…"

Zach sat hunched over in his chair, his elbows resting on his knees, his chin on his knuckles. "I became a cop because I couldn't stand the Hollywood scene anymore. I couldn't stand the injustice. My parents had all this money, but I would drive into downtown Hollywood and see nothing but poverty. My parents gave to charities, but it wasn't enough. They had so much. I thought they could have saved the world with all that money. When I suggested that they try to do just that, they laughed at me. Told me there would always be rich people and there would always be poor people. I couldn't live with that. If they weren't going to save the world, then it was up to me. But I didn't want to use their money to do it. Law enforcement was a way to accomplish my goal.''

"Why the whole world? Why not help one person? You could make a difference that way, too." Delany understood altruism. She also understood how consuming it could be.

"I needed to make a difference with more than just one person. I wanted to even the odds. My parents took more than their fair share. Saving only one person didn't seem like enough." It had become his whole purpose in life, really. He'd felt he needed to save the world in order to justify the life his parents had given him as a child.

"After my brother died," Delany remarked, "I wanted to save the world. I wanted to save everyone who had ever been addicted to drugs. I realized quickly enough that it was an impossible task."

"So now you save kids one at a time, is that it?" Zach asked, eyeing her casts, evidence of where her generous nature had gotten her.

"Sometimes I think 'save' is a really egotistical word. Who am I to think that I have the ability to save someone? I've been lying in this bed for almost two months, and I've come to realize many things. First, I've ignored my own life in an effort to do good. That's not completely healthy. Second, you can't save people. You can lend a hand or an ear, but people will do what they want. It's like trying to make a river run upstream. You can try, but in all likelihood you'll fail. And the constant struggle against impossible odds will only wear you out. It's exhausted me.''

With a nod, Zach acknowledged what she said, but he couldn't give in so easily. "I can't give up. People who have so much need to give because they are the only ones who can."

"But who saves you, Zach? In your attempt to pay off this imaginary debt incurred by your parents, you've forgotten how important you are. You allow guilt to rule your life,'' Delany accused.

He winced at her words, but then turned them against her. ''And what about you? You're lying in a hospital bed because of your guilt.''

"So maybe we both need to put it behind us. Maybe we both need to take more care of ourselves." Delany grimaced. "I guess I'm not in a position to say that. I'm selfish enough to admit that I don't want you to start taking care of yourself quite yet. I still need you.''

Her words sent a thrill through him. As much as he had tried to do his part for humanity, he had never actually felt needed. Not even one drug addict he'd put away had been grateful for his intervention.

"After all," Delany continued, "you rescued me that night. It's only right that you see it through."

"I didn't rescue you," Zach stated harshly, standing abruptly at her words. Talk about having a life ruled by guilt. He felt guilty because he'd lied. But if he told her the truth now, she would assume that that was the only reason he had stayed. It wasn't true. He didn't come every day out of guilt. He came because he needed her to need him. He was useful. He loved her company. He loved the peace that she brought to his life. He loved…

"I'm sorry," Delany apologized, although she didn't know what she was apologizing for. All she knew was that she didn't like the tone of his voice, and she especially didn't like that tone aimed at her.

Hell, he was in love with her. It was going to hurt like a son of a bitch when she found out the truth and then walked away from him because of it. His only hope was to get her so involved in the relationship that she wouldn't be able to walk away. And right now he had plenty of time to do that. Now she couldn't walk away from anything.

"Hello, patient!" Dr. Manuela entered the room, pushing a tray in front of him. "What a beautiful day to take off two casts."

Zach cursed inwardly. So much for time. "That's right. I'd forgotten that today was the day. You must be excited."

Delany wondered about his strange and suddenly pensive mood. "I'm a little frightened."

"The buzz saw?" Zach inquired. Her face had been a picture of terror the last time.

"The buzz saw," Delany confirmed. "And the legs. Once the casts are off, I start my rehabilitation. I'm finally going to know if I'll ever be my old self again."

The doctor set up the tray beside her bed. "We've talked about this, Delany. Your back has healed and you have feeling in your toes. With some proper therapy and hard work on your part, you'll walk again in a few weeks."

"Yes, but will I run? I've asked it before and I'm asking it again."

The lengthy pause was answer enough. "I don't know," the doctor replied. "But it's really too early to say for sure. Let's get these casts off. You're certainly not running anywhere in them.''

Zach walked to the other side of the bed and held her hand while the doctor quickly removed the casts. Her hand strangled his at the sound of the saw doing its work, but then suddenly the room was silent and Delany was left with two bare legs. Looking down at them, Zach observed that both were thin, white and unshaven. In fact, they were the ugliest pair of legs he had ever seen…and the most beautiful.

It had taken time, but she was finally free of the plaster shell that had been a part of her life for the past two months. Delany still wore the back brace, but only as a precaution. Tomorrow her therapy would begin, and soon her recovery would be complete. Zach could only hope there would be enough time to make her fall in love with him. Only a woman who loved him would forgive him his lies.

"They're disgusting, aren't they?" Delany asked, noticing Zach's vacant stare.

"Yep."

"You don't have to spare my feelings. Give it to me straight," Delany demanded sternly, used to Zach's forthrightness.

Zach lifted the sheet to take another look. "Okay, they're not disgusting. They're *really* disgusting."

Delany couldn't help but laugh. "Well, I can't do anything about the pale color or the wasted muscles, but I can shave them. Would you get me the soap and a razor from the bathroom?"

"I don't think soap is going to do the trick. You need some heavy-duty shaving cream," Zach informed her.

"One compliment after another. You really know how to make a girl feel special."

Zach smiled at her retort because he knew she wasn't offended by his remarks. They knew each other too well for that by now. "I'll be back."

A few minutes later, he returned with his purchase from the hospital pharmacy.

"You'll have to help me out of this brace," Delany called to him as Zach retrieved a washcloth and a razor from the bathroom. He also filled her water pitcher with hot, steaming water. The necessary items were placed on the nightstand beside her bed, yet he ignored her request to remove the back brace.

When she protested, he explained calmly, "You wouldn't be able to bend far enough even without the back brace. You don't realize how stiff you are. This time, I'll shave your legs."

"You can't do that!"

"Why not?"

Delany was at a loss for words. Shaving her legs seemed so intimate, so sexual. "They're disgusting, you said so yourself. Why would you want to touch them?"

"I said they were really disgusting. That doesn't mean I wouldn't love the opportunity to touch any part of you. Shaven or unshaven."

Delany gasped a little at his words. It was the first time he had made any sexual overtures toward her, and she thrilled at the prospect that maybe he was finally starting to see her as something other than an invalid. Then he pulled the sheet back again. She took another good look at her legs and groaned. They *were* awful.

Zach didn't seem to mind. He took the hot, wet washcloth and ran it up and down her legs, cleaning off the residue of the cast and gauze. Then, carefully, he lathered on the cream and coated her right leg in a white froth. After a soak, the razor ran up Delany's leg, taking with it the cream and hair stubble.

Delany didn't see how it was possible, but she found herself aroused as Zach performed his duty. It seemed like such a thankless task, but he shaved her legs with as much care as an artist painted. He lifted the leg, inspected the area that he wanted to shave, and then with long, slow strokes of the razor, he made her leg look less and less as if it belonged to a hairy ape. The feel of his hands on her legs, manipulating their position, seemed so intimate. The fact that she was unable to move her legs herself made her completely vulnerable. She was in his care, and it felt surprisingly good.

It took thirty minutes, so methodical was he. But her legs, now wiped clean of the remaining cream, had been downgraded to merely disgusting.

"You do nice work. Have you ever thought about opening up a beauty shop instead of a restaurant? Let me tell you, that kind of shave beats a wax job any day of the week."

"That was fun," Zach boasted as he wiggled his eyebrows, feeling playful now that she was out of the casts. "Maybe we should turn this into a tradition."

Delany liked the implication of his words. "The truth is out. You have a thing for pale, hairy, sickly looking legs. Pervert."

"Your legs are beautiful," Zach whispered. The bed dipped with his added weight, and his hand rested on her thigh just above her knee.

The tone of his voice changed, but Delany didn't know how to handle his sudden seriousness, so she kept her tone light. "How can you say that? Look at them."

"I have, intimately. After staring at those casts for so long, I can't think of anything more beautiful."

A blush crept across her face, highlighting her embarrassment. "Maybe someday you'll let me return the favor."

"Thanks, but I've grown rather fond of the hair on my legs. Don't you want me to have that macho look?" First the romance novels, now his legs. Next she'd be suggesting a nice earring for him to wear.

"I meant your face. I could use a hot cloth and one of those old-fashioned razors. I would hold your chin in my hand and I would be so careful not to nick you." Mimicking the actions she would use, Delany brought her hand up to his face and rubbed the shadow of stubble that had grown in the past few hours. "You could use a shave right now."

Zach pressed her hand to his face. Her touch was so soft, yet it hurt him with its intensity. "Don't." His voice was a whisper, but the command in his tone was obvious.

"Why?" Perhaps her question was bold. Maybe she revealed too much, but she needed to touch him. It wasn't too much to ask, was it?

"Because you're not in casts anymore. Nothing will stop me."

It was odd, Delany thought, that such harshly spoken words could sound so wonderful. "Stop you from doing what?" She wanted him to spell it out for her so that there would be no mistake.

Zach leaned over, his face only inches away. "This."

Zach closed the last few inches quickly and took her lips in a hot, deep kiss. He brought his hand around her neck to hold her in place for his ravishing. It was as sweet as he imagined it would be. Her softness met the firmness of his lips and yielded. He bit their fullness gently, and when that wasn't enough, he commanded her to open for him.

"Let me in. I need to be inside you."

Delany opened her mouth and gave him access to plunder her with his tongue. She felt as if she were lost in the eye of a tornado, swirling around in confusion, unable to touch her feet to the earth. It frightened, yet exhilarated her. She loved him so much. And never in her dreams had she imagined what kissing the man you loved passionately would feel like. For Delany, it was a powerful new sensation.

Zach glided his tongue over hers. Sugar and silk greeted him, surrounded him, until he felt wrapped in her heat. But it wasn't an uncomfortable heat. Instead, he basked in her warmth. She was the sun and she brought life to his body. Soon though, he realized he was getting out of control. Zach's sex hardened and strained against the fly of his jeans. It was a painful enough sensation to bring him out of the kiss.

Delany actually moaned her disappointment when his lips left hers. Her breaths were shallow little pants, and it took all her strength to bring herself under control. Finally, she felt a sense of balance return. It was a good thing her sense of humor returned with it, too. She needed to protect herself with levity. "The casts on my legs stopped you from doing that to my lips? I think you need an anatomy lesson, Mr. Montgomery."

He would have laughed if he wasn't still achingly aroused. He had known it would be like this. Known the frustration would kill him. Zach was just glad to see that he had enough willpower to pull back from the brink. "It's a lot harder to look at you as a patient now."

"I don't want you to look at me as a patient," Delany confessed, touching her tongue to her swollen lips.

Zach sighed. It comforted him to know that the physical attraction wasn't one-sided. But he didn't think she was ready to accept his physical needs. He saw a glimmer in her eye. She was gazing at him intently, as if he was some kind of hero. He didn't want to be her hero. A relationship based on a sense of obligation would mean nothing to him.

"Answer me this, Delany. Why don't you want me to look at you as a patient?"

"That should be obvious," Delany murmured shyly.

"Maybe you've grown attached to me because of the circumstances that led to our meeting. You think I saved you that night. And you see me every day. Maybe it's just..." Zach didn't know what he wanted to say. It wasn't in his nature to be uncertain. He had too much arrogance for that. But this was important.

"You think I've developed some Florence Nightingale crush," Delany accused. Was he trying to tell her that he didn't want her affection? Then why had he kissed her?

"I want you to be careful." I'm a liar and a cheat, Zach added silently.

"Thank you for the warning." Her voice was laced with ice, and Zach knew he had upset her. Damn it, he wasn't any good with stuff like this.

"I'll see you tomorrow." Zach moved off the bed and headed for the door.

"No."

Zach stopped and turned. "What do you mean?"

Delany didn't know what she meant, but she felt as if she needed to prove something to herself and to Zach. "You think I've become too attached because you're

here every day. Maybe it would do us both good if you
didn't come for a while.'' At times, Delany believed
that she either needed to hold on to Zach with everything she had or let him go completely. Perhaps now
was the time to let him go completely and see if she
could make it on her own.

It hurt. More than Zach would ever admit. But if he
wanted to be sure that she was attracted to him because
of who he was and not who she thought he was, then
it might be a good idea. "Well, I guess that I'll see
you...whenever. You have my number at the apartment.
Call me when you want me.''

It was the right thing to do. She had grown far too
dependent on him. Perhaps she only thought she loved
him because of his proximity. If that was the case, then
why wasn't she in love with her doctor? she reflected
bitterly. No, she was in love with Zach, but that didn't
mean she could spend the rest of her life dependent on
him. There was no guarantee that he would stay forever.
At this moment, Delany knew that if he told her he
wasn't coming back, she would be utterly devastated.
Much better that she told him to go. It made her the
one in control. Stupid, but in control. It would definitely
hurt less this way. Only, the pain was so bad now, she
couldn't imagine how it could be any worse.

Tears ran down her cheeks, and as Delany looked
around the empty room, she knew that she might have
just made the biggest mistake of her life.

Chapter 5

"**P**ush. You're not working hard enough, Delany. You've got to push harder," Stan, Delany's physical therapist, instructed.

Delany stared up at him mutinously. She was on a bench that kept her back straight while her legs dangled off the front. The tops of her feet were underneath two cushions that were hooked to the weights on the back of the machine. She was supposed to push upward against the cushions, straighten her legs and thereby lift the weights. All this was done in an attempt to increase her muscle tone so that she'd be able to start on the parallel bars. Delany could barely straighten her legs without the weights pushing down against her. She didn't know how this boy thought she could do it with the added ten pounds.

He *was* a boy, she thought childishly. He could be no more than twenty-two. He was tall, his body perfect, his muscles well defined, his hair blond and his eyes

green. She hated his perfection. She hated that he made
her do things she couldn't, when he so obviously could.
Most of all, she hated that he wasn't Zach.

"Stop shouting at me," she snapped unnecessarily.
Stan hadn't been shouting, but Delany was too irritated
to care at this point. "If I could do it, don't you think
I'd be doing it by now? It's been a week."

Stan knelt beside her, obviously accustomed to such
tongue-lashings in his profession. "Listen, Delany. I
know it's hard. But I've seen your X rays. Your back
is healed, and there's only minimal nerve damage.
There's no reason why you shouldn't be able to accomplish these tasks. You told me you wanted to run marathons again. Well, I'm here to help you do that, but I
can't do it without your cooperation."

He was right, and she hated him for that, too. Weary
of the pain the exertion caused, Delany wanted to free
her legs from their imprisonment. She tried to lift her
feet out from beneath the cushions, but even that small
accomplishment was beyond her. Frustrated, she
pounded her arms against the dead weight that was her
legs, then picked them up and placed them where she
wanted.

She hadn't expected she would be this weak. She
hadn't realized her back would hurt as much as it did.
She hadn't totally understood what Doc Manny meant
when he said she must endure some pain in order to get
results. Beyond that, she hadn't conceived that losing
Zach would be so agonizing.

She missed him so much her teeth ached. Delany was
furious with him for even daring to walk out just because she'd told him to. Why had he listened to her?
He should have known that her words were only an
attempt to salvage her pride. Obviously, he hadn't. Six

days. Six days, and he hadn't even called, never mind about stopping by to see her. The energy that used to get her through the day was gone. Rather than read, she preferred to nap. Rather than eat, she preferred to nap. Her day was consumed by sleep.

Even the therapy she had longed for, to finally get her out of bed, seemed to take more energy than she had to give. This strange man had to touch her, and it revolted her. He lifted her out of her wheelchair, manipulated her legs, massaged them after the therapy was over. All of it made her skin quiver with disgust.

It was because she resented Stan; she resented the therapy, too. Walking was still important to her, but gone was the inner drive that could help her accomplish that task. She was nothing more than a whiny brat, unwilling and unresponsive.

Even though she hadn't even been able to work up a sweat, Stan must have sensed her exhaustion because he only pushed her one more time. "Five more, Delany. Five more lifts, and I'll take you back to your room."

Delany interpreted that statement as back to bed. She craved sleep, mind-numbing sleep. Her eyes wanted to close, blinding her to all the sights she no longer wanted to see. Sleep would bring peace. Sleep would bring Zach. In her dreams, he would come to her, talk with her and laugh with her. While she slept, they could be together.

"Five more lifts," she repeated firmly. The idea of at least dreaming about Zach spurred her on. Delany placed her legs back into position, clenched her hands around the grips that extended from the bottom of the bench, and with as much strength as she could muster, she pushed until her knees came close to being straight. They dropped and the weights fell with a clang.

"Slowly, Delany, you've got to release the weight slowly. You work the back of the legs when you do that. Now come on, just four more," Stan encouraged.

"Please be quiet while I do this," Delany answered, her tone surly. Again she pushed with all her might, and this time she slowly lowered her legs, feeling the pressure of the weights as she did.

Dr. Manuela and Debbie looked through the window of the weight room. Delany's sour mood was evident.

"Poor Stan," Debbie commented. "She's been like this for the past week. She barely even speaks to me anymore."

"So what happened? Did they get into a fight?" Manny asked.

"All I know is what she told me. She said she was growing too dependent on Zach and that she needed some space. Whether that's the truth or not, I don't know." Debbie's heart ached for her friend. Delany loved Zach, and Debbie believed that Zach loved Delany in return. He had been so dedicated to her, and Delany had blossomed under his care. Now that the gardener was gone, the flower had wilted. "Maybe I should call him," Debbie suggested. Maybe communication could solve their problem.

"You assume an awful lot. If he does return, what makes you think she'll make a remarkable recovery?" Manny asked.

Debbie thought for a moment, then shook her head against his cynicism. "You know her, Manny. This isn't her right now. My guess is that Zach wouldn't put up with her laziness. He'd challenge her if nothing else, and Delany is stubborn enough to get well on a challenge."

"Do what you have to. This lady doesn't deserve the emotional pain she's suffering." Manny walked off to make his rounds, and Debbie was left to contemplate her next move.

"I brought dinner," Debbie announced as she rolled in the dinner tray.

Delany looked up from her book with disinterest, then lowered her head once more to her reading.

"It's nice to see you, too."

Delany looked up at her friend, this time her gaze apologetic for her rudeness. "I'm sorry, Deb. I'm just worn-out."

"From what?" It was a bold question, one guaranteed to bring a response.

Delany, under the assumption that perhaps the nurse didn't know where she'd been for the past few hours, answered, "I've been with Stan in Rehab."

"Oh, I know where you've been. I just want to know why you're tired."

The jab hit home, and Delany's face flushed. "What are you trying to say?"

Debbie pushed the tray out of her way and moved closer to the bed so she could confront Delany with the terrible truth. "I'm telling you that if you don't start working harder, you'll sit in this bed, or one like it, for a very long time."

"I tried," Delany defended, knowing in her heart that she hadn't tried at all.

In more of a motherly manner, Debbie sat on the bed and softened her voice. "Why don't you call him? You'd feel much better and then you could get your focus back."

"You think my problem is Zach Montgomery?" Delany barked a laugh filled only with bitterness. "I've been on my own for years. Never have I relied on a man for anything, and I'm certainly not going to start now."

"Would it be so bad?" Debbie questioned. "Would it kill you to have someone here to help shoulder the burden? That's usually why people get married. Life's too hard to take it on by yourself. So you find someone you love and then the two of you take it on together."

Delany's eyes grew hard. "That sounds nice, Deb. But what if you don't find someone to help you? It's not a given in this life that you'll find a mate. It's also not a given that if you do find that person, he'll stay. I've learned to go it alone, and I won't stop now."

"He would have stayed if you hadn't told him to go. Swallow your pride. Call him." Leaving Delany to ponder those words, Debbie left the room.

And it was enough. Delany chewed her lip, wondering for the thousandth time if she hadn't made the biggest mistake of her life. She didn't know what had possessed her to tell him to leave. Perhaps it was the realization that she needed him. Needing someone frightened her more than she'd ever been before. She'd been a self-reliant child by nature. Her parents had given her life, and Delany had taken it from there.

Her brother, Michael, had been the child they fussed over and pampered. Perhaps they'd pampered him too much. Everything had been done for him, so he hadn't done for himself. Michael had never known what it meant to be responsible for his own life.

Delany had to be grateful then that she didn't have a dependent streak in her. Only now, she realized that independence came with a price. A very lonely price.

Call him, her heart whispered.

Delany rejected that idea. She couldn't risk it. Couldn't risk her heart. What if he said no? Debbie was right, though. Hard work was the only cure for what ailed her. Stubbornness would have to be her motivation. Independence, her rallying cry.

Zach wasn't coming back. He didn't love her the way she did him. So what would compel him to come back?

He missed her. This feeling was new for Zach. Traditionally, he left people without looking back. He had learned to suppress his deeper emotions and exist on a more superficial level. It was easier to leave his family, easier to change undercover roles, easier to avoid pain when those close to him died. Unfortunately, this kind of shallow life had cost him. He had forgotten who he was.

Hence, this leave of absence from his job. To discover himself, he needed to let down the walls he'd built and look deep inside. In the process, he had let Delany sneak through the barriers. His feelings for her were the first real emotions he'd felt in a long time, aside from his one lapse of reason that had ended by Zach taking a bullet. It felt good to live on a deeper level. More substantial. Emotions brought exhilaration and excitement. Along for the ride, however, were agony and despair. Quite a combo.

With the TV remote, Zach mindlessly flicked through the channels. Black-and-white movies, sitcoms, infomercials, rock videos passed before his eyes in a blur until he found a college football game that he hoped would hold his attention. The apartment came furnished with all the amenities and for that Zach was grateful. It would be easier to leave when the time came. All he would need to do was pack his clothes and go.

So why wasn't he going anywhere? It wasn't as if he didn't know the answer to the question; it was just that he didn't want to acknowledge that answer. He wanted Delany. He loved her. And he couldn't see beyond that.

Time for a new question. What was he doing *here?* She'd told him to leave, and so he had left. Last question. How did he get back?

Several possibilities flashed through his mind. The most appealing idea was simply to march back to the hospital, tell her that she had behaved like a child and kiss her senseless. Pride stood between him and that particular idea. Zach wasn't fool enough to let pride keep him from claiming the woman he wanted. He was just arrogant enough to wait and see if she would claim him first.

Zach wanted Delany to call him.

Testing her in this manner wasn't fair. But to kick him out of her life simply because he questioned her devotion to him was also unfair. Not that he had questioned her devotion, only the reasons behind it. Which brought to mind yet another test he had in store for her. Eventually, Zach was going to have to tell her what he had done that night. Confessions were supposed to be good for the soul, but Zach didn't buy that. His confession, if accepted poorly, would rip his very soul from him. His deception would shake the foundation of the tenuous relationship they had built.

Zach needed to know if their relationship would survive the earthquake. If she called him, he would have his answer. If she called him, he could plant their relationship on top of the San Andreas Fault, and they would survive.

If she called him.

* * *

The phone stared at her, taunted her, mocked her, if such a thing was possible. It took all of her willpower not to throw it against a wall or smash it on the floor. It beat like a heart in the silent room. *Bump-ump. Bump-ump. Call-call. Call-call.*

He'd told her to call when she wanted him.

She wanted him. What she didn't want was to admit that she'd been wrong. She didn't want to feel as if she was crawling back to him. She didn't want him to think that he was that important to her. Which was ridiculous because he *was* incredibly important to her. And he had to know that by now.

Delany reached for the phone and set it next to her. When had all this complexity entered her humdrum life? Wake up. Teach. Help kids. Run. Eat. Sleep. Simplicity had been her trademark. During the past weeks, she'd fended off gangsters, struggled with ruthless weight machines and battled the elusive love monster.

Love was a monster. With hideous teeth that latched onto a heart, love pulled and pushed and prodded Delany in directions she had no intention of ever going. Only now she was there. Her choice was simple: stay or go back. Delany refused to retreat.

Quickly, before she could change her mind, she punched with impatient fingers the numbers she had memorized long ago. Those numbers would lead her back to Zach.

Impatiently, Zach clicked off the TV. He couldn't sit on his butt waiting for something that might never happen. He wouldn't visit her, but he wouldn't waste his time, either. If nothing else, a movie might take his mind off Delany for two hours.

Keys in hand, Zach pulled on his coat and opened

the door to leave. He couldn't get out of there fast enough. Not one more minute lost, he promised himself.

Then he heard the phone ring.

It was a long-distance company calling. They wanted to make him part of their family of friends. Zach wasn't biting. The answering machine could pick up the call. He was out of there.

Beeeep. "…Uh…I…Goodbye."

The sound of the click resonated through the small studio. Zach pounced on the phone, but he knew it was useless. The call disconnected. The caller now was lost to him.

Had it been Delany? The voice sounded feminine, yet there was so little of the message to tell. It had to be her. Zach picked up the phone to call Delany, knowing it had to be her, but a kernel of doubt held him back. What a perfect excuse. Someone called, and it sounded like you, so I thought I should call just to check. If their positions were reversed, Zach wouldn't believe that obvious lie. He needed proof.

A hit of a button, and the message replayed. Zach listened intently. This time, he heard something else. Some background noise filtered through the stilted words. Still unable to make it out, he turned up the volume of the machine and once again rewound the message.

"…*Dr.* Uh…*Manuela*…I…*Please report*… Goodbye."

"Gotcha!" Zach whispered. He removed the tape from the cassette in case she dared to protest.

Sunlight filtered through the windows of the rehab center and bounced off the shiny metal of the weight machines. The glare was enough to cause Delany to lose her concentration. Her arms gave out first, and without their strength to hold up her body, her legs buckled beneath her.

"Damn!" The curse left her lips before she could prevent it.

"Don't let your frustration get the better of you," Stan advised. He got behind her and with powerful arms lifted her off her derriere once again into position over the parallel bars. "Maybe you're not ready for the bars."

Delany locked her elbows, leaning forward slightly so that her arms supported her. It was a good thing that the hospital food didn't agree with her. Her weight loss was coming in handy. Naturally, it was easier to blame the food rather than the actual cause of her lost appetite.

She'd gone to bed thinking of him and she'd woken up this morning in the same condition. Had he gotten the message? Had he known it was her? Delany shook her head. Now wasn't the time to dwell on any thoughts other than those of recuperation. Last night she'd promised herself that she would walk again no matter what, and that was what she planned to do.

Over her shoulder, Stan, whose hands were still resting gently on her waist, ready to catch her if she fell again, showed his concern by gently squeezing her.

Flashing a daring smile she didn't necessarily feel, she tried to reassure the young man. "I'm ready for the bars. Did I ever tell you what my name meant?"

Cautiously, she bent her knee, lifting it slightly while at the same time dragging it forward. Once it was set, she allowed some of her weight to rest on the leg, knowing that the more she did, the sooner her legs would be able to hold all of her weight.

Encouraged by her improved attitude, the therapist

offered a reply. "I figured it was Irish for stubborn mule."

Delany exhaled sharply, a cross between a laugh and a groan of pain as her muscles protested the extra effort. "Descendant of the challenger. My father said I come from a long line of rebellious Irish warriors who loved to challenge anyone and everyone. He said it was my legacy to take on the demons of the world." Delany struggled to lift her other knee and dragged it forward past her planted leg. Gingerly, she let her arms relax slightly. "This is just another demon that needs to be challenged."

Stan stood behind her, but kept far enough away to give her the room she needed. It was almost as if he sensed she no longer needed the safety net he provided. He moved out from between the bars and watched silently as Delany challenged those demons.

"Just a few more steps and then we'll hit the Jacuzzi," Stan called out.

A tremor shook her arms. Her muscles protested, but Delany would give them no quarter. Her melancholy had cost her too many days, and she was determined to make up for it. Bend. Lift. Drag. Set. Now the right leg. Bend. Lift. Drag. Set. A few more, she told her screaming muscles. Just a few more.

Without warning, her elbows buckled, and although Delany struggled valiantly, her legs couldn't support the weight. She knew she was going to fall, and she loathed the humiliation of it. Suddenly, there were two arms to catch her and keep her an inch off the floor. Those same arms propped her up until she stood, then moved quickly so that one arm supported her back while the other moved behind her knees to lift her into the air.

Shocked that Stan would be so presumptuous, she opened her mouth to protest.

Instead, the breath left her as she raised her head and found herself staring into Zach's eyes. Her thoughts flew in a thousand directions. In a daze, she wondered if she weren't back in her dreams. One of her wonderful dreams. Then she brought her hand up to touch him. She felt the rough stubble of hair on his cheek scratch her palm. It wasn't a dream.

"You're supposed to let me fall. It's good for my motivation. The more I fall, the less I want to." Her voice was a whisper, the flutters in her stomach not allowing her to speak any louder.

"I could never let you fall. Not as long as I was there to catch you." Zach settled her more comfortably in his arms and turned to the muscular blond therapist Zach had witnessed touching Delany, his hands around her waist. "Where does she go now?"

The therapist grinned. "The Jacuzzi first, and then I need to give her a rubdown."

A return smile graced Zach's face, only it wasn't filled with any warmth. Instead, the smile held a certain message. It said, "Over my dead body will you touch one hair on her head."

Zach's actual words were a little more civil. "You know, kid, I happen to have a great deal of experience with the kind of therapy you're talking about. I'm sure I could do the rubdown if you gave me a few pointers."

"I'm afraid that's not possible, sir. You're not a licensed physical therapist, while I am. It would be against hospital policy. However, I can assure you that Miss Sheridan is just another patient to me. You should have no doubts on that score." Stan attempted to hide another grin.

"Please, Zach, you're embarrassing me. Stan's doing his job. Why don't you wait for me back in the room? I had Debbie pick me out a new mystery novel. You check it out while I finish up here." Delany would have been more than happy to remain in Zach's arms forever, but the sweat on her body was chilling her. As much as she wanted Zach's hands all over her body, she didn't want them there in a medical capacity.

For a few seconds, Zach stubbornly considered putting up more of a fight. A quick glance at Delany's pale face convinced him that she needed more from him now than a show of macho bravado. Ignoring Stan, he maneuvered his way around the sports equipment to a door that was marked Bath. As soon as he pushed it open with his shoulder, he could hear the bubbles of the Jacuzzi.

Stan followed with Delany's wheelchair. He came up beside the couple and silently indicated that Zach could put Delany down and be on his way. Zach shot the young man one last quelling look that dared him to enjoy the sight of Delany's body, then left.

"That is one tough boyfriend you have, Delany," Stan commented as he prepared Delany for her dunk.

Boyfriend. Delany blushed with an inner warmth. "Yes, he is a rather formidable b-boyfriend." She stumbled slightly over the unfamiliar word, but she couldn't help the smile it brought to her lips, nor the glow that suddenly lit up her eyes, nor the tears that began to run down her face.

"Are you okay, Delany? You pushed yourself too hard this time, didn't you?" Stan accused gently.

Not about to admit her feminine weakness and the fact that she had been crying simply because she was

so happy, Delany murmured agreement and placed herself in Stan's capable hands.

Zach sat impatiently in his old familiar chair, holding
the book Delany had told him about. It was one he had
read and knew Delany would enjoy. Irrationally, he was
bothered by the idea that he hadn't been here with her
to see her enjoyment with the other books she'd read
since his departure. Delany wasn't a passive reader, nor
a passive listener for that matter. Every turn of the page
brought a new expression to her face. The characters
became more real to Zach because they seemed so real
to Delany. She laughed out loud at the funny parts,
sucked in her breath during the frightening parts and
sighed softly during the sad parts.

Intensity. The word came suddenly to Zach, and instantly he knew it described Delany perfectly. She lived
intensely, worked intensely, read intensely. That meant
she probably would love intensely, as well. It worried
Zach.

He had taken this time off work to get his bearings,
to try to remember who the hell he was. It wasn't fair
of Zach to give Delany only half of himself when she
was someone who would give him everything.

"Come here often, stranger?"

Zach picked his head up at the sound of her husky
voice. Her hair was piled on top of her head to keep it
from getting wet, but several tendrils had escaped the
bun and fallen around her face. The steam had curled
them, forming ringlets all around her face and neck. Her
eyes sparkled and her skin was flushed from the heat.
She looked like a delicately carved cameo. A portrait
from a long-ago age. Zach's breath froze in his chest,
causing an ache he had never felt before.

No, he didn't know who he was. But there was no rule that said you couldn't create yourself. Be something you wanted to be. Zach looked at Delany and knew what he wanted to be. He wanted to be the man who was worthy of her. A tall order, but one he dedicated himself to fulfilling.

"Well?" Delany queried. Zach stared at her with unreadable eyes. It was as if he was making a pact. The question was only with whom was he making it.

"Nothing. I suppose I've missed you."

"You suppose?" Delany smiled at her own cockiness. Normally, she wasn't so bold. She had no reason to be because there had never been anyone in her life who had made her feel so confident. Zach was different. He had stayed with her. More importantly, he had come back to her.

"Aren't we acting the queen today? Very well, Your Majesty, the truth—I did miss you. Now it's your turn," Zach countered, willing to give her what she wanted as long as she gave something back in return.

"My turn?" Delany questioned, her eyes alight with mischief and innocence combined.

Zach stood and bore down on her, intent on extracting from her that which his ego demanded. Bracing his hands on either side of her wheelchair, his face loomed before hers.

"You know what I want to hear," he threatened softly.

"Maybe I do, and maybe I don't," Delany whispered, anxious to see how far he would go.

She didn't have to wait long. Before she could finish her sentence, Zach's lips pressed down on hers. It was a ferocious kiss. He let her know with his lips and his tongue how much he had missed her. Delany in turn placed her hands behind his head, holding him to her so that she could let him know, also without words, how much she had missed him.

She felt his tongue plunge past her teeth to duel with her own. Their breaths mingled. His rough stubble scraped her cheeks. Her fingers entwined in his silky locks. It was the most perfect kiss she had ever experienced.

With a sigh, she forced herself to release him when he pulled back. "I missed you so much." It was as if the words had been pulled from her lips forcibly by his own.

"I know you did. I just wanted you to say it." Zach moved behind her and pushed her chair closer to the bed. In one scoop, he had her in his arms and then on the bed. With another motion, he covered her with the afghan. "You should probably sleep now. You've had a long morning."

The last thing Delany could think about was sleep. Her body didn't listen. The muscles in her arms and legs were smart enough to know they would be called upon again that day. They demanded rest.

"You'll stay?" Delany's anxious eyes met his. She couldn't bear to wake up again and have him gone.

"Of course I'll stay. Somebody's got to keep Stan in line." Zach pulled his chair next to the bed and picked up the book from her nightstand.

"You're not jealous?" Delany accused. Zach was too confident to be jealous. He was simply letting her know that she was special to him.

Zach arched a brow, but didn't answer. She was right; he wasn't jealous. Jealousy would imply that he was worried about something happening between Delany and her physical therapist. Zach knew instinctively that

Delany's emotions were monogamous. If the way she looked at him was any indication, Zach knew that he had put his affections into the right hands. Only time would tell if that look remained after he told her the truth about who he was and where he had been the night she was injured.

That night. Hell for her, yet the start of heaven for him.

"So tell me, how has the search for your restaurant been going? Surely you've found something by now." Delany's question was actually twofold. Yes, she wanted to know if he had found the perfect place, but she also wanted to know if he would remain in Tacoma indefinitely.

"Actually, I do have a lead on one place. It's in the warehouse district. Take your nap now and I'll tell you all about it when you wake up." Zach, for once, told the truth about his search for a location. With nothing to do while he was away from the hospital, he had turned up a few spots that he thought, with a little effort, might make a nice tavern. If there was a college campus on the way, that was one old building that would be prime real estate for a bar-and-grill-style business. He didn't know when he'd truly begun to think about opening a restaurant, but suddenly the idea wasn't so much a lie as it was a legitimate possibility.

It had been the job with the DEA that had kept him in the dark about his true character. Always under cover. Always a mask in place. Perhaps the only way to really find himself was to leave the job for good. It was a thought.

"Zach, I hate to be a pest..."

"Uh-oh, not another chocolate fix," Zach teased, remembering Delany's one and only weakness.

"It's been so long. I was too embarrassed to let Debbie know about my addiction."

"A Butterfinger?"

Practically drooling at the thought, Delany nodded her head. "A Butterfinger."

With a laugh, Zach was on his way to the vending machine. It was just a few feet down the corridor across from the lobby and telephones. Zach took the spare change from his pocket and fed the machine.

Not once did he turn and recognize the young man in blue on the phone.

"I'm tellin' you, O.G., it's him," Enrico insisted. "I came to the hospital to visit a brother who's recoverin' from his wounds from that last 'slob' attack. And then I see him comin' out of some room." Enrico held his hand up beside his mouth so as to modulate his voice. He didn't want to gain the attention of the traitor. At least not yet.

"You're tellin' me the pig is there?" O.G. exclaimed. He began to clench and unclench his right hand. The hand that was now missing a thumb because of that pig. Anger raged inside his body. Once his L.A. contacts discovered that he had given up the name of their contact in Seattle, they acted swiftly. O.G. had been kidnapped at gunpoint by the most unforgiving group of drug dealers it had been his misfortune to meet. He was about to lose each of his fingers, one at a time, before they finally shot him to death.

Fortunately for him, some of his gang who were still loyal had followed him. Armed as they always were, they were able to knock off the dealers before they got to finger number two. Still, his thumb was not the only thing he'd lost. Despite the fact that he'd escaped with his life, he returned to his hood only to find that he'd already been replaced. The dealers in L.A. were not about to give up the Tacoma market. They sent one of the Crip leaders from L.A., who had recently been released from prison, to assume the title of O.G. The majority of the gangsters, all under the age of fifteen, readily accepted the change of command. Once you were a part of the nation, it didn't matter what city you came from. Since the Crip nation had begun in Los Angeles, it was like having a celebrity O.G.

His thumb, his gang, his pride...all gone. It was the pig's fault. Police, FBI, DEA—it didn't matter the farm you came from. The only thing that mattered was the way his bacon was going to taste when fried.

"Find out why this pig is there. Follow him. I want to know where he goes, who he sees, when he eats. Everything."

Enrico, too loyal for his own good, was happy to oblige. "You are the Original Gangster, man. O.G. You own him! He's gotta pay. Let me be the one to make him pay."

"No," O.G. burst out. Then, his tone calmer, more deadly, he grated, "He's mine. And before he goes down, he's gonna know the one who did it to him."

Chapter 6

"That's it, Delany, just a little more," Stan encouraged. "I want you to work hard, but not kill yourself."

Delany shot Stan a quelling look, then concentrated on the floor. More accurately, she concentrated on her feet that were connected to her legs that weren't making the progress she expected them to make. In the three days since Zach's return, she'd been simultaneously more focused and completely distracted. Zach spent every morning observing her therapy. He would often help to motivate her in ways that Stan couldn't. Her determination to walk increased tenfold.

Her mind, however, began to shift and sway, sometimes whispering things to her that she wasn't prepared to deal with. Almost two weeks of therapy had gone by and she could still barely move her legs. Granted, her efforts that first week had been dismal.

She worked hard to make up for that loss of time, yet she still got nowhere. What if she wasn't able to recover? What if she had to spend the rest of her life in braces and a walker? She was a marathon runner. She was a challenger. She wasn't an invalid.

There was also Zach to think about. What was she going to do about him if she could never be the person she used to be? Would he even continue to pursue a relationship with her if she were permanently crippled? Finding a mate for life was something close to impossible today. Finding a mate with this kind of strike against you would be like winning the lottery. It happened. It must happen. Millions of people with disabilities didn't deserve a life without love.

Only Delany hadn't been lucky in love even as a single healthy person. She questioned the notion that her luck would improve now that her health had failed her. Zach deserved more than a slug who could barely walk. He was a wonderful guy, handsome and virile. He deserved the best. Delany saw the braces. They weren't the best.

No, she scolded herself. She couldn't let herself think that way.

"Delany, you're losing your focus. Your arms aren't going to support your weight forever. Keep moving." Zach stood at the end of the parallel bars with his arms crossed over his chest. He kept them there to stop himself from reaching out to her. Every time she groaned against the strain, he ached inside. He watched as the sweat pooled on her forehead while she struggled to bring her legs back to form. It hurt him more than she could know.

"Try to put a little more weight on your legs, Delany," Stan instructed, noticing that her arms were indeed trembling again.

"Do this, do that. Now I know how my students

feel," Delany grumbled. She made a pact with herself to cut down on the nagging the next time she saw them. The truth was that Stan was right. Her arms were starting to tremble and she needed to release a little of the pressure soon or she would collapse again. Like a child on the monkey bars at recess, she wanted to move but was afraid that the slightest shift in position would send her falling. If she stayed where she was for much longer, the result would be the same.

Gently, she let her elbows bend and attempted to stay on top of the movement. The arches in her feet began to tense, anticipating the stretch she forced upon them. The muscles in her calves cramped slightly, and her back began to protest. The pain was hell, but it was better than the numbness. So Delany endured.

Hunching forward, she lifted her arm and slid her hand down the bar. Her legs bent and moved more easily after three days of work; that much credit she would give herself at least. They remembered what they were supposed to do. All they really needed was some practice and a little added strength. Next she moved her other hand. Her legs cooperated, and for a brief moment, she began to feel as if things were once again under her control. This time with a bit more confidence, she took her next step and allowed her legs to do even more of the work, her arms less so.

One step. Two steps. "By Jove, I think she's got it!" Stan declared happily.

Delany turned to smile, but the slight shift in balance brought her joy to a crashing halt. This time, Zach was too far away to make the grab, and the floor rushed up to meet Delany. She tried to brace her fall with her arms, but her muscles, too sore from all the strain, gave way underneath her, and her bottom hit the mat with a decided thunk.

Immobilized, she didn't say or do anything. Both Stan and Zach rushed to her side, but the damage to her pride had already been done. Her face red, her eyes suddenly swollen, she managed with Zach's help to move herself into his lap so that her back was supported by his chest and her now useless arms could rest on the strength of his.

"How about a few minutes alone, Stan? Then you can take her away and do your thing with the hot tub and the massage." Zach could see that it was Delany's pride that hurt more than anything else right now. He knew because he'd fallen on his butt a few times himself during his rehab, and every time, he had hated himself for doing it.

Stan seemed reluctant to let his patient out of his sight, but he finally acquiesced. "Not too long. I don't want those muscles to cramp up on her," he warned.

Sitting on the floor, they watched Stan leave. The room seemed incredibly quiet. Usually there were several people working out in the gym with their different therapists, but Delany had asked for the early-morning sessions to work with the bars as she hoped to avoid falling in front of a crowd of people.

"You told me that falling was good for you. It made you tougher," Zach reminded her, happy to let her head fall against his shoulder. Maybe it was a bit chauvinistic, but he liked it when she leaned on him. Even if it was for only a little bit of time. Delany was far too independent to allow herself to be taken care of for very long. So this time was special.

"I don't want to be tough anymore. I'm tired of being tough." It was a surprising revelation for her to hear herself admit that. Was it true? And if so, how long had she been tired? "Since my brother," she said, answering her own unspoken question.

"What about your brother?" Zach prodded. The time for her to release her anger had come.

"My brother messed up, and my parents couldn't deal with him. They couldn't deal with his addiction, or his death. Somebody had to deal with it. Somebody had to take care of my father when he couldn't cope with Mother's death." Her voice was soft and strangely flat, as if she was seeing her life story for the first time. Like a spectator, she watched herself falling over and over again, then, all alone, picking herself up.

Zach closed his arms around her and brought his lips to her ear. Softly, he nuzzled her neck and tasted her sweat mixed with her sweetness. It was a gesture of comfort, not one of desire, but it felt better to him than any sexual embrace he had ever given in his life. "Tell me, Delany. Tell me all the times you had to do it by yourself."

"I had to make the funeral arrangements, all three of them, by myself. Since their deaths, I've spent every holiday by myself. It wasn't fair that they all left me. It wasn't fair that all I tried to do was help Cici, and those monsters hurt me. I can't walk because of them. I have nightmares because of them. All I tried to do was help. I don't want to help anybody anymore. I'm tired of caring about everybody else and their needs. I'm so tired."

She didn't cry or sob. She felt selfish and whiny. Guilty, too, because she blamed her parents for dying. However, for the first time in years, Delany felt free of the burden that she never realized she'd been carrying.

Turning to see his reaction, Delany asked, "Do you

hate me for that? For suddenly feeling so sorry for my-self?''

"You're just human, Delany. For a while there, I wondered. It seemed like every thought you had and everything you did was for other people. I didn't know whether to kiss you or canonize you. It's not right to give all your energy away, to give all of yourself away. You need to think of yourself. And right now, while you're hurting, you need to think only of yourself.'' If Zach was smart, he would listen to his own advice. He wasn't going through the physical pain anymore, but he hurt nonetheless. He needed to get his own act together. Not spend his days nursing someone else back to health.

He owed her. It was as good an excuse as any, yet he didn't buy it. He loved her. But that still didn't ex-cuse him from avoiding the issues in his own life. When he was with her, when he helped her, he was healing himself. Every day he came closer to knowing who he was because she constantly showed him sides of himself he didn't know were there.

"But it was all so useless. I don't even know where Cici is. Dan said he looked everywhere, but there's still no trace of her. She might have already been initiated. She might be one of them by now. I might not ever fully recover, and it was all for nothing.'' The idea that she might lose the use of her legs, and Cici, too, was overwhelming. Only it didn't make her sad. Furious was a better description.

Her anger sparked her eyes to life, and Zach felt a sudden tension grip his body. His time of being needed had come to an end. It had been sweet while it lasted. He looked forward to the time she would need him again and found himself wishing it would be soon.

"I want to get up." Determination rang out in Delany's voice.

Zach hesitated. "Stan will be back in a minute. You need to cool down for a while. A bath and a massage, and then you'll be ready for the pool by this afternoon."

"I want to get up." Before Zach could stop her, Delany struggled to get out of his lap. She wished it had been possible to stay within his arms forever, but it wasn't.

No use fighting the inevitable. Zach helped her back into position over the bars. "If Stan sees me, he'll ban me from the therapy room."

At that moment, Delany couldn't have cared less about Stan and what he thought. It was a freeing thought. Who cared what Stan wanted or didn't want? It was her life, her body. She could do with it what she wanted. She had no intention of pushing herself to the point of harm. She just didn't want to end the day on a fall.

"A few steps and then Stan can have me," Delany grated as her arms once again rebelled in protest.

"Watch what you say. I think he enjoys your company far too much for a man who's seen you naked." Zach smirked, but he was only half kidding.

"I wear a suit in the tub, and a towel during the massage, Greeny." She chided him because there was no need for him to be jealous, but at the same time she secretly reveled in his possessiveness. His comments also helped to take her mind off the pain. Just a few steps; that was all she would need.

Moving her arms and her legs in sync, she was able to lift her legs and take two steps into Zach's waiting arms. With a heavy sigh, she fell against him and allowed herself to borrow his strength. For her, he never seemed to run out.

Quickly, Zach lifted her against his chest and deposited her in her chair.

"I did it. I had to." Delany willed him to understand.

"I remember how it was. I remember that the goals I set for myself always surpassed those of the therapist. Only my goals mattered to me. I needed to prove to myself that it wasn't going to end with a—" Zach stopped abruptly. A bullet. Zach hadn't wanted to give the drug dealer the satisfaction of thinking that he'd won some kind of victory by taking Zach out of law enforcement. His refusal to give up had been as important to his recovery as his doctors had been. The words would have to be left unsaid for now. He wasn't ready to tell Delany the truth. He didn't know if he was even willing to remember it.

Before Delany could question him about what he'd left unsaid, Stan came through the door with a determined look of his own. "Let's go, Delany. I've got to have you rubbed down, fed and rested if you're going to be ready for the pool this afternoon."

"The pool is a cakewalk compared to the bars." Her buoyancy in the water made her feel as if she were once again in control of her body.

Stan, however, had other ideas. He wiggled his eyebrows and assumed a fake German accent. "Not zo fahst. Today I ahd zee veights to your legz."

"No, no," Delany dramatically protested. "Not the weights. Anything but the weights."

Stan laughed at her response and moved behind her chair to take her to the tub room.

"I'll see you back in the room?" Delany asked. After

three days, she still needed to reassure herself that Zach wasn't going anywhere.

"I've got an errand to run, but I'll be back as soon as possible." Leaning down, Zach kissed her on the lips as if he'd been doing it forever.

An uncertain gleam appeared in her eyes, but only for a moment. He'd be back. She knew he would. "I'll see you tonight."

"I don't know that I can help you, Mr. Montgomery." Dan Banks leaned across his desk, his face sympathetic. "Cici hasn't been in school since, well, not since the night of Delany's...accident. I've checked with her friends, adults she's close to... Nothing."

Zach cursed under his breath. He had warned the girl of the consequences if he ever saw her again in the company of Crips. Delany was right. She had done it all for nothing if Cici was now a part of that life. "If there was any chance that she wasn't with her brother on the streets, do you have any idea where I might look?" Zach wasn't prepared to fail at this point.

The principal leaned back in his chair, seriously thinking about the question. "There are two possibilities. I checked with both of them, but maybe we need to check with them again. She used to bag groceries for Mr. Gonzales down at the Stadium Bag and Save. That's not too far from Tacoma General."

Zach reached for a pen on the desk before him, pulled off a sheet of paper from a notepad close at hand and began to jot down the information. He knew the grocery store. It was where he'd been buying his staples. "What's my other choice?"

"The Browns. They were her sponsor family."

For a moment, Zach looked up, his expression curious. "Sponsor family. Like foster parents?"

Dan shook his head. "No. Actually, it was a program
Delany started. She paired up wealthy, socially con-
scious families with deserving children. If the student
met the criteria, passed all the tests and Delany's personal interview, then she matched the youngster with a
family, usually alumni, that would pay the school tuition."

"A scholarship program," Zach summarized. He remembered Delany had mentioned it.

"It was more than that. These families just don't
write a check. They act more as mentors to the students.
For instance, the Browns have invited Cici over for dinner, taken her to the movies with their kids. They've
shown her what a normal family could be like. For kids
who come from the Hilltop, it's something they've
rarely experienced. An excellent program. Unfortunately, we don't have enough families for all the deserving students out there, but Delany's motto was 'One
at a time.'"

A soft laugh escaped Zach. He thought it somehow
ironic that his own personal motto had been "Save the
world." Delany's idea suddenly made more sense to
him. "Sounds like she did a lot of good here." Zach
recalled meeting Patti when he'd dropped by the school
before. She was living proof of the work that Delany
did.

"She did more than teach. She saved lives. I mean,
she literally saved lives." Dan's expression grew
thoughtful at his use of the past tense. "She is coming
back, isn't she?"

Zach stood, his hands smoothing down his jeans. "I

can't answer that question for her. I can tell you this. She needs to have a life, her own life, I mean.''

"No one ever forced Delany to do what she did," Dan replied defensively.

"No, you're right. Delany wanted to do it. But you let her." Zach walked out of the office without waiting for a response.

Mr. Gonzales was a short, balding man who gazed out over his store as if it were his empire. He stood on a stepladder in the corner and watched as his checkers checked and his baggers bagged. One of the stock boys pointed him out and Zach immediately had the sensation that the man took his job far too seriously. All the guy did was manage the place.

"Mr. Gonzales," Zach called as he walked up to the man on the stepladder. The man turned and looked at him, his first expression being one of annoyance at having been disturbed. Then his expression altered when he recognized Zach as a customer in need of his assistance.

"Is there something wrong with your purchase?" he asked, stepping down from his perch. He barely reached Zach's shoulder now that he was standing on the floor.

For a moment, Zach was confused by the question. Then he looked at his hand and remembered the yellow bag of treats he had picked up for Delany.

"No, I just wanted to ask you a few questions about a girl you know. Her name is Cici Delores. She used to bag groceries for you, I understand."

The manager's face underwent another transformation. This time, his expression was completely closed. Zach had enough experience in law enforcement to know when a witness was intentionally clamming up.

"Look," Zach explained, "I'm a friend of Delany Sheridan's. She's worried about the girl, and I want to put her mind at ease."

"How do I know you're really Delany's friend?"

Waving one of the candy bars in the air, Zach made his point without words.

Mr. Gonzales caved in instantly. "You're looking for Cici?"

"Yes."

"I lent her my car so she could get out of town if she had to. The buses aren't safe because her brother's friends are always riding them." Mr. Gonzales suddenly looked around as if checking to make sure no one was within earshot of their conversation.

Zach wasn't surprised. Many people had the impression that gangs consisted of a bunch of punk kids. Zach knew better. They were a lethal organization that killed often and without remorse. Mr. Gonzales was right to be cautious.

His tone slightly lowered, Zach continued his questioning. "Do you have any idea where she might be. Or do you think she's left the state?"

"The Browns."

"Her sponsor family?"

"They live on Federal Way. I'll give you the address. She might not still be there, but that's where she was headed." Mr. Gonzales sped down one of the aisles toward a door marked Employees Only. Zach followed. Once back there, Mr. Gonzales wrote the address on a slip of paper and handed it to Zach. "Listen, I know this sounds ridiculous, but make sure you aren't followed," Mr. Gonzales instructed. "Something happened that night. I don't know what—Cici wouldn't explain—but she's afraid. If the gang is out to get her, they will. They've already been around here, looking for her. I don't want to be responsible if anything happens to that girl.''

"I'll be careful." Zach took the address and mentally thought out the route he would take and the circles he could make to check and see if he was being followed. He didn't want to be responsible for leading the gang to Cici, either. Delany had given too much of herself for this girl's sake already.

"I lost him."

O.G. slammed his good hand down on the card table in front of the spot where a sullen and somewhat chastised Enrico now sat. Beer bottles rattled and then fell to the floor.

"What d'ya mean you lost him?" O.G.'s rage had been slowly building ever since the moment he discovered that the pig was still in town. Ostracized from his nation, hiding out in a one-room apartment inside a condemned old house, O.G. had nothing left to do but grow more and more angry and plan his revenge. Somebody had to pay. He would never get his gang back. If any of the old L.A. contacts ever saw his face again, he was as good as dead. His livelihood, his money and his authority were gone. Somebody was going to pay.

"I followed him like you said, and then he started to make weird turns, like he knew I was back there. The next thing I knew he was gone, man. Gone." Enrico prepared himself for more anger to be thrown his way. O.G. had been nothing but angry lately. His leadership had been stripped from him. His gang members numbered only three—Enrico and two other useless kids who decided to stick it out with him. He wasn't going to like losing the pig on top of everything else.

"He's a cop. DEA probably. I told you to be careful. Now he knows he's being followed." Damn. Surprise would have been a good thing to have in his corner. Easier to lead a pig to the slaughterhouse when the animal thought he was going for some grub.

"I was careful. I don't know how he knew I was on his tail. Besides, it don't make no difference. He goes to that hospital every day to see the broad. He'll be there waiting for us whenever we want to take him out." Enrico stood and removed his pistol from the back of his sagging jeans as if to show how much heart he really had.

"Sit, you idiot. I can shoot him any time I want. That's not how I want it to be. Pain. Real physical pain is what I want that pig to feel. Tell me about the woman he visits."

Enrico suddenly realized what he had not told O.G. "That's right. Catch this, man. She's the same broad from that night."

"What're you talkin' about?"

"You know, the night we were goin' to initiate my sister, Cici. The woman comes and says no, take her instead. So the boys had a little fun, and now he sits with her in the hospital."

O.G. absorbed the information while he clutched his right hand in an attempt to soothe his missing thumb. "Good to know, Enrico. Maybe the pig doesn't like to see the ladies get hurt. Maybe we take her and the pig comes to us."

"Yeah," Enrico sighed. He had a score to settle with the teacher himself.

Revenge was cool. He might die, but the cop who was responsible for his missing thumb would die, too. There was a chance, a small one, that if he nailed the pig who blew the contact, maybe the brothers in L.A. would forgive him. If not, the Crip nation was large and expansive. Other cities would welcome him as O.G. First, though, he had business to take care of.

"Go back to the hospital. Watch her. Watch him. Report." Commands that were kept direct and simple were easier to follow, especially for Enrico. His sister had gotten all the brains.

"Watch her," Enrico repeated. "My pleasure."

Delany was anxious. It was after eight, and there was still no word from Zach. She wondered if she'd been too confident before when she believed his return was certain. Perhaps he had changed his mind, realized that he was better off without some whiny invalid who loved nothing more than to cry in his arms.

Stop it. You're only human, she told herself. If Zach couldn't accept that, then he was no one she wanted to be around. But she did want to be around him. There were moments when she thought that was all she wanted. It never occurred to her that love could be so all-consuming. When had she stopped being Delany and become part of a whole that seemed to include Zachary Montgomery? It was an awesome concept.

If there were nagging doubts and suspicions, then she put them aside. He had told her that he'd found a location for his bar and grill, but they'd never returned to the topic. It wasn't that Delany didn't believe him. It was just that she couldn't believe him.

Delany grimaced in self-disgust. She didn't want to doubt him. But there were too many questions left unanswered. Why had it taken so long to find a location? Did he really plan to open a restaurant? What had his life been like before he came to Tacoma? And why

Tacoma? Questions. All questions and no answers. And then there was that look in his eye. Guilt, maybe, but more apologetic. Many times, Delany had sensed that there was something Zach wanted to tell her, but couldn't. A secret that he held.

It was terrible to think it, but Delany suspected that Zach was hiding something from her, something important. It was easy to ignore when he was just a helpful stranger. It got harder to ignore when he became her friend. Now that she was in love with him, her suspicions wouldn't go away.

"Who are you, Zach?" she whispered to herself. "More importantly, what are you?"

Just then, the door swung open as if her thoughts had summoned him.

"Are we still seeing visitors?" Zach's broad shape filled the door, and instantly the room was filled with his presence.

"You're a visitor I'll see any time," Delany confided with a smile. Now that he was back, it was simple to shove her doubts to the back of her mind. Live now; worry later.

"That's good to know, but how about a little extra company tonight?" Zach waved to someone on the other side of the door and motioned for whoever it was to come in.

Curious as to who it could be, Delany craned her neck. It stunned her to see Cici walk through the door, but it thrilled her more.

"Cici." Delany wanted to shake the girl silly, then hug her until she cracked.

"Hi, Ms. Sheridan." Cici walked closer to the bed, but hesitantly as if she was uncertain of the welcome she'd receive. When Mr. Montgomery had shown up on the Browns' doorstep, Cici wanted to hide under the nearest rock. Guilt plagued her every move, despite what Mr. and Mrs. Brown had tried to tell her.

"Are you all right? Did you get home okay? Of course not," Delany responded, answering her own question. "If you went home, Enrico would have been waiting for you."

"I went to stay with the Browns. Mr. Gonzales let me borrow his car, and then I just took off. I left your car in front of your apartment building. Your manager has the keys," Cici explained, hoping that Ms. Sheridan wouldn't think she'd stolen the car. For added measure, Cici added, "He told me to take the car that night." She pointed at Zach, who moved around the bed to relax in his now-familiar chair.

It had been a tiring day for him, driving all over looking for the girl. Not only that, but he still had to deal with the knowledge that someone had followed him. It could have been a gang member looking for Cici, but he didn't think so. How could any of her brother's friends know who he was or why he would be looking for the girl? No, it was unlikely that whoever had been trailing him was searching for Cici. More than likely they were after him. So who were "they" and why were they following him? It wasn't as if he hadn't done a million things to warrant someone coming after him for revenge. Zach was just curious about who it was this time.

Delany, oblivious to Zach's pondering gaze, chuckled at Cici's thoroughness. "It's okay. I know. I told you take the car, too, remember? I'm glad you're safe. Do the Browns understand the situation?" Delany wondered if they knew how much danger was truly involved.

At that point, Cici realized it was going to be a long explanation. She sat on the edge of the bed and began to recount the details of the past few weeks.

"All I was going to do was ask for some money to leave town, honest," Cici declared, knowing exactly how much danger she had put the Browns in. "But then Mr. Brown pulled me inside and made me tell him the whole story. He didn't make me go to the police or nothing."

"Anything," Delany corrected, still a teacher at heart. "Go on."

"He said he knew how dangerous it would be for me to be seen in Tacoma, so he was going to let me stay in his house until things cooled down. Mr. Brown was terrific, and so was Mrs. Brown. They stayed up the whole night helping me work through my problem. I felt so guilty, Ms. Sheridan."

"There was nothing for you to feel guilty about. I'm an adult. I made my own decision to go there that night. What happened to me was my fault, not yours," Delany finished emphatically. Guilt was a powerful emotion, one she didn't want Cici to drag behind her for the rest of her life.

"That's what Mr. Brown said. But you wouldn't have been there if it hadn't been for me and my stupid brother. I can't help remembering the way he looked. He wouldn't stop hitting you, even when I begged him. He's evil, Ms. Sheridan. I mean, it's like he likes to hurt people. I didn't realize it until that night."

Cici recalled telling her teacher about her loyalty to her brother and how he'd always been there for her and her mom. The truth was, he'd been there for himself. He'd put food on the table for himself to eat and left Cici and her mother with the leftovers. Enrico paid the rent because he needed a place to sleep. He didn't care if someone else slept there with him. He hadn't really done anything for her, certainly nothing to warrant her loyalty.

"Then you understand why you have to get away from him and his so-called 'brothers.' He never did deserve any of the loyalty you had to offer him." Delany believed now that Cici could walk away from her brother and never look back.

Cici nodded in agreement and reached out to hold Delany's hand. "I don't know what I'm going to do. I can't stay with the Browns forever. I feel bad enough as it is, taking their charity the way I have."

"It wasn't only charity that made Mr. Brown take you in that night. It was caring. You don't recognize it because you've never seen it before. Take their help. They've got plenty of it to offer," Delany instructed. The Browns were good people. They wouldn't let Cici down.

Cici gave her teacher a quick kiss on the cheek. "You're wrong, Ms. Sheridan. I've seen caring before. You were the first one to teach me, and I'll never forget it."

"Who was the second president of the United States?" Delany quizzed.

In a heartbeat, Cici replied, "John Adams. I won't forget my history, either. I promise." Laughing at the fact that Delany could still be a teacher while she was flat on her back, Cici backed off the bed.

Zach, who'd been silently listening to the entire exchange between the woman and girl, stood, ready to drive Cici back to Federal Way.

"Mr. Brown is waiting for me downstairs. He figured you'd be tired of driving back and forth, so he said he'd

meet me here.'' Cici waved goodbye to Delany and was
on her way out the door.

"I'll make sure you get to his car safely," Zach informed the girl, acting out of both politeness and caution. If someone was following her, he didn't want to
take any chances that they had picked up his trail. "I'll
be right back," he told Delany, then headed out the
door behind Cici.

He had done it for her. She'd said she didn't want to
believe that she had sacrificed her well-being for nothing, and he'd sought to prove to her that she hadn't. It
was the most precious gift anyone had ever given her.
Looking toward his chair, as if to visualize him there,
she smiled at his goodness.

Zach had his secrets, but Delany would never doubt
his character. Whatever he was hiding, she would eventually know, but she wasn't worried about it anymore.
Nothing he could tell her would shake the trust on
which she'd built her love for him. And it was a love
that would last forever. He was the one, the magical
one. She suspected as much when she first heard his
soft snores fill the room and saw him slouched in the
very same chair that was now empty.

That's when she saw it. Something yellow peeked out
from under the chair. It looked suspiciously like a yellow plastic bag. A yellow plastic bag that might contain
the most succulent, chocolaty, peanut-buttery-tasting
candy ever. There was nothing she craved more than a
Butterfinger! He'd remembered her favorite treat, and
he was going to surprise her with a whole bag.

Now that was love.

There was only one problem. They were under the
chair, and she was way up on the bed. Most likely he
would have to wait for Mr. Brown to arrive. Then, of

course, he would stay and chat with the man. Thank him for letting Cici come and visit. Zach would ask if there was anything he could do to help, offer any advice he could give, because that was the kind of man he was. At this point, it was going to be at least twenty minutes before she got her chocolate fix.

To walk over to the chair and get them herself was obviously impossible. Sure she had managed a few steps on the parallel bars, but walking to the chair would mean taking at least two steps solo. And that was just to get to the chair. Then there was the return trip.

Dr. Manuela. Zach might stop and talk to Doc Manny. They would talk football and other sporting events. Debbie might stop by and decide to shoot the breeze with him. Now Delany was looking at another ten minutes before she got her hands on the sweets.

Two steps. Perhaps "impossible" had been a harsh word to use. "Improbable" was more like it. Actually, the more Delany judged the distance from the bed to the chair, the more she thought it was doable. Slowly, she pulled off her covers and swung her legs to the floor until her toes touched cold tile. Using the bed for support, she gripped the edge of the metal frame and allowed her legs to absorb some of her weight. Her feet ached, her muscles protested, her back creaked, but then she was standing. Not steadily, but standing unsupported was an achievement. Cautiously, she held out her hand trying to reach for the chair arm to use it as another support. It was too far away. She was going to have to take one step freely without holding on to anything.

For a second, she thought herself insane. Life and limb were literally being risked for a candy bar. However, it wasn't the candy bar, and Delany knew it. It

was the idea that something she wanted was out of
reach. The candy all but dared her to walk to it, claim
it, and eat it. As a descendant of challengers, Delany
never backed away from a dare.

Unable to actually lift her leg, she more or less slid
it forward. Once her right leg was securely in position,
she encouraged her left leg to catch up. One small step
for woman. One giant leap for candy!

Twenty minutes later, Zach returned to the room to
find Delany all snug in her bed, munching on a large
piece of chocolate. If the brown smudges around her
lips were any indication, it wasn't her first piece. Without a word, she merely smiled at him and continued her
chocolatefest.

"I think you're ready to go home."

Later that night, Delany closed her eyes and dreamed
of freedom and marathons…and Zach. All the events
that had happened during the day drifted through her
mind. It was such a relief to know that Cici was well
cared for. Delany felt rather self-satisfied. Not only had
she rescued Cici from the gang, but she was going to
walk again. They had taken nothing from her.

The gang walked away empty, but Delany had found
the love of her life as a result of their maliciousness.
All things considered, everyone had won except for Enrico and his friends. That knowledge thrilled Delany.

If only her stomach didn't ache so. Well, what do
you expect when you eat a bagful of chocolate bars?
Delany chastised herself silently. If she was awake the
whole night, she had only herself to blame.

Creak.

For a moment, Delany stopped her internal groaning.
It sounded as if someone had opened the door to her

room. Naturally, it was Debbie. Her face turned toward the door, Delany was about to request something to settle her stomach. Thank goodness Debbie was always checking up on her, Delany thought. One unaided walking trip was enough for her that night.

Only it wasn't Debbie. In the darkened room, it was difficult to make out a face. A young man stood in the doorway of her room, the door held open by his shoulder.

"Can I help you?"

Immediately, the shadowy figure was gone. Delany thought back to her paranoia after the attack. She remembered thinking that there were gangsters in every corner, waiting for her, ready to pounce. She had once imagined them outside her door.

"Don't be ridiculous," she commanded herself. It was somebody who got lost. Somebody looking for a family member. So what if the hairs on the back of her neck stood straight up. It didn't mean anything.

The last thing Delany saw before she drifted off into slumber was a logo for the Los Angeles Raiders. Briefly, Delany wondered what made her think of the skull and crossbones. Before she could put her finger on it, she was asleep.

Chapter 7

"It's official," Debbie declared. "Dr. Manuela is going to sign the release papers."

For a moment, Delany didn't know what to think. She'd been in the hospital so long, she was almost afraid to leave. It had been over a week since the Butterfinger incident, as Stan liked to refer to it. Never in his career had candy bars given someone the will to walk. There was a first time for everything, Zach informed him.

Regardless of what inspired her to walk, the fact was that Delany was now legitimately walking. She still had uncomfortable moments when she lifted her legs, and it hurt to keep her back in a completely upright position. More accurately, Delany resembled a hunchbacked, shuffling old woman rather than a young walking one. But she was walking! And she was improving daily.

Stan balked at the idea of discharging her at this stage of her rehabilitation, but as soon as Zach had put the idea into her head, she couldn't let it go. It wasn't so much that she wanted to be home; it was just that she wanted to be out of the hospital. She wanted real food, and her own clothes, and more than anything, a change in scenery.

The only thing she didn't want was another Butterfinger candy bar. After eating practically the whole bag in one sitting, Delany believed it would be a while before that particular candy ever tempted her again. She thought about her stomachache and the visitor it had conjured up. The more Delany thought about it, the more she believed she had dreamed him up as a result of all the chocolate she had eaten.

"There is only one condition," Debbie added, trying to read Delany's expression.

"What's the condition?" Delany asked, still unsure of her decision.

"Well, actually, there are several. Dr. Manuela will run down the list for you and let you know what you will need to do. I, on the other hand, have a few conditions of my own. One, you must promise to call me often."

"Without a doubt. I wouldn't have made it if it hadn't been for you, Deb," Delany confided seriously.

Debbie, refusing to get sentimental, continued with her list. "Two, you simply must invite me to the wedding."

"Debbie!" Delany cried, frantic that Zach would choose just that moment to walk though the door.

"Relax, he's down the hall arguing with Stan over your release. He's got this crazy idea that he can take care of you as well as, if not better than, Stan. Naturally, Stan refutes the claim. You know how sensitive physical therapists are. It's the hands, I say. Soft hands, sensitive natures.''

"You're incorrigible, you know that?" Delany's heartbeat returned to normal. Nothing drove a man off quicker than the M word. It was ludicrous even to think it. They had only known each other a relatively short time. Delany was still trying to decipher Zach's secrets. The idea of marriage was so far from her mind, it was laughable.

All right, it wasn't that far from her mind, but the rule was, when you made a wish, you didn't tell anybody or else it wouldn't come true. Delany kept her wishes secret, even from herself.

"Why pretend like it isn't a possibility? You love each other. It's not as complicated as you would like to make it," Debbie asserted. "I don't know why young people today have to turn every moment of their lives into such a big production. Sometimes you have to accept things as they are.''

Delany would have liked nothing better than to agree, but it *was* complicated. There were still things about Zach she didn't know. His past was a blur, his present was vague, and his future was totally obscure to her. Not only that, but she wasn't a hundred percent herself. With Zach's life filled with so much uncertainty at the moment, was he prepared to take on the challenges of a girlfriend who still needed a cane to walk?

In retrospect, Delany realized that the hospital had been a very safe environment for them. The isolation of the small room lent itself to the intensity of their relationship. How well would they get along now that they had the whole world to contend with? Delany hoped that nothing would change, yet in a way she hoped that everything would change...for the better.

"I really think it's too soon to let her go," Stan protested even while he held the door open for Zach, who entered pushing a wheelchair in front of him. Apparently, they hadn't quite reached an agreement over Delany's readiness.

"Well, I say she's ready, and Doc agrees with me. And so does Delany," Zach argued. He left Stan and found Delany dressed in a pair of comfortable sweatpants and sweatshirt with St. Joseph's printed across her chest.

Her chest. Zach gazed for a moment at the words. The letters seemed to reach out and grab his attention. For a second, he found himself fantasizing about what lay underneath the sweatshirt. It wasn't as if he hadn't noticed Delany in a sexual manner before, but with all of her extensive injuries, he had forced himself to push that aspect from his mind. For a time anyway.

Now she was coming home with him. She didn't know it yet, but Doc had given his permission for her to be discharged on condition that he stay with her and monitor her progress for the next few weeks. She was ready to leave the hospital, but she wasn't ready to fend for herself just yet.

Zach had planned it all in advance. He telephoned Mort to ask if the cabin he had on Anderson Island was available. Mort, believing that Zach was using this time to recuperate mentally from his own shooting, was happy to do anything that would enable Zach to return to duty. Uncharacteristically, Mort confessed that Zach was missed and that he was the best damn agent he had ever worked with. Zach was grateful for the praise, but he was even more grateful for the cabin.

"You're sure it won't be a problem, Mort? I know

how you and your wife like to get away every now and then.'' Zach confirmed that he had Mort's complete agreement. He hated to have to ask for anything, but this wasn't for him. It was for Delany.

"I told you, anything you need to get you back to work is yours. Watch the rug in the living room, though. It's Navajo and it's new. Also, I should tell you that it will be pretty isolated. The island usually doesn't start to get active until after Memorial Day. We're a month off from the season. Even the country club across the cove will seem deserted.''

"Actually the more secluded the better,'' Zach admitted. There were things that Zach needed to discuss with Delany. On a secluded island, the chances of someone calling the police when the fireworks began were slim.

"So when are you coming back?'' Mort asked bluntly, tired of pussyfooting around the question.

There was only silence, and then a slight cough.

"Damn,'' Mort muttered. "That's what I thought. It's that girl, isn't it?''

Zach didn't know what to say, how to explain. "I don't know if it's her or me. If she's the one, you know…the one, it's not fair to give her only part of my attention. The job can't take less than one hundred percent. Somehow, I think there has to be another way.''

"To save the world, you mean,'' Mort clarified. "That was always your problem, Zach. You see crime fighting as a moral obligation rather than an exciting job with some perks. Sure it's great to catch the bad guy, but you'll never catch all the bad guys. No one ever has.''

"I wanted to. Now I know I can't do it all at once.

There is something to be said for starting from the bottom up.'' Delany had taught him that.

Mort chuckled. "Boy, she really must be something. Have fun at the cabin. The key's under the planter in front.''

"Not very original for an agent,'' chided Zach.

"Not everyone's James Bond. Do me a favor and keep in touch.'' It was Mort's way of saying that he would miss him.

So now Zach had the release forms and a place to be released to. Delany wasn't fully recovered, but she looked good. Her cheeks glowed with health, her hair shone, her eyes sparkled, and her deep breaths made the letters on her chest move, which in turn caused a sudden tightening in Zach's groin. He'd been waiting for this, he realized.

He'd also been waiting for the doctor to give her a clean bill of health so he could officially tell his libido it was okay to go into overdrive. Briefly, he allowed himself to fantasize about making love to her, and the image became so powerful that he was forced to physically shake the idea from his head.

He stood in the room with Debbie, Stan and Delany, and they all peered at him as if they were waiting for him to do something. Had he been caught staring at her chest?

"Where's the doc?'' Delany asked. The funny expression on Zach's face made her curious. He looked as if he hadn't eaten breakfast and it had just dawned on him that he was hungry.

Zach propelled himself into action and pushed the wheelchair closer to Delany's bed. Although she didn't need it anymore, the hospital refused to allow patients to walk out under their own steam.

"He's on his way. You look cute." Zach vocalized the thought that struck him the moment he walked through the door.

With not a smudge of makeup to speak of on her face, her hair pulled back into a ponytail, and sweats that made her look ten pounds heavier than she was, Delany had to wonder what he meant. "If you think this is cute, wait until you see me in my gym clothes." She wiggled her eyebrows in an attempt at humorous flirting.

Again his stomach tightened in desire, and Zach had to cough quickly to cover the reaction so that it wouldn't be so obvious to everyone else in the room. The idea of seeing her legs encased in tights and a leotard made Zach want to groan. Because the thought of legs in tights led him to think about bare legs. That thought naturally led him to think about what was between her bare legs. That thought made him really want to groan.

Dazedly, he wondered if he had always wanted her this badly or if this was a new feeling. Hell, he wondered if he had ever wanted anyone this badly. Then it occurred to him that he had never had to wait so long to make love to a woman who appealed to him. The waiting had made him more anxious, that was certain. But in the process of waiting he had come to care for her deeply. He loved her. It was his loving her that was going to make their lovemaking so special. It was also going to make it hot!

"Are you hungry?"

Delany's question startled Zach out of his reverie. "Yes. Very." It was the truth.

Delany shrugged her shoulders and replied, "Well, maybe you should get something from the cafeteria before we leave."

"I think it will take a little more than that to satisfy my hunger." The innuendo was lost on Delany.

Debbie, however, understood exactly what he meant. "Come on, Stan, let's leave this couple alone." To Zach she said, "Dr. Manuela will be here in a minute, so don't go getting any crazy ideas." She chuckled at his attempt at an innocent expression and then pushed Stan out the door.

Delany was still confused. Perhaps it was because she was preoccupied. Leaving the hospital? She still couldn't quite believe it.

"Am I really going home?" she asked, shocked at how fast everything was moving.

"No. Not home," Zach responded. He was about to elaborate on that point when Dr. Manuela walked into the room.

"I hear someone is going home today," Manny announced, release papers in hand.

Delany took the papers with trepidation. "I guess I'm a little nervous. But if you say I'm ready, then I must be."

The doctor nodded with a congenial smile. "I don't have to tell you that there's still work that needs to be done. You'll have to meet with Stan on a semiregular basis, and I've included a list of exercises you need to do every day. I feel that I'm leaving you in capable hands or I probably wouldn't have let you go so soon." Manny stressed the point that she wasn't completely recovered yet.

"Capable hands?" Delany looked toward Zach. The doctor presumed an awful lot if he expected Zach to move in with her so that he could watch out for her. "I do live alone, Doc Manny." Delany wanted to make it clear to the doctor, but she also wanted to let Zach know that she didn't expect anything more from him than what he had already given.

"Not for the next few weeks, you don't." Manny glanced at Zach for confirmation.

Zach nodded his head. "I haven't told her yet."

"Told me what?" Now Delany knew how children felt when adults spoke about them while they were in the room but didn't give them a chance to chime in.

"I'll let you explain, Zach. I've got rounds to make. Delany, I'll see you at the next runathon. I think this year I can beat you." With a farewell smile, Doc Manny left the room.

"Explain what? Have I ever mentioned what a control freak I am? I don't like the idea that things were decided without my knowledge." Delany slid her legs off the bed into the soft moccasins that Debbie had left out for her to wear home. Zach had already taken all of her other personal belongings to the car. He never doubted that Delany would be released today.

Standing up to Zach felt good. She barely reached his shoulder and she couldn't quite reach her full height, but with her arms akimbo, she was a force to be reckoned with once again.

Laughter filled his chest as he watched Delany transform herself from patient to tyrant in an instant. "You are formidable, aren't you?" If it was possible, his desire for her doubled at that moment.

"Talk, Mr. Montgomery, before you see just how formidable I can be."

"Dr. Manuela wouldn't let you leave unless I promised to stay with you for a while. It's that simple." Zach moved away and grabbed the cane that was leaning against the other side of the bed. He returned to her and attempted to put her in the wheelchair so he could escape with her before anybody stopped him.

But she warned him off with her hand and informed him regally, "I am not ready to sit yet. You may think it's simple, but I have a very small studio apartment. I can't imagine you'd even fit through the door." She exaggerated, of course. He'd fit through the door. It was the bed that he would never be able to squeeze into. At least not with her in it. The thought was enough to send the blood rushing to her cheeks and various other parts of her body.

Now that her legs worked, it appeared that other parts of her anatomy were returning to life, as well. How could she have forgotten how attractive he was? It had been easy to love him chastely. When he acted toward her as nothing more than a caring friend, it was simple to forget how masculine he was. No longer was she an invalid or a patient. She was a woman. Vaguely she wondered if he found her at all attractive. She'd thought he had a certain virile charm from the first moment she saw him. The first moment he saw her, he'd told her she looked horrible.

"Nothing to worry about. I'm not taking you home."

Now she needed to sit. Gingerly, she sank once again onto the hated chair. For the last time, she thought. "Is it going to be a surprise, or can I know where you're taking me?"

"Have you ever heard of a place called Anderson Island?"

"Sure. I've never been out to that island in particular, but all those islands in Puget Sound are pretty much alike. You have to take the ferry out there, don't you?"

"Yes, and there are only two ferries a day. We'll have to hurry to make the six o'clock. A friend of mine owns a small cabin there. It's nice and secluded. A good place to heal without all the distractions of your daily life. There's an inlet not far from the cabin. You can take your walks along the water."

"Exactly how small is the cabin?" Delany hoped she wasn't obvious. She wanted to know what the situation was going to be. Were they going to be lovers? Or did Zach see her only as a responsibility? Perhaps in his mind he would never see her as anything else. She would forever be confined to the role of friend. She didn't know if she could stand it.

"It's small."

They were going to be lovers. She should have been nervous at the idea. Instead, all she could think about were his kisses. Every time he touched her, he took her to a place she had never known.

Making love with Zach would be like touching a rainbow. All the colors of the spectrum would float across her body and through her mind. It would be magical.

"How long a drive do you think it will be?" Delany asked nonchalantly.

"It will be as short as I can humanly make it," Zach answered not so chalantly.

"They're leaving," Enrico told O.G. over the phone. "She's dressed and they're leaving the hospital. For good, it looks like. He took all her stuff out to his car already."

O.G. absorbed the information. He knew he would have to act soon if he was going to act at all. No telling when the pig might decide to leave the area. Besides, it was time for O.G. to move on himself. The money had run out, and there were other markets to be conquered. He could either pick another city where the Crips were already established, or he could move on to some suburb and create a whole new hood. The burbs were an expanding market for drugs. Eager yuppies searched for a quick fix; high school kids wanted to be bad. All of that added up to easy money to be made in a small, rich town. Wherever there was a need, O.G. would be there to supply it.

Leaving was not an option until he finished with old business first. The cop was a loose end who needed to pay for the pain he had caused. O.G. briefly considered having Enrico off him before he left the hospital. It wasn't what he originally planned, but it would be easier and cleaner to have someone else do it.

O.G. had never claimed to be brave. Survival was his only skill. His right hand loomed in front of him, and he grimaced. No one ever realized how important the thumb was until it was gone. He couldn't pick up a beer with his right hand. More importantly, he couldn't hold a gun with it, either. No, he decided, this was something that he should do himself. Even if he only managed to shoot the pig to death with his other hand, he wanted him to know that O.G. was the one who'd put him away.

"Don't do nothin'. Stay on his tail. Follow him and see where he takes her. Then come back and tell me. Together, you and me will take this guy out." O.G. smiled at the idea of watching the look on the cop's face when he realized death was inevitable.

Enrico hung up the phone, then slowly turned to watch the man wheel the woman along the hospital floor and out the door. "Soon, lady. Soon, I'm going to finish what I started on you." It was a promise.

* * *

Delany turned her head briefly as a black jacket caught her eye. "Raiders," she murmured.

Above the sound of the wheels squeaking on the hospital floor, Zach didn't catch what Delany had said. "What was that?"

"It's nothing. A few nights ago, someone accidentally came into my room. He was a young man, and I think he wore a Raiders jacket." Delany didn't want to make too much of the incident. Her days of being afraid were over.

"Did he look familiar?" Zach thought back to the car that had followed him. Something didn't add up. Who was after them? What did they want?

"I didn't get a clear look at his face. It's nothing."

"I'm sure you're right." Only he wasn't sure about anything. Zach let the issue drop.

"So, how long do you think it will be before you teach again?" Truly, it was the last thing Zach wanted to discuss, but he needed something to take his mind off the growing pressure between his legs. They still had another fifteen minutes before they even got to the ferry.

Delany debated the issue silently. Part of her was eager to return, to get back to her normal life again. The other part of her was afraid of what it would mean if she went back not quite whole. What would her students think if they saw her with a cane? What would they feel when they discovered that it would be a long time before she jogged her usual three miles a day? Delany also couldn't overlook the fact that she hadn't missed teaching as much as she thought she would. Granted, she'd been preoccupied both with her recovery and

Zach. There was no reason that she should have been thinking about school.

The rest had felt good. In fact, it felt so good she wondered if the best idea for her right now would be to take a sabbatical for the remainder of the year. She would be able to start fresh in September, and her body would once again be up to the task.

"I think I might take the rest of the year off." Her words were hesitant as if she was testing the waters.

Zach glanced quickly in her direction. "Sounds like a good idea. It seems to me you were probably burned out before the attack on you ever happened."

With a scowl, Delany retorted, "You didn't even know me before the attack."

Zach couldn't argue. "It seems to me, from what you've told me, from what Cici said, from what Doc Manny said about your racing, that you worked too hard. Not a good hard anyway. There's only about a month and a half left of school. You need a break. Now is the best time."

Zach believed everything he'd told her; he just didn't believe that was the only reason he didn't want her to return to work so soon. They needed time together before the demands of her job came between them. It wasn't that he didn't want her to work. In fact, he respected her a hell of a lot more for it. But it seemed to him they were at a turning point. They could go either way. If he had her complete attention, Zach believed that his odds were better that she would come to see things his way.

Right now, desire was at the forefront of his mind. Images of their making love in a soft, comfortable bed were the only things he wanted to see. Unfortunately, there were other things to consider. Zach couldn't forget

that he still had to tell her the truth. How Delany dealt
with the truth would make all the difference in their
future. If she didn't have her teaching to turn back to,
to use as an excuse, she might be more willing to stick
it out and deal with him.

"Is that why you left?" Delany asked, her eyes
watchful of Zach's expression while his eyes were
pinned to the road in front of him.

The question startled him. For a moment, he wondered if she knew the truth. Then he realized that it was
impossible for her to know that he had left the DEA.
Yes, he'd left because he was burned out. Soon he
would explain it all to her. Now was not the time.
Maybe it was chauvinistic, but Zach's gut told him that
if he slept with her first, she would be less likely to run
away from him. For most women, sex was a form of
commitment. For Delany, he knew that would be true.
The more committed to him she was, the better chance
he had to win her forgiveness.

"The police force. Is that why you left?" Delany
asked again, not sure of what his silence meant.

"I left the force because all of a sudden I knew it
was time for me to move on. Yes, I was burned out.
Although I believe that it was my fault. It wasn't the
job that did me in. It was my dedication. I carried too
much on my back until it finally started to crush me."
Honest, he was being completely honest.

"Don't you ever want to go back, though? Can you
just stop wanting to help people? How do you ignore
that part of you?"

"I don't know. I guess I looked at it as if I'd done
my part. That maybe I was off the hook." Only he
wouldn't be. Delany's point was valid. If Zach did go
through with his bar-and-grill idea, would he ever find

the satisfaction he had found in the DEA? It was a discomforting thought.

"No one put you on the hook, Zach. You put yourself there, just like you burned yourself out. Just like I burned myself out. For people like us, I don't think there is any finish line. I think we have to keep going. People are always counting on us." Delany knew she would teach again, and she also knew she would continue her scholarship program. But the answer lay in moderation. She no longer would let her concern for other people dominate her life. She would no longer feel guilty when she took time for herself. And she would no longer give all of herself away. She needed to save a little bit for herself...and for Zach.

Her gentle smile caught his eye. Zach reached out to clasp her hand with his own. "You are a special lady, you know that?"

"I think we're special together," Delany corrected.

"Yes, we'll be special together." Zach's meaning had changed, and his grip on her hand tightened.

"Is it all right to admit that I'm scared?" Delany wondered aloud, knowing exactly when the conversation had shifted.

"Yes." Zach thought it was perfectly fine for her to admit that she was scared. He was, too. He'd never confess it, but he couldn't remember a time when making love to someone had ever meant as much as he knew this was going to mean to him.

The remainder of the trip was completed in silence. The tension was too powerful to overcome with idle chatter. Delany rested her head against the back of the seat and enjoyed the view. Zach drove the rental smoothly and it wasn't long before they reached the dock. Delany watched the ferry sail into view. It was a

windy day and the water looked choppy, but that was
of no concern to Delany, who had taken the various
ferries around the area more times than she could count.
Zach drove the car onto the ferry and she could almost
feel the water below, lulling her to sleep. Forcibly, she
opened her eyes; there wasn't a single moment she
wanted to miss with Zach. Today was special. Today
was the day she made love, real love, for the first time.
Before her eyes closed one last time, she realized how
lucky she was.

Sunlight drifted in through the window so brightly
that Delany actually felt her face burn. With a groan,
she moved her head away from the light, trying to go
back to sleep. But it was too late. She was all too con-
scious now and left with no choice but to get up. She
reached out her hands experimentally, expecting to find
Zach's hand close by in the car seat next to her. It was
only then that she realized she was lying in a bed and
not in a car seat at all.

With her energy suddenly restored, Delany managed
to prop herself up on her elbows and take a look at her
surroundings. It was morning. She was in a small room
with a rocking chair in the corner, a dresser adjacent to
the bed and a small television on a stand directly in
front of the bed. All of the furniture was cedar. A patch-
work quilt on the bed added a touch of color to the
room. But no Zach.

What had happened to her? It was supposed to have
been the night of her life. It was supposed to have been
magical, wonderful, and very sensual. Instead, it was a
complete and total blank.

"Hey there, sleepyhead." The door opened and Zach
poked his head through. He didn't walk all the way in,

but kept his hand on the doorknob, ready for a quick escape in case she was still sleeping. Once he saw that she was awake, he stepped into the room. He wore jeans and a shirt as if he'd been up and showered for some time now.

"I fell asleep." As if that was news to Zach. "Why didn't you wake me up? How did we get here?" Delany attempted to shake the fog from her head, but it only made her dizzy.

With an indulgent smile, Zach sat down next to her on the bed and brushed the blond wisps from her face. "You conked out in the car on the ferry ride over. I put you to bed, and you slept the whole night through. I didn't realize how tired you'd be. We didn't check out of the hospital until late. You didn't get your usual nap. You're still recovering—"

"Oh, stop making excuses for me. You must be terribly disappointed. I wanted last night to be...special."

"It was special," Zach whispered, his lips close to hers. Then he drew the sleepiness from them with a gentle peck. "I watched you sleep for a while. You were so peaceful. I was happy to share that with you. I crawled into bed beside you and held you all night long."

Delany's eyes linked with his and she saw that he meant what he said. Holding her all night had been special to him. "I love you." She didn't know if it was the right time to make such a confession, but for the life of her she couldn't have stopped the words.

Zach kissed her again, only this time harder, more insistently. His hand wrapped around her head while she in turn circled his neck with her arms. His tongue slipped into her mouth and he tasted her sweetness. He felt weightless, energized. Or was it love? Whatever it was, he wanted more. With his strength, he lifted her body against his so that he could press his mouth more fully against hers. He felt the smoothness of her teeth. He inhaled her breath, felt its warmth mingling with his own.

His hand burrowed into her hair, and he let his fingers run through its length. Silk. Soft silk caressed his fingers. Made his nerve ends tingle. Could her skin be half so soft? Zach couldn't imagine anything softer, but he was willing to find out. Last night, he hadn't wanted to disturb her slumber, so he had removed only her moccasins and socks, allowing her to sleep in the sweats. Now the comfortable clothes deprived him of what he wanted most.

"Lift your arms," he commanded, his voice not soft and warm, but intense and harsh. He was too aroused, too needy. It would be wise to leave her now and regain some control over himself before he made love to her. She wasn't ready for the power of his desire. But he couldn't do it. Too late, he wanted to tell her. It was time to go forward.

Delany didn't question the tone of his voice. She wasn't in control of herself anymore; she hadn't been after the first moment his lips touched hers. And she didn't care. Obediently, she raised her arms and the sweatshirt was lifted from her. Her bra was undone and tossed aside, and she felt herself slowly being lowered. Zach guided her descent with his powerful hands, careful with her still-fragile body even in the grip of his desire.

Hovering over her, he tossed off his own shirt, then with slow, controlled movements he brought his slightly furred chest to rest against her smooth breasts. His nipples puckered at the first hint of her soft skin, and like a cat in heat, he rubbed himself over her.

"Zach," she breathed, although she didn't know where the breath had come from. Her hands reached out to stroke his back, but what began as a gentle caress ended when her fingers tugged deeply at the muscles of his back.

Desperately, she wanted the feel of his lips on her once again, but instead she was compelled to find contentment as his lips brushed her neck, her shoulders and the delicate flesh between her breasts. Oh, how content she was!

"More," she demanded. Delany didn't know what that entailed, but she was feverish with need. Her body ached, and for the first time in months, it was a pleasant, joyous ache. Her stomach fluttered, her face flushed, and inside she felt hot and moist and...empty.

With a grin that bordered on mischief, Zach began to patiently apply his lips and tongue to every part of her body. He tickled the back of her knees with his fingers. He made her giggle with delight as his tongue dipped into her belly button. He made her gasp in shock when he pulled down the front of her sweats and kissed her intimately. Then he waited for her gasps to subside and started again.

"I can't take it," she moaned. She was on some unforeseeable edge, but rather than pull back, she wanted to plunge over the side.

"You said you wanted more. We haven't even begun yet." Zach stood then and stripped off his jeans. Delany boldly admired the virile and physically powerful man before her. She felt compelled to reach out and touch his sex, now engorged with desire. It was hot to the touch, and she pulled her hand back from the flame.

Zach caught her hand and returned it to his heat, partly because he couldn't stand to be without her touch and partly so that she could know him as intimately as he knew her.

Soon the teasing became too much for him to bear. Zach leaned over and began to tug further at the waist-band of her sweatpants, being careful as he slid them down her precious legs. Then he gently pushed those legs apart so that he could kneel between them and gaze down upon her.

"I feel so vulnerable," she confided. Instinctively, she tried to move her legs together only to have her soft inner thighs come into contact with his hard and hair-roughened thighs. A wave of sensual pleasure swept over her and she found a compulsion to arch her back and offer herself to him.

"It's all right to be vulnerable with me." And it was. Unbeknownst to her, Zach had placed protection under one of the pillows in the hopes of what the night might bring. Efficiently, he applied the condom and then low-ered himself so that his body came into contact with hers from chest to toe. He took care to keep most of his weight on his elbows, not wanting to cause her any pain.

Delany sensed his caution and was dismayed. She wanted to share the wildness she felt simmering beneath the surface of his skin. She wanted him to be as uncon-trollable as she knew she felt. "I won't break," she whispered as she placed soft kisses around his mouth and on his earlobes, enticing him to give her more of his weight.

Tremors moved up and down his spine, and he had to resist the urge to thrust his hips against her. Despite her words, Zach knew that she needed gentleness from him at this moment. Slowly, but irrevocably, he moved forward until his manhood met her heat. Her body softened in degrees to make room for him. Like a tease, her body offered itself to him, then resisted him when he pushed forward.

"You're so tight," he murmured, trying to back off and give her time. But she gripped him harder and smothered him in heat. He wanted to explode, but he wasn't ready to give up possession of her body.

Delany shifted her hips forward, seeking more of what he had to offer. Restlessly, her inner thighs scraped against his flanks, then gripped them tighter, as if with the meager strength of her legs she could move him closer to her. "I feel so full. I never thought I could be this complete."

"Not yet," Zach told her urgently. One rolling surge, and he slammed his hips against hers, firmly planting himself inside her. Together they sighed at the intensity of the completion. Zach savored the feelings, both physical and emotional. This was perfection. This was love.

Desperate to prolong their loving, he tried to withdraw, hoping to regain some composure once he had left her. But the slightest movement on his part caused Delany to tighten her thighs again. She intended to hold him in place forever.

"Don't leave me," she begged.

"I can't now. I won't ever." With those words, Zach thrust forward again. And then again and again until he didn't know when mere pleasure had ended and sheer ecstasy had begun. He heard Delany sob beneath him and he hoped fervently that he hadn't hurt her. But he was too far gone to even know or understand what had happened between them. All he knew was that she couldn't leave him now. She couldn't leave him ever. He had entered her body. But she had possessed his soul.

Chapter 8

"Don't cry. It's all right, I've got you." Zach held Delany as they lay on their sides, her back pressed against his chest, her legs twined around his. She rested her head on one arm while his other hand tried to wipe the tears that wouldn't stop falling from her eyes.

"You must think I'm such a sap, but it was so beautiful. I never really imagined it was true, you know." Delany hiccuped the words as she attempted to control her sobbing.

"What was true?" Zach wondered, reassured now that he hadn't hurt her.

"Making love. I never thought it'd be like what everybody said it could be. I thought all the movies and the books were fiction. But it's all true. It's so powerful and beautiful." She rambled, she knew, but she didn't have the will nor the inclination to stop herself. "You probably just want to go to sleep now. I read something that said there's a physiological reason why men get tired after sex, so you don't have to try to stay awake just for me.''

Zach chuckled at her innocence. ''It's about nine o'clock in the morning. I don't think I'm ready for a nap quite yet.''

''Morning. The sun is shining. All the lights were on and I didn't even care.'' Delany felt she should have been embarrassed by that idea, but she wasn't. On the contrary, she was quite willing to spend all the daylight hours in bed with this man.

''If it had been midnight, I would have turned on all the lights. I needed to see your body. I needed to know if you looked as soft as you felt.'' Zach emphasized his point by reaching down to caress her breast while his lips grazed her shoulder. Delany didn't have to peek over her shoulder to see his eyes and know that they enjoyed the view.

''You've already seen my legs. Up close and personal,'' she teased. She still remembered how taken aback she was when he offered to shave her legs for her.

Zach shared the memory. ''If you only knew how much more I wanted. All I could think of was where your legs led to. You would have been shocked. I was having licentious thoughts about a patient in a hospital. I didn't win any morality awards that day, I assure you.''

''You were a perfect gentlemen, too perfect at times.'' Delany would have preferred him to be less stingy with his kisses.

Perfect. The word triggered memories in Zach. He recalled a time when he believed Delany to be perfect. Her dedication, her courage, her selflessness—all smacked of perfection. Now he knew her weaknesses.

Her stubbornness, her temper, her craving for chocolate all spoke of her human frailties. Delany was only human. She was an exceptional person to be sure, but she had her flaws like everyone else.

Zach felt he came nowhere near to being exceptional himself. What kind of man allowed the woman he loved to be beaten? Granted, he hadn't loved her then, but now that he did, his crime seemed so much worse. It was time to tell her.

The thought stung like a thorn in his side. It wasn't as if he didn't know that he had to tell her. It wasn't as if he'd forgotten the truth. Last night, the idea of making love to her took precedence over all his other thoughts. Reason told him that after making love to her, she would be more committed, more attached to him. With the connection firmly established, he would be able to hold on to her even after she learned the terrible truth.

Technically, that connection was complete. It was time to tell her.

Zach felt Delany snuggle into him, her bottom rubbing against his sex, causing it to swell. Later, his body whispered to him. Later you can tell her everything. Let me enjoy this for a little while longer. Let me be joined to her one more time. Zach was at a loss to defy his body's needs. He kissed her gently on the shoulder and rolled her over carefully so that once again he hovered over her.

''Tell me again.''

Delany knew instinctively the words he wanted. She knew how wonderful it felt to say them. She could only imagine the joy it must be to hear them. Some part of her mind cautioned her that Zach was holding back. He hadn't said the words, and Delany had the impression that there was a very significant reason as to why he hadn't. It wasn't that he didn't love her. She knew in her heart that he did. She knew by the gentle way he touched and kissed her. She knew by the way he so fiercely protected her. She knew by the way he took care of her. His actions said more than his words ever could. So why couldn't he say the words? What was he hiding?

"I love you, Zach."

It would be all right, he thought as he lowered his lips to hers. If she loved him, then she would forgive him. All thoughts of what might lie ahead left Zach as he began to immerse himself in the satisfying pleasure of making love to Delany.

"You're sure they're on that island," O.G. asked, as he gazed at the ferry that would take them across to Anderson Island.

"Positive," Enrico answered, anxious now that the moment was so close at hand. O.G. could have the pig. He wanted the teacher that thought she was so much better than him, the teacher that made Cici think she was so much better than him. His baby sister thought that way because of that interfering bitch. She would have to hurt for that. She would have to die for that.

"How many ferries after this one? I don't want to give them the chance to get off the island once we're on. This kill needs to be done quickly and in private."

"No problem," Enrico assured him. "This is the last ferry of the day. Another one doesn't come until mornin'. Too late for them. Check it out, man, this boat is private. There's practically no one gettin' on this ferry 'sides us."

O.G. nodded in agreement. The timing was perfect. There was no place for the pig to go. He had him trapped. Powerful sensations ran through O.G.'s body. He was a hunter and the cop was his prey. The excitement was real. This was more than an anonymous drive-by kill. This was man against man. O.G. had no doubt that he would win such a contest. The key was conscience. O.G. didn't have one. Whatever had to be done in order to ensure the kill, O.G. would do it. The cop wasn't as fortunate. Apparently, he was a sucker for wounded birds. O.G.'s original plan to take the girl hadn't panned out. That didn't mean she couldn't be useful. In fact, O.G. planned to make good use of her.

"What do you want for dinner? How about something easy like spaghetti?" Delany was in the kitchen scrounging for food among the cabinets. She glanced at her discarded cane and smiled. It felt good to stand even if she could only manage it for short periods of time. Delany knew her use of the cane would be short-lived. It was more of a nuisance than anything else. Unfortunately, without it her legs would soon start to tremble slightly, and her back would begin to ache. While her freedom lasted, though, she intended to enjoy it.

Zach hadn't answered her question. He was taking a shower, his second of the day after a long morning and afternoon of making love. Again, Delany smiled. It had been the most beautiful day of her life. Zach had made her a huge brunch of eggs, fruit and biscuits and had served her in bed. They ate, read, talked, and they loved. Time evaporated, and suddenly it was past seven o'clock and the sun was gone.

Now it was time for Delany to do some cooking of her own. Only Zach wouldn't answer her question. "Zach," she shouted. It was a tiny cabin. Even if his ears were filled with shampoo, he should still hear her.

Her students didn't call her the Mouth for nothing. Delany left the kitchenette and walked down the small hallway that ran between the living room and the bedroom. The bathroom door was closed, but the water was off. "Zach," she called a little more softly, suddenly concerned. "Can you hear me?"

He heard her. Zach stared at the mirror in front of him now covered with steam. His features were blurred, and he thought it was a truer reflection of his soul. It was time to tell her, and she wanted to know if spaghetti was acceptable for dinner.

"I'll be out in a minute. There's some beer in the fridge. Why don't you grab us a couple?"

Delany sensed something was wrong. His voice was strained, harsh. It seemed impossible after such a long day of loving and a hot shower that anyone could sound more tense. Knowing that she wasn't going to get the answer immediately, she put off dinner for the moment and went to fetch some beers.

A few minutes later, Zach, now dressed in crisp jeans and gray T-shirt, joined Delany in the living room. Delany herself was snuggled on the couch, beer in hand, as she finished the last few pages of the book that they'd been reading together in the hospital. She wore another sweat suit, this one a brilliant blue to bring out the blue of her eyes. The colorful suit stood out against the neutral colors of the cabin. Mort had redone the living room, it seemed, to match the new rug. The beiges and browns of the desert scenes contrasted with the green foliage outside.

Zach spotted his beer waiting for him on the counter, a glass next to it. He ignored the glass, twisted off the top of the beer and took a few large gulps. It seemed silly to think that a few swigs of beer would give him the alcohol-induced courage that he needed, but it was worth a try.

"I can't believe he did it," Delany muttered.

Zach moved to sit in the chair across from the couch. His belief was that it would be easier to tell her the truth from a distance. "Did what?"

"The psychologist. I can't believe he killed his own wife. I thought it was the boyfriend all along." Delany plunked down the book, slightly irritated that her assumption had been wrong. "There wasn't one clue. Not one lousy clue anybody could have found in here that would have led them to the psychologist."

"The insurance policy was a clue," Zach added, putting off the inevitable one more time.

"Too obvious," Delany muttered. She refused to give the author any credit for misleading her. "It was a dirty trick."

Speaking of dirty tricks, Zach thought, wondering how that phrase would work as an opening to their conversation. Somehow, he didn't think it would go over so well.

"What is it?"

Interrupted in his musings, Zach met Delany's eyes directly. Honesty lay deep within those crystal-clear blue eyes. His deception was going to hurt her.

"I have something to tell you."

"Oh, my God, you're married," she moaned. Delany had watched enough television to know that every tragic conversation between a man and a woman began with those very words.

"I'm not married. I'm not a criminal. I'm not gay."

"Obviously." He'd spent all afternoon proving that last point. So, if he wasn't any of those things, what exactly was he?

"I'm a liar." It said everything, and nothing at the same time.

Delany shook her head, refusing to believe him. Ironic since he spoke the truth. "Zach, you're the most honest man I know."

Zach laughed harshly. "How can you say that? You really don't know me. You can't know if anything I've told you is the truth."

"It isn't about words, Zach. It's about character. You wouldn't have stayed with me if you weren't an honorable man, an honest man. Come to think of it, you wouldn't have stopped to help me in the first place if—"

"I didn't."

"Didn't what?" a confused Delany questioned. His muscles tense, Zach stood abruptly, then finished the remains of his beer in a couple of gulps.

"I didn't stop to save you," Zach began. He headed for the kitchen on the pretext that he was tossing away his bottle. Truthfully, since truth was what he was aiming for now, he wanted to escape her penetrating gaze. Please don't let me lose her, he begged silently once more.

"So you stopped after it was over. The point is you stopped."

"Stop making excuses for me," he ordered, his voice raised. "I saw the whole thing happen, Delany. I was in an apartment on the third floor of a nearby building trying to get a gang leader to give up the name of his drug contact. I looked down and I saw it all happen. At first, I thought it was an initiation. Then I saw your long hair. You were trying to crawl away. I knew you were in trouble. But I waited until I got the name of the contact before I came to help you." The last sentence rushed out in a breathless sigh. Like a shaken soda, the pressure inside Zach was intense. Now that the bottle was open, the foam spilled over the side.

Stunned, Delany tried to make sense of what he'd said. "You told me that you left the force."

"I left the L.A.P.D. when I was twenty-six. I became an undercover agent with the Drug Enforcement Agency immediately after. I've been working with them for the past eight years. I was under cover the night you got attacked."

"The restaurant?" Delany asked, dealing with one lie at a time.

The worst over, the truth came more easily now. "When I told you that story, there was no restaurant. I took a leave of absence to stay with you, and I had planned to go back. Now, I don't think I ever can. I've just started to realize who the hell Zach Montgomery is, and I'm not willing to give that up. A few weeks ago, I contacted a real-estate agent to help scout for locations for a small bar and grill. So what was a lie has now become a reality."

"How long?"

Zach shook his head, not understanding the question.

"How long?" she shouted. The sense of betrayal was immeasurable. "How long did you wait?"

"I don't know. It seemed like forever. Two minutes."

Again Delany was confused. "Two minutes?"

"He wouldn't give up the name. I had to have the contact's name." Zach turned and rushed toward Delany, who still sat on the couch. Kneeling in front of her, he took both her hands in his as if to convey the intensity of his words through touch.

"My last assignment before this one, I was under

cover with a gang down in Texas. Same kind of role. I was trying to expose their contact, a cop with the border police who allowed the gang members to pass at night with the drugs. I was close, this close." Zach released her wrist and pinched his fingers closed to demonstrate his point. Flashes of memory flooded him, and his back began to hurt all over again. "Then this kid walked in. Some stupid kid who ran from the cops and dropped his stash.

"The O.G. was furious," Zach recalled. The story spewed from him. "He was going to shoot him right there in front of me. And the kid, I think the boy wet his pants. He stared down the barrel of the gun and murmured some prayers. I couldn't let him do it. I couldn't let that gangster shoot him. I knew it wasn't my problem. This kid was just another gangster who sold drugs to kids younger than he was. But he was kid, and I couldn't watch him die. I grabbed the O.G.'s arm at the last second and the shot went wide."

"They knew you were a cop," Delany filled in, imagining the rest of the scene. "You didn't get hurt in a car accident, did you?"

"Dealers usually don't show concern when gangsters get knocked off. It happens every day. I tried to explain my way around it, but it was no good. I jumped out a window and took a bullet in my back. Luckily, there was a uniformed cop close by. When I came around, they told me that the gang had relocated. The only thing they left behind was the body of that kid I tried to save."

"I'm so sorry, Zach." She ached for him, knowing that for him, his efforts had been in vain.

"Nothing. I blew my cover, lost the name of the traitor cop, was almost paralyzed, and it was all for nothing. If I had kept my mouth shut, at least I could have made some good come out of the situation. The kid would've still died, but hundreds like him might have had a better chance without drugs infesting their neighborhood. Instead, I sacrificed everything for one kid.''

Zach glanced up at Delany from where he knelt; her expression was hard to read. "I couldn't let that happen again. I couldn't risk everything I was doing to save you."

"What did you do after he gave you the name?"

"As soon as he gave me the name, I was out of there," he mentioned offhandedly, curious as to why she asked. What did it matter what happened after? "I ran down the stairs, hoping I could get you into your car before they opened fire. But the cops came, and everyone scattered." Zach was ready for her condemnation now. He deserved it. He only hoped that they could work beyond the pain and the betrayal.

"You said you saw me. Was I talking to Enrico then?"

"No, you were on the ground. One of them pulled a gun. Why do you ask? What's the point? I waited two minutes, maybe three, until I did anything. I know you'll hate me for that. What I want to know is, will you ever forgive me for it?" Zach stood then. He was pleading with her and he didn't like it. She wouldn't want someone who begged, and he refused to do it. "You shouldn't have been there, Delany. What I did was wrong, I know that. But I also know that we stopped a major source of drug distribution that night. I can't be sorry for that. I won't be."

"Who asked you to be sorry?"

The tone of her voice was expected; the question was

not. "How can I not be sorry for what I did, for what I allowed to happen?"

Delany stood then, too, her legs shaky, but not from weakness. "What did you allow to happen? You did your job. You looked out a window, saw me on the ground, waited until you got the information you needed and then came running after me. You risked too much doing that. If someone had seen you help me, your cover would've been blown. Your information would have been useless."

Zach released another sigh. This time, the pressure released inside of him was even greater. "You understand."

"Yes, I understand perfectly."

"So you're not mad." It was almost too good to be true.

"I'm furious," Delany corrected.

It was too good. "I don't understand. You said you knew why I did what I did."

"I do, but you don't. Zach, why did you stay with me?"

He couldn't guess where the questions would lead. His only choice was to follow along. "I stayed because I cared for you. I know it's a lousy time to say this, but I love—"

"Don't you dare," Delany shouted. She didn't want to hear the words, not now when she knew they weren't true. "That's not why you stayed. You got into that ambulance, and you stayed with me at the hospital because you felt guilty. Guilty!"

He refused to lie again. "At first. Yes, I did feel guilty."

Delany grimaced ruefully. "It's ironic. You sacrificed your work for that boy, for me. But you don't feel guilty

about that. You weren't worried that you were going to
be fired. You sat with me night and day all because of
two lousy minutes.''

"I could've stopped them before they hurt you.''

"No, you couldn't have stopped them. You didn't see
me until I was already hurt. Beyond that, you couldn't
have stopped me from going. I am the only one responsible for what happened to me. Remember, that's
why I didn't involve the police. That fact has been the
only thing that has kept me sane. That and you. Or at
least the image of you.''

It was beginning to make sense. "You're angry because I lied. I had to. You wouldn't have let me stay if
you knew.''

"No, I wouldn't have let you stay so you could ease
your guilty conscience. I wouldn't have been your pet
project.'' Her legs began to tremble as the realization
of what was about to happen hit Delany full force. She
was going to lose him. In truth, she never had him. She
sank into the pillows of the couch.

"That isn't why I stayed. I told you, at first I might
have felt responsible, but later I felt more.''

"Stop it. How could you have felt anything for me
when you were so busy condemning yourself. You're
an honest man, Zach. I know you don't believe that,
but it's true. You said you wanted to save the world,
but you never could. You couldn't because you'd always put the needs of the one before the needs of the
many. For that I love you.''

"You still love me?'' Zach wondered aloud. The
words should have elated him, but something in her
eyes bothered him.

"I do love you. That's why it's going to hurt so much

to leave you." She couldn't stop the tears then. The sense of loss was almost too great to bear.

Zach was incredulous. "Leave me? Why the hell would you do that? You love me and I feel the same way. As long as you can forgive me, there's nothing to stop us from being together."

"It's the forgiveness you want, Zach, not us. You want me to say it's all right. It's okay that you blew your cover to try to save that boy's life. It wasn't your fault that they killed him anyway. And it's okay that you almost blew another assignment. It wasn't your fault what happened to me. You're off the hook. You were never on it."

Off the hook. Zach remembered a time when he felt as if he dangled on some hook of guilt. He also recalled a time when he believed that he owed Delany something. When had that feeling changed into something different, something stronger? It did change, didn't it? For a moment, Zach wondered if Delany was right. Only for a moment, though.

"That's not true."

"Oh, Zach," Delany sighed in anguish, "how can it be anything but true? I believe you when you say that you lost yourself in the job. You don't know who you are at all, do you? You think you're so tough, but you're a pussycat underneath. You feel too much. Responsibility. Guilt. That's what made you stay. That's why I have to leave."

Delany stood with as much dignity as her shaky legs would allow and left the room. Tears fell unchecked down her face as she made her way unsteadily to the bedroom. Once there, she was brought up short by the sight of the bed where she had spent the afternoon. All afternoon, Delany had made love. All afternoon, Zach sought forgiveness.

In the corner, Delany spotted the bag that Zach had packed for her before they left the hospital. It was empty, which meant Zach had already stored her items away in the dresser. Her mind commanded her to immediately take the steps that would remove her from this situation. Her heart commanded her to crawl into a ball and attempt to stop the pain.

Knowing her mind was in firmer control than her heart, Delany followed the former's dictates. She reached down, lifted the light bag and placed it on the bed. The drawers were opened to reveal her sweats folded neatly.

Zach came to the bedroom door to find her removing her clothes from the drawers where he had placed them only last night. His thoughts were murky and confused. He couldn't imagine that what he felt for Delany wasn't real, but he couldn't be certain. She seemed to know him better than he did. Since he wasn't sure who he was, he began to think that maybe she did have a better perspective on his motivation. Her leaving, however, was out of the question until he was positive.

"You can't leave."

Delany didn't look up. Her eyes were flooded with tears she didn't want to show him. "I've already told you why I must. I won't repeat myself."

Her stubbornness displayed itself through the rigidness of her back, something she had only just begun to be able to do again. It angered Zach like nothing else she'd done.

"You are so damn righteous," he accused. He spoke to her back. "You think you know me so well. You think you've got it all figured out. What if you're wrong?''

Delany turned to face him. "If you only knew how badly I want to be wrong."

"So what if you are? What if my staying had nothing to do with guilt? What if I love you desperately? You're going to throw it all away. Everything we might have is lost because you think you're so damn smart."

Zach thrust his hands through his hair as his frustration bubbled over. He saw the pain in her eyes at his words, but he couldn't make himself stop.

"An angel. That's what I thought you were once. I didn't know what to do with someone so perfect. You intimidated me. Humbled me. Here you were so courageous and brave. You're not courageous at all. I scare the hell out of you, don't I? Don't I?'' he barked. In this he was right.

"No," Delany denied. "I wanted you to love me."

"Here I am. I'm standing in front of you telling you that I love you. You don't believe it because that knowledge frightens you to death. You're so busy trying to be right, you won't look at your part in all of this. You don't know what the hell a real relationship is. From day one you've been on your own, so you don't know what it means to give a part of yourself to anyone. I'm the one who doesn't really know me? You know me better? Then the opposite is true. You don't know what's inside you. You can't figure out what's swimming around in your head, so it's easier to take it all out on me. You see, Delany, I know you better than you know yourself. Tit for tat." Zach stood now, his arms akimbo, as if to brace himself for the coming salvo.

"Go to hell," Delany returned. Anger surged within

her. How dare he tell her she didn't want the only thing in this world she did? Whisking the bag from the bed, she attempted to leave, but Zach stood like a rampart in front of her.

"Get out of my way. I'm leaving."

"No, you're not."

If possible, her face glowed hotter. "I've said all I needed to say, and I've listened to everything I'm going to listen to. Now get out of my way."

The force of her voice stunned Zach, and he wondered if he had crossed over some invisible boundary in her mind. Or maybe he'd simply hit too close to the mark.

Resigned, he informed her, "You can't leave because there's no way to get off the island. The next ferry isn't until seven in the morning."

She could have hit something. Preferably Zach's face. "I can't stay here with you. I won't sleep in that bed with you again."

Her disgust evident, Zach retaliated in kind. "I wouldn't want your charity. I'll sleep on the couch." He stormed past her and removed a pillow from the head of the bed. Then he left the room, slamming the door behind him.

Once he was gone, Delany tried to bring her breathing back under control. Her knees gave out beneath her, and she sank on top of the bed, clutching her overnight bag like a security blanket. What had happened? It was as if all they'd said between them had been some odd dream. Perhaps she was still sleeping. If only she could wake up now, she could laugh off the whole thing as a bit of indigestion. Zach would tease her for eating too much before bedtime. Then he would kiss away the remnants of the dream and everything would be right with the world.

Only she wasn't asleep. Nothing was going to wake her from the fog she wandered through. Her fault! He accused her of being afraid of their relationship, when it had been all him. He had lied to her from the very beginning. He'd even told her that he hesitated before he came to her rescue.

No, that wasn't fair. Zach couldn't have done anything to help her. It would be pointless to explain it to him because he refused to look at the situation logically. On the third floor of an apartment building, he would have been powerless to prevent the attack. Who did he think he was—Superman?

As she played his words over again in her mind, her anger surged once more. Zach cried intimidation because she was such an angel. Well, what was he? It wasn't all right for her to be perfect, so why was it expected of him? Delany knew she wasn't perfect. She'd stopped trying to be years ago. With Zach's help, she had even begun to forgive herself for her brother's death.

Zach was the one who refused to ease up on himself. Zach searched for forgiveness, but he would never find it until he forgave himself first.

What if you're wrong...? What if I love you desperately?

It wasn't something she could allow herself to believe. It would leave Delany too vulnerable if she thought for a minute that he hadn't come to her out of pity and a warped sense of obligation. Because if she let herself love him the way she knew she did, and he realized that she was right, the pain would kill her.

"So what does it feel like now?" she asked aloud of

the empty room. It feels rotten, she admitted silently. Delany couldn't imagine being in any greater pain. But something else frightened her even more. To live with Zach, to love him and have his children would be the greatest joy she had ever known. To lose that joy would destroy her.

Delany had survived a great deal in her short life. She considered her fortitude to be considerable. She wasn't willing to test it again. Needing to escape the small room, she moved into the living area. She saw a man's jacket by the door. But it would suit her needs. Without a glance in his direction, but aware of him just the same, she shrugged into the jacket.

"Where do you think you're going?" Zach sat on the couch, his elbows on his knees.

"Outside. I need some air."

"It's too dark, and you're not strong enough yet."

The absolute authority of his tone rankled her, but she refused to challenge him. To engage Zach now while she felt so exposed was wrong. If he wore her down, convinced her of his arguments, she'd end up believing him, she knew. That would be a mistake. Zach had proven himself to be a very adept liar. She couldn't risk accepting his version of things, even if he thought they were the truth. It would devastate her in the end.

"I'm just going to the shore. The moon is out and I'll be careful." Delany didn't wait for a response. She opened the door and threw herself into the night air, embracing for a moment the sensation of freedom.

"Your cane..." Zach called, but she had already left.

Zach watched her go, knowing he should stop her, but he hoped the walk would clear her mind. He'd been a complete and total fool. Perhaps she would forget that once the clean air filled her senses.

It was supposed to have been an apology. Zach had worked it all out in his head while he showered. All he had to do was confess that he'd seen her that night. Tell her about his job. Then wait it out while she screamed and raved at him for being a scumball, for letting her get hurt, for lying to her afterward. When her ranting died down, he would kiss her neck, her lips and then her breasts, whispering all the time that he loved her. Her anger would dwindle like a fire that had burned all its kindling, and the incident would be forgotten.

Perfect.

Only, as Zach knew from experience, plans rarely worked out as planned. Hell, every plan he had ever thought of went astray somewhere in the end. This last plan of his simply followed suit.

She'd gotten ticked over the wrong thing. Zach believed that was when things began to change course. Delany didn't hate him for the two minutes that he'd hesitated. She hated him because she believed that he had taken pity on her. She accused him of seeking forgiveness and was convinced that all he wanted was for her to absolve him of his guilt.

Knowing that in a sense she was right, the more Zach thought about it, the more he realized that her anger was probably justified. He wouldn't have wanted to be anyone's charity case. If the boy Zach had tried to save had come to his hospital room every day because he felt guilty for what Zach had done for him, he would have told the kid to scram. Only Delany hadn't known why he was there, so she'd never gotten the opportunity to tell him to get lost.

Great. He realized why she was angry, but it was too late. He'd already accused her of being a perfect angel. Told her it was her fault they were fighting because she was afraid. If she never spoke to him again, he couldn't blame her. But she had to talk to him again because, whether she believed it or not, he was in love with her.

Zach refused to give up just because of this mistake. His whole life had been nothing but a series of mistakes, and he'd fixed them, one after the other. This was simply one more thing on the list. A sense of well-being filled Zach. He was in control. All he had to do was convince Delany that he was for real, that their love was for real, and that this mistake, like so many others he'd made, would be forgotten.

Zach decided to track Delany down. It was only fair that he let her know in advance that his persistence would know no bounds when it came to making her realize his love. He stopped himself short of the door. Perhaps it would be best to let her cool off some more. It was mild out tonight. A brisk walk might go a long way toward helping her clear her mind.

The water reflected the moon's glow. Light danced across the ripples.

Plunk. Delany tossed another rock onto the water's surface only to watch it disappear as it sank below the light. So much for skipping stones. The rock's plummet was actually quite prophetic. Delany herself felt like she was drowning.

Why her? she wondered. Why didn't she deserve any happiness? She'd fought for the life of her brother. She'd struggled to save her parents. She'd battled for her students' lives. Why wasn't she allowed to love? Why didn't anyone love her for who and what she was?

Pathetic, she cried silently. She hated the wave of self-pity that overcame her, but she wallowed in it anyway. All she wanted in this world was Zach, and he was going to be denied to her. She deserved a little pity. Who would it hurt after all? No, she wouldn't hurt anyone, she reflected bitterly. It seemed to be her lot in life to be the one who was hurt.

Her anger began to blaze once more. Zach had no right to hurt her. She hadn't done anything to him; she hadn't asked anything of him. He'd pushed his way into her life, made her fall in love with him, and then he'd had the audacity to tell her that she wasn't allowing him to fall in love with her because of her fear.

Bull.

Delany wanted to charge back into that cabin and tell him to go to hell again. Then she wanted to wrap herself in his arms and tell him to make everything better. A contradiction to say the least.

Fight.

Delany didn't know where the uninvited thought came from. Somehow it managed to push itself to the forefront of her mind. The night she was attacked she remembered how the Crips closed in on her. She remembered the pain that she received at their hands, and how extreme it was. She also remembered how she'd tried to fight them.

Descendant of the challenger. Her name's meaning came back to haunt her. Maybe if she wanted Zach, it was her responsibility to fight for him. Maybe she should challenge him. If he came to her first out of guilt and then stayed with her out of pity, maybe now it was time to persuade him to get to know her without all that baggage. A clean slate. If they had been two strangers who had met, what would have happened? Would the connection have been as intense?

With all her heart, Delany had to believe that the answer was yes. Zach and she had connected from the very first. If they had a fresh start, perhaps they would connect all over again. This time, though, they would both be on an equal footing.

It was a promising thought. Delany stood and dusted the dirt from her backside. Zach wouldn't know what hit him. After all, she hadn't been named Delany for nothing.

A noise from behind her stopped Delany in her tracks. It sounded as if someone was walking along the path that circled the inlet. She supposed it could've been someone from the country club across the water out for a walk after a heavy dinner. But the club was empty; its windows were all blackened. The hairs rose on the back of her neck.

It might be someone from one of the cabins that dotted the cove. Delany shook her head at her paranoia. Since the attack, she'd envisioned Crips behind every door. It was ridiculous to think that she wasn't perfectly safe on the small island. Besides, Zach was only a shout away.

Nevertheless, Delany began to pick up her pace. It wasn't easy as her legs weren't up to such a workout. Something inside her, however, refused to allow her to slow down. Again, she heard the noise of crackling branches behind her. In her mind, she began to estimate how far away she was from the cabin. If she ran, would the muscles in her legs be able to support such a pounding? Delany couldn't say for sure, but when the noises behind her began to sound closer, she attempted the impossible.

She began to run. Pushing her legs beyond their endurance, she only hoped that, after years of running, her legs would somehow instinctively carry her away from the danger. Her back protested as her feet made contact with the ground. Speed became impossible as her muscles began to cramp and her feet turned to lead.

A branch smacked her ankle, and before she realized what was happening, Delany was facedown on the damp grass.

"Za—"

A hand clamped over her mouth, aborting her shout. Ruthless arms lifted her from the ground, and she felt herself pressed against what she took to be someone's chest. Relying on her self-defense training, she struck out with her leg, aiming for her attacker's instep. But after the run, her legs were limp from overexertion. Her kicks did nothing more than irritate the person who held her.

From the corner of her eye, she saw someone emerge from the thicket of trees she had just fled through. Although he was a stranger to her, she knew instantly from the blue rag he wore over his head who he was. Fear stabbed her heart, but she forced herself not to succumb to panic.

"What's the matter, sweetheart? It looks like your legs don't work so good no more. Maybe my boys were too rough with you." O.G. smirked at the woman. She was afraid, and he loved it.

"We didn't hurt her enough, man. I'm gonna teach her what real pain is tonight."

Delany recognized the voice instantly. Enrico. Apparently, he wasn't satisfied with what he and his gang had done to her the first time. It sickened her, but it also gave her strength. Enrico was nothing more than a depraved child. He needed the security of a group because he couldn't function alone. To beat up a woman was weak. To need a group to do it was pathetic.

If his hand wasn't still firmly placed over her mouth,

she would have told him that. Even without saying the words, Delany heard them inside her head. They gave her courage. She was stronger than her attacker. With that knowledge tucked inside her, she believed she had control over her situation, despite the fact that she was being held prisoner.

"Where's the pig?"

Obviously, O.G. wasn't the brightest man in the world. He'd just asked a question of someone who wasn't allowed to speak. She hoped his stupidity continued.

"Man, take your hand off her mouth so she can answer," O.G. instructed. He wanted to kill the pig now, his impatience goading him into error.

Delany prayed her eyes wouldn't give away her victory. As soon as she felt the hand move away from her lips, she breathed in deeply.

"Zaaaachhhh..." she screamed as loudly as was humanly possible.

Chapter 9

The shrill scream echoed through the night. Immediately, Zach rushed over to the door. Then he stopped. There was something about the quality of the scream that didn't fit. Delany wasn't simply calling for help because she'd fallen. There was terror in her voice.

Deciding not to take any chances, Zach ran to the bedroom. Frantically, he opened all the drawers in the dresser. Earlier, when he'd been unpacking, he'd seen a metal strongbox. Zach instinctively knew that it was where Mort kept his gun—he'd told Zach that he had one for the house, one for the cabin and one for the job. Despite his many weapons, however, Mort was a fanatic about gun safety. Mort had teenage boys he needed to be concerned about. He always kept his guns under lock and key.

Zach spotted the metal box in the bottom drawer. It had a padlock on it that could only be opened with a key.

"Damn," Zach muttered, running a hand through his hair. Where had Mort hidden the key? He would need to keep it close at hand so he could get to it easily, but somewhere his boys wouldn't think to look.

Damn, he swore again, this time silently. Zach didn't have time to search the house. He needed to get to Delany. For a moment, he considered going without the gun, but then he reconsidered. If it was who he thought it was, he was going to need to be armed.

O.G. was the only logical enemy. He was the most recent victim of Zach's deception, other than Delany, of course. And after what Delany had told him about the stranger in the hospital doorway, it made even more sense. O.G. was after revenge. Zach couldn't say that he blamed him. Being forced to live your life in fear because you ratted on your drug contact was not an easy thing to forgive.

It was Zach's hope that O.G. would've been taken care of by the people he betrayed. Unfortunately, they hadn't finished the job. Zach shouldn't have been surprised. O.G. got to be the Original Gangster because he ducked more often and with more success than any other gangster. He must have ducked again. Unfortunate for him because now it was Zach's turn to take a shot at him.

This time, there would be no place to duck. That was Delany he held out there. Because he touched her, because he made her afraid, for this he would die.

Zach stared down at the strongbox once more. Time spent searching for a key was useless. An idea came to him. With the box in hand, Zach raced for the kitchen. He'd spotted a wrench earlier that morning when he'd repaired a leaking kitchen faucet. The plumbing job would have to compensate for the demolished box.

The wrench was exactly where he'd left it. Zach began to hammer the lock with maniacal blows. Despite the sturdy look of the lock, it came apart easily with the force of Zach's blows. He tossed the lock aside and found the gun within, along with a new box of ammunition. It was a simple revolver, which would put him at a disadvantage if O.G. packed an automatic. Zach wasn't worried. One shot was all he would need.

Zach pushed the gun into his sweatpants, grateful the elastic waist was tight enough to support it. Slowly, he opened the front door of the cabin and stared out into the dark night. The moon was bright and would provide him with sufficient light to stalk his target. Crouching low, he moved stealthily across the grass, heading for the trail that would lead him to the shore. Instead of using the trail, he remained in the thicket of trees that bordered the path and moved parallel to it.

Twigs crunched beneath his feet. Zach stopped. He removed his sneakers and left them on the trail. His socks were quickly soaked by the wet ground, but Zach paid no attention. He was virtually silent as he moved through the trees now, and that was all he cared about. A few yards in front of him, he spotted movement through the trees. Instead of the two figures he expected—O.G. and Delany—there were three.

"I need to speak to a Mort Dietz."

"Who may I ask is calling?" the late-night receptionist inquired.

"My name is Cici Delores. I'm a friend of Mr. Montgomery. He told me that if I ever needed help with a situation, I could call Mort Dietz. Well, I need help."

Cici needed a lot of help. That afternoon, she had faced grave danger in order to visit her mother. The woman was a drug addict, but she was still Cici's mother. Cici wanted to at least let the woman know that she was safe. The Browns had discouraged her, knowing that if one Crip spotted her, Cici's life would be in danger. Cici's determination overcame their reluctance.

Despite the threat of danger, the reality was tame. Cici made her way inside the apartment complex where she used to live, and no one spotted her. She carefully planned her time. Before dusk, the streets were usually free of any Crip activity.

The apartment smelled of stale smoke and Scotch. The dinginess, the dirt, the despair in the tiny one-bedroom apartment that she used to call home was all too familiar to Cici. She marveled at her luck at having the Browns to watch over her. The Browns and her mother were as different as fire and water. Cici knew what it meant to be part of a family now, and she prayed that she would never have to come back to this.

Her mother sat on the worn couch, avoiding the side where the spring poked through the cushion. Unexpectedly, she was more coherent than usual. It was obvious that she'd been drinking most of the morning, but that was easier to deal with than a crack high. She wore a smock that hid a once-trim figure and a blue kerchief over hair that once gleamed. It was a sad way to end one's life.

"Hi, Momma, it's Ci. I came to let you know that I'm okay. I didn't know if you were worried or not." Cici sat on the floor in front of her mother. She hoped some of her words would seep through her mother's alcohol-fogged brain.

"Your brother wuz lookin' for ya," the inebriated woman drawled, her words slurred and expressionless.

"Sez he's gonna get thas teacher of yours. Never did like her. Thought she wuz sooo high'n'mighty."

Alarmed, Cici pushed for more information. "How could he get her? He doesn't even know where she is."

What appeared to be a laugh erupted from the older woman's throat. "You don' know. You think you're the only smart one in this family. But my boy is smart, too. He's real smart, street smart, ya know."

"No. How is he smart, Mom?" Cici tried to keep the bitterness from her voice. Years of bringing home straight A's, trying to make her proud, and the woman talked about how smart Enrico was. What kind of mother resented her child's success? A mother who never knew what success was, Cici supposed.

"He tol' me all 'bout it. Tol' me how he was gonna hurt her. Tol' me 'bout how he found her at the hospital and then followed her. Anderson Island's the place. He lef' arready. He's gonna get her, too." Cici's mother continued to ramble, but no one was left to hear her.

As soon as Cici realized that Enrico knew where Ms. Sheridan was and that he'd followed her, she rushed from the apartment. Cici hopped into the Browns' car and headed for the north end of Tacoma where she was unlikely to run into any gang members. Once there, she pulled into a convenience store and found a pay phone.

The night she had visited Ms. Sheridan in the hospital, Mr. Montgomery had walked her out to see that she got safely into Mr. Brown's car. He'd given her the number of his office in Seattle and told her that if Enrico or any other Crip gave her trouble to contact Mort Dietz. All she had to do was mention that she was a friend of Mr. Montgomery, and Mr. Dietz would come to her rescue.

To Cici, it sounded too good to be true. After all, she

wasn't anyone special enough to warrant first-class treatment from the DEA. She couldn't imagine ever needing them, but she kept the number anyway. She was glad that she had. She wasn't the one who needed help, but Ms. Sheridan and Mr. Montgomery did.

Now she was speaking with some operator who was about to cut her off.

"I'm sorry, Miss Delores, but Mr. Dietz is in a meeting, and he cannot be disturbed," the receptionist replied.

"You don't understand," Cici cried urgently. "This is about Mr. Montgomery. I think he's in trouble. I think there are some people who are after him."

It must have been the desperate quality of her voice, but somehow the receptionist knew not to dismiss the young woman so quickly. "Hold the line."

What seemed like a year passed before another voice came over the phone. Cici had been feeding quarters into the hungry pay phone to keep the line open. She was down to her last one when a gruff male voice barked in her ear.

"What do you know about Zach Montgomery?"

Cici struggled to remain calm and explain the whole story without sounding like an imbecile. "My name is Cici Delores. Mr. Montgomery helped my teacher when she was attacked by a gang. He stayed with her while she was in the hospital and everything. Well, I know for a fact that those gang members have been following Ms. Sheridan and they know where she is. And if they know where she is, then they know where Mr. Montgomery is."

"Gang members," the man repeated. Cici was prepared for him to cut her off on the assumption that she was a raving lunatic. She didn't know what she would do if he did. Wrong. She did know. Ms. Sheridan had risked her life for her. Cici could do no less.

"Please believe me, Mr. Dietz. Mr. Montgomery gave me this number in case my brother ever came back to hurt me. He's a Crip and he's dangerous and—"

"Crip?" Mort snapped. "Is that who's gone after Mr. Montgomery?"

"Yes," Cici shouted. There was a spark of recognition in the man's voice.

Mort cursed under his breath. Apparently, the Crips from Los Angeles hadn't dealt properly with the traitor in their midst. O.G. was after Zach, then. What for? Revenge. Idiot, Mort thought. If the gangster had any sense, he would have been on the first bus to New York. Instead, the ex-gang leader hung around and was after one of his best agents. Ex-agent, Mort corrected. It made no difference. Zach was first a friend, then an agent.

"Do you know where they are?" Mort had lent Zach his cabin. It was on a fairly remote island. Was there any chance that O.G. knew where they were holing up?

"My mother said something about Anderson Island."

Damn, they did know. "Mr. Montgomery took Ms. Sheridan there to help her recover. I'll send people right away. Thank you, miss. You've been a great help."

The line was abruptly disconnected. Mr. Dietz wasn't wasting any time. Help was on its way. Cici wished she could be sure that they would get there in time. All she did know was that Enrico had a head start. A big one.

Waiting was not an option for Cici. She had one more call to make to the Browns, and then she needed to get down to the dock and wait for the ferry. It might be futile, but Cici couldn't stand by and let her brother hurt Ms. Sheridan all over again.

* * *

"Where's the pig?" O.G.'s thumbless hand smacked her across the face. His four remaining fingers left angry welts on her cheek.

"Coward," Delany muttered, her contempt for these men growing each second.

"What did you say, bitch?" Enrico asked from behind her. Ruthlessly, he pinned her arms to his chest.

"O.G. Is that what they call you? Original Gangster?" Delany spat. "It's more like O.C. Original Coward. It's what you both are. You go after the helpless in gangs. You carry weapons and shoot people in cold blood. You beat up women. Let me ask you a question. Have you ever once faced someone in a fair fight? Ever?" They were bold words that would probably earn her a few more slaps for her trouble, but Delany was infuriated with these thugs. Besides, it felt much better to be enraged than it did to feel frightened.

"Ya, I'm gonna face him tonight. I'm gonna face the pig and do to him what he done to me." O.G. displayed his crippled hand and grinned maliciously. "Do you think he'll cry, or do you think he'll squeal like the pig he is."

"I think he'll kill you." It was a simple statement of fact. Although it wasn't obvious in the dark night, O.G.'s face paled slightly.

"Man, what are we waiting for? He's got to be in the cabin. Let's go get him." Enrico didn't like her last comment. So much so that he wanted to knock the guy off as soon as possible and then get back to his hood. He was safe in his hood, relatively speaking.

O.G. wasn't sure whether or not the cop had heard the scream. He didn't want to take any chances that he was waiting for them in the cabin. He'd rather have the cop come to him. That way he, not the cop, would be in control.

O.G. pulled out the gun he kept tucked in the low, sagging waist of his jeans. He held the semiautomatic to Delany's head and pushed the barrel of the gun between her eyes. He anticipated the fear she felt. It made him feel powerful.

The cold metal stung Delany's skin. It was an odd feeling to be so close to death. She waited for her life to flash through her mind. But all she could see was Zach. She remembered the first time she'd heard him snore. The first time she'd seen him smile. And she remembered how he'd been earlier that morning—gentle and loving. If she were to die, she could only hope that somehow he would live. He would carry the memory of them together with him for the rest of his life, and in some small way that meant that they would be together for as long as he lived.

"The pig got a gun?"

Delany didn't answer. The hesitation caused O.G. to push the gun harder against her forehead. Her mouth dried instantly, and even if she had wanted to say something, she would have been unable. What could she say? If she told them that he was armed, would that make them think twice about going to the cabin? If she told them he wasn't, would they relax their guard? Delany hadn't seen Zach with a gun, but that didn't mean he didn't have one. It was more than likely that if he was an agent with the DEA he would have to be armed at all times. However, if he had resigned from his job, perhaps he no longer carried a weapon. The gun pressed even harder against her head, forcing her to answer.

"I don't know," Delany whispered. It was truthful if nothing else.

"You don't know nothin'," O.G. snarled. "I should probably kill you now and be done with it."

"Wait, man," Enrico interrupted. "I want to have some fun with her. I've been waitin' to get my hands on her again. We got some unfinished business."

Viciously, Enrico threw Delany from his grasp. The sudden freedom caused her to stumble forward. Her legs, unable to adjust to the imbalance, buckled beneath her, and she was sent sprawling. She turned over quickly, expecting Enrico to pounce on her as soon as he could.

He hovered over her, a malicious grin on his face. Delany thought briefly that she would rather face the gun in O.G.'s hand than face Enrico unarmed.

As he bent down toward her, a sudden explosion rocketed through the night air. Delany looked up and saw that the grin was gone. In its place was a dribble of blood. Before she had a chance to understand what had happened, Enrico started to topple. She stiffened as she prepared for the impact of his body. Suddenly, a hand pulled Delany to her feet by the back of her sweatshirt and jerked her out of the path of the falling body.

"Another shot and she dies," O.G. warned. He had reacted instantaneously. The loud gunshot meant the pig was close. He grabbed the woman and used her as a human shield. The gun in his left hand pointed at her temple while his right arm threatened to cut off her oxygen as it wrapped around her neck.

Zach held his position behind a clump of trees in front of O.G. He wasn't sure, but it still looked as if O.G. didn't know exactly where he was. Damn the coward for acting so quickly. Zach should have been able to get off two shots before Delany was threatened again.

O.G. was so immune to the sound of gunfire that the noise hadn't startled him at all.

"I mean it, pig. Back off or the bitch gets it." O.G. tightened his grip around Delany's neck and dragged her slowly along the path, toward the cabin.

Delany struggled to catch her breath while at the same time she struggled to move her legs.

"Move it, or I'll shoot you right now. Don't try nothin' stupid like falling. You're keepin' him from shootin' me, but you're also keepin' me from shootin' him. If you ever want to see your boyfriend alive, you'll do what I tell you to." O.G. never once looked behind him. He risked a guess that the shot had come from the direction of the water. So if he could get them back to the cabin, he would once again be in a position where the pig would have to come to him.

Delany squinted against the darkness, trying to locate Zach. O.G. lied. He couldn't have Zach in his sights. If she couldn't see him, then he couldn't. But Delany couldn't be sure, and she wasn't willing to take that kind of risk with Zach's life.

"I know you're out there, pig. Don't try nothin'." O.G. had reached the front door of the cabin. He was faced with the dilemma of how to open the door. If he used his right arm, she might duck, and the cop would get off a shot. Same thing if he took his gun away from her head for a second. O.G. didn't know how close the guy was, but there was no reason to test it.

His hands occupied, he decided to use his foot. Kicking backward, he slammed his foot against the door. He felt a slight give, which encouraged him to try again and again. Finally, the door swung backward. He pulled Delany inside with him, then quickly slammed the door shut.

Once inside the cabin, O.G. felt secure. Enrico was dead, but he had no plans to meet the same fate. The cop would have to come to him. And the cop wouldn't know what was happening inside the cabin. He'd start to get edgy about his girlfriend. That edginess would be to O.G.'s advantage. Without a clear head, he couldn't think. If the cop couldn't think, he was dead.

O.G. released Delany immediately, but still held the gun on her. "I want you to pull those blinds down," O.G. instructed, pointing at the large window in the living room that overlooked the beach.

Delany saw O.G.'s hand tremble. He was nervous and that was good. For a brief second, she considered rushing him in an attempt to get control of the gun. If she'd had full use of her legs, she would have been able to land a side kick into his stomach or a straight-leg kick at his wrist. Either one would have caused him to lose the gun. Only the two of her legs together could barely support her weight. She had no chance of resting all her weight on one leg while she used her other leg to strike.

"Now!" he barked at her.

Gingerly, Delany shuffled to the window and slowly lowered the blinds. She stared out into the black night once more, hoping for a glimpse of Zach. She saw only darkness.

Mort felt the wind push through his hair as the boat sped across the water. Two other boats, filled with Seattle police officers, followed behind him. Time was running out for Zach. It was taking too long to get to the island. Mort had no way of knowing what kind of head start the gang leader had on him, but he knew it was significant. He could only hope that Zach had kept his wits about him.

He thought of the gun he kept in the bottom of his dresser drawers in the bedroom. The key was in a small dish on top of the book shelf in the living room. Zach might not have any idea the gun was there, but it might be his only hope against the gang leader, who was undoubtedly armed.

"Can't you make this boat go any faster?" It was more a command than a question.

"I'm up to full speed now, sir," replied the driver, who had already pushed the boat past its limits.

"Just get me to that island," Mort shouted over the sound of the wind and the waves. Get me there in time, he added silently.

Zach knelt down in the grass, maintaining a position behind some bushes while he observed the cabin. Delany lowered the blinds, most likely at O.G.'s command. The overhead light was on, but the blinds were too thick to see any shadows moving behind them. Zach was now ignorant of everything that happened in the tiny cabin. Damn!

He had to hope that O.G. was too busy planning his next move to even bother with Delany. He also had to pray that Delany wouldn't try anything foolish. Briefly, Zach entertained the thought of leaving to call for some backup, but it was a useless idea. Help wouldn't get here until it was too late, and Zach had no intention of letting Delany out of his sight for that long.

He needed to put a stop to O.G. now. The odds were even now that the boy was dead. Zach felt that his chances were remarkably high.

Boy. Zach glanced back over his shoulder at the body

that now lay dead on the wet grass. He had hated to do it. To kill one so young. But there had been no choice. The boy was a fool. A kid who got into trouble way over his head.

No, Zach wouldn't feel guilty over him. That boy, that thug, had beaten Delany unmercifully before. Who knows what he would have done to her this time? Zach refused to regret the killing. It was either the kid or Delany. The kid never had a chance.

His focus returned to the cabin. Zach weighed his options. An open frontal attack would leave Delany too vulnerable. O.G. would have time to grab her and hold her at gunpoint once again, or even have time to shoot her if he chose. Zach couldn't storm any castle walls tonight. That left a sneak attack. The cabin had only one door. It had a large window in the living room, a small window over the kitchen sink and another large window in the bedroom. There was no way he could get through either the living-room window or the kitchen window. That would essentially be sneaking into O.G.'s lap.

The bedroom window wasn't much better. The bedroom was only a few feet away from the living room. If the door was open, O.G. would immediately hear any noise coming from the back of the cabin. Zach cursed Mort for being able to afford only a small vacation home.

It was a ridiculous thought. And a time-consuming one. Zach had to think methodically. His time was limited. The more time Zach wasted, the more time O.G. had to plan. It was better to act now while he was still reeling from the death of his fellow gangster. Nerves were on edge, adrenaline pumping through O.G.'s system. Now was the time to catch him off guard.

If only he could see where O.G. was, then he might better plan his attack. The blinds in the living room had been closed; more than likely the other windows were now shielded, too. O.G. wasn't as stupid as Zach had once believed. Zach amended that thought. O.G. was stupid, but he was a survivor.

Once again, Zach's eyes roamed the cabin for any possible point of entry that would take O.G. by surprise. There was no basement; there was no attic. Attic. Zach glanced up and checked the rooftop once more. No, there was no attic, but there was a very quaint fireplace in the living room. Mort always insisted that a fire was the only way to keep the wet chill of Seattle's winters at bay. Where there was a fireplace, there was a chimney.

Thank heaven for the stories of Santa Claus. Zach now had his point of entry. The next task was to get on the roof and determine if he would be able to fit down the chimney. The likelihood was slim. Still, he thought of other ideas he might be able to put into practice once he was up there.

Removing the damp socks from his feet so as not to slip, Zach began to move toward the cabin, always keeping a tree in front of him in case O.G. picked that moment to look out the window.

"What's your boyfriend doin' anyway?" O.G. complained. An attack was imminent. O.G. felt sure of that; he just wanted to get on with the fight. Time to live or die. As soon as the pig fired one shot, O.G. would know his location. One shot was all it would take. "Maybe he doesn't think you're worth the trouble."

"Zach's going to hurt you for what you've done to me. When he's pounding on your face, I'll try to stop

him before he kills you, but I can't guarantee anything.
Zach is uncontrollable when he's mad."

Delany hoped her words penetrated the gang leader's
thoughts. The more fearful he was, the more nervous
he was, the better chance she had of catching him off
guard. It was the only way her limited strength would
succeed against him.

It wasn't that Delany wasn't confident about Zach's
abilities. He was a law enforcement agent after all, and
skilled in the art of defeating men of O.G.'s caliber.
However, she couldn't rely on him to save her. She
wasn't some heroine in a fairy tale who needed to be
rescued by the dashing prince. Delany trusted that Zach
would do everything he could to save her. But she was
also going to do everything she could to save herself.
To cower before this coward was beneath her.

"Prepare to be challenged," Delany muttered. From
her seat on the couch, she watched as O.G. paced back
and forth from the kitchen to the living room.

"What did you say?" O.G. heard her muttering, but
the words were unclear. He was overreacting and he
knew it. The broad was powerless against him, so it
didn't matter what she said. O.G. wanted respect,
though. He held the gun. He waited for the pig. He was
the one who decided if she lived or died. He deserved
her respect.

"What do you think you're going to accomplish?"
Delany responded, ready to mete out her own punish-
ment. "You know these hostage situations never work.
Zach is probably calling the police right now. In about
an hour, this cabin will be surrounded by a SWAT team.
You'll tell them you want a helicopter and safe passage
off the island. They'll storm the cabin. Kill you and
rescue me. I've seen it a dozen times on television."

O.G. snarled at her brave words. "You don't know nothin' about real life. Right now I decide if you continue to breathe or not. Right now you need to say your prayers, little lady, in case I decide to pull this trigger and do away with your words for good." O.G. matched his words with a deed. He moved in front of Delany and pointed the gun in her direction.

"Not so brave, are you? Now you know who's in control."

"So tell me what the plan is. Tell me how you think you're going to get out of this alive," Delany flung back. "If you kill me, your chances are nil. I know it, and you know it."

"I can make him think that your dead body is a live, unconscious one, so don't tempt me. All I have to do is wait for your boyfriend to make his move. Once he's dead, I'll have no problem gettin' off the island." O.G. returned to his pacing. Time passed, and as much as he hated to admit it, the woman was right. Hostage situations rarely worked well for the hostage taker. If the pig was calling in help, the best choice to make was to leave the cabin, find him and kill him before he made it to a phone.

O.G. balked at that idea. The plan was to make the cop come to him, not the other way around. That was before Enrico got shot through the back, though. Maybe now it was time to consider other options.

No way. O.G. wasn't into this commando stuff. He knew about smash and grabs, drive-bys and drug deals. Chasing a cop through the woods was not his style. His only choice was to stay put and hope that the cop was made nervous by the idea of O.G. holding his girlfriend. A nervous cop was not a smart cop.

* * *

The brick chimney was built adjacent to the cabin, almost as an extension. The best way for Zach to reach the roof was to crawl up the chimney. The bricks provided him with edges to grab onto as well as toeholds for his feet. The sharp brick cut into his bare feet, but Zach paid little attention to the pain. With his powerful arms, he was able to reach the roof in seconds. Once on top, he looked down the chimney and knew that his assumption had been correct. There was no way he would fit. It was time to put another plan into practice.

With carefully placed footsteps, Zach moved over the part of the roof that covered the living room until he reached the edge. Gently, he lowered himself onto his stomach, his head hanging over the roof. The distance to the large window was only about three feet. That meant if Zach lowered his body down and hung on to the roof with his fingertips, his feet would land directly in the middle of the window. Perfect.

Zach lifted himself stealthily and began to search the roof for something that would cause the proper distraction. Once again his eyes focused on the chimney. Retracing his steps, he made his way back to the chimney and gave it a closer look. He noticed that one of the bricks on top looked to be loose.

He began to move the brick back and forth to work it free. Chunks of concrete gave way, and in a few minutes the brick was out. The tricky part was the timing. O.G. would have to be preoccupied by the disturbance long enough to give Zach a chance.

The plan was to toss the brick down the chimney. Not only would it cause a lot of noise on the way down, but it would cause some ashes to scatter once it hit bottom. O.G. would check it out, assuming that Zach was up to something. Then Zach could race to the edge

Undiscovered Hero

of the roof. He would hold tight to the roof's edge, then propel himself forward. His momentum should be enough to break the window and gain entrance. O.G. would naturally be stunned by the sudden explosion of glass. His confusion would give Zach plenty of time to draw his gun on the gang leader.

Perfect. It was the most perfectly stupid plan Zach had ever devised. There was no way it was going to work, but there was also no way it could fail. Zach's only other choice was to go for the police. The police would only turn the situation into a major confrontation. Zach didn't like the idea of Delany being subjected to a prolonged hostage rescue. It was too chancy. Too many things could go wrong, and Delany would be the one to suffer. Zach's only option was to get to her now, while O.G. was still jumpy.

Zach held the brick high over the chimney and let it drop. As soon as the brick began falling, he raced toward the edge of the roof. His only thought—*please let this work*.

O.G. heard the noise come from the wall. It wasn't until he looked around that he realized there was a fireplace. He got down on his knees and tried to look up the chimney, but he couldn't see anything. He barely pulled his head out in time as the brick came slamming down to the ground, spreading ashes and dust everywhere.

Delany's attention was captured by the noise, as well. She couldn't imagine what it was, but she knew that Zach must have had something to do with it. Instinctively, she moved closer to the fireplace.

O.G. inhaled the ashes and dust and began to cough

frantically. "Son of a…" he shouted, trying to remove the soot from his eyes.

An instant later, the sound of breaking glass startled him out of his coughing fit. Glass sprayed everywhere, and O.G. assumed a bomb had exploded inside the cabin.

As soon as she heard the glass shatter, Delany crouched on the floor and shielded her face from the flying shards. She didn't want to lose sight of O.G., though. Zach was providing a distraction. All she needed to do was take advantage of it.

When Delany glanced up, she saw that O.G. was on his hands and knees on the ground. His hand still clutched the gun, but it wasn't pointed at her. She was about to make a grab for it when a sharp command aborted her plan.

"Back off, Delany," Zach ordered. On his knees and surrounded by broken glass, Zach held his revolver on O.G. The gang leader was still trying to understand what had just happened. "Drop the gun," Zach barked. He wished he could stand, but his feet were too badly cut when he shattered the glass window.

O.G. looked up, his face covered in blood from a hundred tiny scratches the glass fragments had inflicted. He looked down at his hands, his left one clutching the gun, his right one minus a thumb. The anger and pain all came back to him in that instant. Knowing he was going to die, but hoping to take the pig with him, he lifted the gun and attempted to aim it in the right direction. Only he didn't know what direction that was because of the blood dripping over his eyes.

The sound of a gunshot reverberated through the small cabin. Delany was forced to cover her ears. The sound seemed so loud, so explosive. So final. Then there was only silence. Delany saw that O.G. was dead. Blood now bubbled from a hole in his chest. Then she turned and looked at Zach.

He knelt on the floor, his eyes expressionless, his face marred by tiny scratches. He was the most beautiful sight she could imagine. He lowered his gun then and turned to Delany.

"Are you okay?" His voice was gruff with tension and shock.

Delany could only nod in response. She stood up to walk over to him. That was when she saw the blood spilling from his feet. She screamed. Then as she watched, frozen with horror, the blood drained from his face, leaving it drawn and ashen.

"Zaaachhhh!"

It was too late. He never heard her.

Chapter 10

"**Y**ou're sure that he's going to be fine? There was so much blood," Delany sobbed. The only thing that supported her was the strong shoulder of Mort Dietz.

Dawn had already debuted outside the hospital lobby windows. But she had only just received word that Zach was going to be all right. Exhaustion had finally taken its toll after the long night. Zach's crashing through the living-room window seemed days ago, not just hours ago. Delany remembered it all with a shudder.

After Delany realized that Zach had fainted from loss of blood, she bolted into action. First she removed the major pieces of glass from his feet, then she wrapped bath towels around them to stem the bleeding. Large, cushy green towels quickly became drenched with his blood.

Delany knew that time was about to run out. She hurried to get the phone and call for help when the front door burst open. Thinking she was under attack again, she reached for the revolver Zach had dropped when he passed out. Her arms straight out, she prepared herself to kill anyone who would try to stop her from helping Zach.

"Don't move," she shouted to the man who had entered first. "I'll blow your head off. I swear I will."

"Not with my own gun, I hope. It would be terribly embarrassing." Mort Dietz entered his once-quaint cabin to find glass everywhere, a shattered window, soot blackening all his furniture and two bodies that bled profusely onto his new Navajo rug. He also found one terrified woman who held a gun on him and looked for all the world as if she was prepared to carry out her threat. He raised his hands high above his head as he approached her.

"Don't come any closer," she commanded. "Who are you?"

"My name is Mort Dietz. I own the cabin. I'm a friend of Zach's. You've got to let me help him. He's losing too much blood." Mort kept his tone gentle, yet persuasive.

Delany knew he was right, but how could she trust him? Behind him, more men entered, men who all wore black. They could've been officers, or something else.

Her confusion and mistrust were apparent, so Mort added, "I've got some identification in my back pocket. Let me pull it out and I'll prove who I am."

Delany nodded curtly and watched carefully while the man removed his wallet, then displayed a badge. On the other side of the badge was an identification card that showed his picture. On top of the card, Delany read Drug Enforcement Agency.

"You worked with Zach." She believed him now

and lowered the gun. She backed off so that he could check on Zach's condition for himself. "It's his feet. He crashed through the window with his feet. I don't know why, but they were bare. I think he might have cut an artery. We've got to get him to a hospital." The words fell out of Delany's mouth in a rush. She didn't know if she was making any sense, but something must have gotten through. Mort Dietz called in his men and together they lifted Zach and carried him to the car they had waiting outside. Delany followed along, and in a few minutes they were on a speedboat headed back to Tacoma.

An ambulance was waiting for them at the dock. As Delany rushed alongside the men carrying Zach, she was distracted by the sound of her own name.

"Ms. Sheridan!" Cici had slept in her car all night, waiting to catch the first ferry of the day.

Delany was torn. Zach needed her, but somebody had to tell Cici that her brother was dead. Delany turned to Mort and asked, "Please sit with him in the back. I have to tell this girl that her brother is—"

Mort looked over Delany's shoulder and spotted the girl running across the dock. "Is that Cici Delores? Tell her thank-you for me. She called and warned me about her brother's plans. If we hadn't gotten there when we did, Zach might have bled to death. Don't worry, Delany, I'll make sure Zach gets to the hospital. We'll meet you there."

Grateful for the man's understanding, Delany turned to meet Cici. On the water, behind Cici, Delany spotted another boat headed for the dock. She knew it carried the bodies of O.G. and Enrico.

"They found you in time," Cici blurted, short of breath from running. "My mother told me where Enrico

went and what he wanted to do to you. So I called Mr.
Dietz for help. Mr. Montgomery gave me the number,
but I never thought I'd have to use it. Who's in the
ambulance?'' Cici watched it pull away as another van
pulled into the parking lot. The word Coroner was written across it.

Delany, in a state of shock from all that had happened, attempted to control her shaking body. ''Cici,
you're going to have to be strong,'' she instructed. The
words were meant to help herself, as well.

''Is somebody dead?'' Cici asked.

''Zach was in the ambulance. He was hurt trying to
save me. He's lost a great deal of blood, but they've
got him stabilized. I think he's going to be okay.'' Delany heard her voice crack, and once again she tried to
bring herself under control. Cici didn't need her to be
hysterical right now. Cici herself was going to be hysterical soon enough.

''Tell me what happened, Ms. Sheridan. Where's Enrico?'' Cici saw Delany look beyond her to the water.
Cici turned her head to follow the direction of her gaze.
They saw the motorboat pull up to the dock. They saw
men lift two lifeless bodies from the bottom of the boat,
then hand them over to two others who waited with
stretchers and heavy black bags. Turning back to her
teacher, Cici knew the answer to her next question. But
she had to ask it anyway. ''He's dead, isn't he?''

The young face betrayed all the emotions the girl felt.
Delany empathized. She, too, had watched her brother
die, powerless to help him. Delany had learned the hard
way that you couldn't control other people's lives. You
could offer guidance, help and love, but in the end you
couldn't force anyone to do what you wanted them to
do just because you knew it was right. That was her

lesson. Delany's brother had made his own choice. So had Cici's.

"I'm so sorry, Cici. I'm sorry he had to die. Not for him, but for you."

"I stopped loving him a long time ago, Ms. Sheridan. I'm sorry he had to die, too, but it was inevitable. If it hadn't been this, it might have been a drive-by of some gang rumble. Enrico chose his road and now he's dead because of it. It's his own fault."

Astounded at the girl's maturity, Delany wrapped her arms around her and offered her all the strength she had left. It was a small gesture in the face of such a loss, but it was all Delany had to give.

After a few minutes of absorbing the strength that Delany gave so freely, so selflessly, Cici pulled back and said quietly, "Come on, I'll drive you to the hospital. Mr. Montgomery needs you."

Delany allowed Cici to tug her along to her car. When she sat down in the passenger seat, Delany felt as if the weight of the world had been lifted off her shoulders. She was exhausted, but she knew she couldn't sleep until she saw Zach. She had to witness his recovery with her own eyes. She had to let him know that she was there for him despite their personal problems.

As they drove away from the dock, Delany recalled Mort's words about Cici's part in the rescue. Delany tried to smile at the girl, but she no longer had the energy to do even that. Regardless, the warmth and gratitude in her voice were unmistakable. "Mr. Dietz told me that you warned him about Enrico. You saved Zach's life. In the time it would have taken to catch the ferry off the island, Zach would've bled to death." Delany felt herself shiver at the thought.

"I'm no hero, Ms. Sheridan," Cici replied, her eyes steady on the road ahead.

"Oh, yes, you are. You're the most heroic person I've ever known," Delany whispered, her head lolling against the cushion that supported it. She closed her eyes, reminding herself silently that she needed to stay awake. Zach needed her. When he was feeling better, they were going to have to settle their differences. But for now, those issues could wait.

At the hospital, Mort told her that Zach's condition was stable, and Delany's first instinct was to allow the sleep she'd held at bay for so long to overcome her, but she couldn't. She needed to see Zach first. She wanted to feel the beat of his heart under her palm and to feel his breath on her cheek so she would know that Zach was truly alive. What they'd said to each other before was written on the wind. Forgotten.

"Please, I've got to see him," Delany told Mort as she feebly attempted to push her way past him.

His arms held tightly to her own. "He's sleeping right now. The doctor said it would be best to let him rest."

"No." She tried to convey to the man holding her how imperative it was that she be with Zach. "You don't understand. I need to be with him. He was there for me, and I've got to be there for him. I won't wake him. I only need to sit with him, hold his hand."

Mort was helpless against her entreaty. Moving aside, he allowed Delany to pass. She entered the quiet private room. Zach was under the blankets. He had an IV hooked up to him to replace the valuable fluids he'd lost. Under the blanket, the shape of his feet were pronounced, from the bandages, Delany presumed.

His breathing was deep, and Delany knew that he was sound asleep. She pulled up a chair next to the bed and clutched his hand in her own. He never stirred. Delany had to smile at the irony.

"Can you believe it?" she whispered, not wanting to wake him, but needing to talk to him all the same. "Here we are, back in the hospital. We just got out of this place. Only now our positions are reversed."

Zach slept on peacefully.

"I wish they weren't. I'd give anything to be where you are if it meant you'd be okay. You've done so much for me, and now I can repay the favor." Delany rested her head against the bed so she could see their hands linked together. "We've got a long way to go, Zach, but I think we'll get there." Delany finally allowed exhaustion to overtake her, and she drifted off to sleep hunched over the bed.

Later that afternoon, Debbie entered the room and surveyed the soundly sleeping couple. Delany, despite the soft sighs that belied the depth of her sleep, looked uncomfortable with only her head and chest supported by the bed. Leaning over her friend, Debbie gently shook Delany by the shoulder. "Delany. Wake up, hon. We just got that back healed. I don't want to see all of Stan's hard work go to waste."

The gentle shake was able to penetrate Delany's muddled dreams. She lifted her head, and her eyes came into focus. After a moment, so did her brain. She was in the hospital, but she wasn't *in* the hospital. She was with Zach because he was injured saving her life. The horrible memories returned in a flash. O.G. would've shot Zach if Zach hadn't been so quick on the trigger. That thought alone was enough to send Delany into a panic.

With a large stretch, she worked out the cramps and the aches in her neck and back. Delany looked at her friend. "He's going to be fine." Delany knew it, but she wanted Debbie to affirm it.

"Yes, he's going to be fine," Debbie reassured her, happy to oblige. "Doctor Manuela said he'll need to stay off his feet for a few days to give the cuts and lacerations some time to heal. Other than that, he'll be as good as new. There wasn't any serious damage done to the muscles. There was just a lot of blood. The stitches will come out in no time."

"So much bleeding," Delany recalled. It was a horrible experience to watch the blood drain from someone's body.

"Don't get her started, Deb, or she'll faint on me." The husky voice emanated from the bed, and Delany instinctively turned toward the sound. Zach's chocolate brown eyes were open and alert. For the very first time, Delany really believed that he was definitely going to recover.

"I'm not the one who fainted at the sight of blood. That was you," Delany teased in an effort to hide her relief now that the fear was gone.

"Never. Besides, real men don't faint. We just pass out." Zach may have been down, but he hadn't lost the fight.

"Well, then, you passed out," Delany agreed, humoring him. "Big time."

"All I want to know is when I'm going to get rid of you two. It's not healthy to spend so much time in a hospital," Debbie warned them, then smiled at their expressions. "Okay, I get the message. I'll be back to check on you later, Zach. And you, too, Delany. Don't forget you're not exactly a hundred percent, either."

Debbie exited the room, leaving the couple to themselves.

As soon the amicable nurse was gone, Delany wished that she hadn't left. The silence between them was daunting. Now that the threat of danger was gone, they were back to their original problem before the gang leader had found them. Only the more Delany thought about it, the more she felt that she had overreacted. But that was because she'd fallen in love for the first time in her life. It wasn't important how Zach had found her; it was only important that he had. His reasons in the beginning might not have been pure, but at least he'd been honest about it. After almost losing him, Delany didn't care anymore about the details. All she wanted was him, no matter how she got him.

She opened her mouth to tell him exactly that when he stopped her.

"I think you should go."

Delany was dumbfounded. "What do you mean? I'm not going anywhere. I'm going to stay here and take care of you, like you did me."

Zach sighed deeply, the expression on his face grim. Instinctively, Delany knew he didn't like what he was going to say next, but he was going to say it anyway. "You can't stay with me. It would mean repeating the same mistake we've already made. I don't want you here because you think you owe me. You're staying out of pity just like you believe I did. What happens next time one of us needs the other? Do we keep score? Do we spend the rest of our lives doubting the other's motives, constantly wondering if we're only there for one another because of some kind of payback?"

Delany protested immediately. It was ridiculous to think that she was here for that reason alone. Hell, she'd told him she loved him. Didn't that mean anything to him? "How can you think I'm only here as some kind of payback?"

"How could you think that I stayed with you all that time out of guilt?" Zach's eyes locked on hers, communicating with her more than his words did.

For a moment, she was at a loss for words. "But originally, you—"

Zach interrupted, "Yes, originally. But aren't you the slightest bit glad that you have this opportunity to repay me? Aren't you grateful for the chance to set us back on some sort of equal footing?"

Yes. It was humiliating, but it was true. Delany *was* grateful for the opportunity to do for Zach what he had done for her. Of course she wouldn't wish this upon him. She wouldn't have him hurt for the world. But at the same time, she felt that his being here did make them equal.

"I guess we're equals now," she agreed. Perhaps he would see the positive side to that.

Zach muffled a small groan as he shifted his weight to sit up, his feet jarred by the movement. He needed to face her eye to eye, not flat on his back. Which only proved how warped they both were when it came to their pride. Once settled, he faced her again. After a pause to organize his thoughts, he began.

"Yes, we are equals. Love shouldn't be about that. You don't need to repay me for what I've done. I stayed in the beginning because I felt guilty. Maybe you were right, maybe I did want you to forgive me…for a lot of things. That feeling ended so quickly, though, Delany. I think it ended the minute you opened your eyes. I told myself that guilt was my only reason for staying, but I lied. I do that. I'm a very skilled liar." Zach gave her a crooked smile.

"Yes, you lie. But you're not really a liar. You're honorable," Delany countered, defending him against himself.

Her words touched him, or more accurately, her vehement tone touched him. She really did love him. She needed to know that he also felt the same way, that he wasn't sending her away from a lack of love. It was an overabundance of love that pushed the words out of his mouth. "I lied to you, and I lied to myself. The truth was that your eyes made my gut tighten. Your laughter made me happy. Your pain made me want to cry. I hate to cry. From the first moment I touched your hand, I knew you were different from anyone I had ever met. So maybe I told you I stayed out of guilt and pity. Maybe I even believed it myself for a while. That was a lie, too. I stayed because I fell in love with you."

Tears rippled down Delany's face. His words made her so happy, yet also nervous because he said them as if it was the last time he would speak such words. "That's why I'm here, Zach. I'm here because I love you."

"If you love me, then you'll leave."

Delany shook her head. "I don't believe that. I was going to tell you that nothing we said to each other on the island makes a difference anymore. It doesn't matter what your reasons were, or what mine are now. We love each other. That's all that counts."

"No." Zach felt a sadness settle over him. "It sounds nice on a greeting card, but it doesn't work in real life. I can't have you here because I don't want our relationship to be about equal footing, or pride, or who did what to whom first. You need to accept the fact that I stayed with you because I loved you. The only way you can prove to me that you really believe that is to leave. You'll show me that you can accept my love without any conditions. I can love you, and give to you, and you don't have to give anything back to me. That's what it's all about, not this equality bull.'' Zach's tone was fierce.

Perhaps it was his ferocity that shook Delany to awareness. Zach wanted her to leave so that she could prove to him that she accepted his love. To her it didn't seem like Zach got much from the deal. ''How do I prove to you that I love you?'' Delany asked.

''I know.''

''Do you?'' she questioned doubtfully. ''Do you have any idea what I feel for you? How could you know that you've brought color back into my world? How could you guess that when I lay in that bed day after day, your face was the first thing I thought of when I opened my eyes and the last thing I thought of before I closed them? How could you know?''

Zach brushed his hand across her cheek, drying the wetness he found there. ''I know,'' he simply repeated.

''I don't want to leave. Who will take care of you?''

''I've taken care of me for a long time. Please, Delany, it's important to me. You are so wonderful, so full of warmth and goodness. I need to know that for a while you needed me. Being there for you was my gift of unconditional love. Accept it, and then we really will have a fresh start.'' Zach felt her reluctance, but he also knew she would do what he asked.

''What happens after I leave?''

Zach wished he knew. What he was doing here was not without risk. ''We go to our separate corners and try to get our bearings. You've been through too much in the past few months. You need to go back to your life and remember what it was, and then decide if you still want me in it.''

''You, too?''

''Me, too. After a while, when this is all behind us, then we'll know if what we've got together is real, or only circumstance.'' Zach knew now, but he wanted to give Delany time.

Delany knew now, but she wanted to give Zach time. ''I'll be at school. I've got a runathon coming up soon.'' Her decision to take the remainder of the year off now seemed pointless. She'd wanted the time to be with Zach. If she wasn't going to be with Zach, school was as good a place to be as any once she was fully recovered. There would only be a few weeks left of the school year, but she would see the year out.

Zach nodded, pleased that she was going to cooperate, yet missing her already. ''I've got a restaurant to build.''

Delany nodded in return. She leaned over him and pressed her lips to his in a bittersweet parting kiss. She felt their firmness beneath hers, and for a moment the breath left her body. His tongue darted across her lips, and Delany opened her mouth to receive him, needing to feel him inside her body one more time before she left. She challenged him with her own tongue. Penetrated his mouth, stormed his defenses and dared him to let her go. After one last taste of her mouth, he pushed her way.

''You've got more willpower than I do,'' Delany muttered as she pulled away from him, her body aching with regret.

''I've got more to lose,'' Zach returned, though his body experienced the same turmoil as hers.

Without any more words between them, Delany left
the room as silently as she'd entered.

Delany left the hospital that day, feeling as if her
heart had dropped into her stomach and broken into a
million pieces. Briefly, she considered asking Doc
Manny if he would repair it, but somehow she knew
that there was no operation for what ailed her. All the
platitudes she had ever heard, about time healing all
wounds, and love conquering all, were slaps in the face
to her.

Love was a terrible, aching pain, and anyone who
said differently was a liar. The hollowness she felt
wasn't going to go away, or mend, or heal. Losing Zach
was like losing a part of herself. Only if she found him
again would she be whole. The worst part about it was
that Delany knew where he was, but she could do nothing about it.

So she returned to her apartment, replaced the pictures that had been taken from her shelves and the robe
that had been taken from her closet. The colorful afghan
she kept close to her at night. To wrap herself in its
warmth helped her imagine that it was Zach's arms that
kept her warm. It never worked, but she refused to pack
away his gift.

Nights were the worst. At bedtime, she gazed up at
the ceiling and relived all the times she had spent with
Zach. Her body would tighten with desire when she
remembered their passionate lovemaking. Vividly, she
recalled the feel of his hands on her flesh, his lips on
her breasts and stomach. Her body wanted him almost
as badly as her soul did.

Delany wondered if Zach was reliving their passion,
as well. She wondered if he slept at night or if he, too,

lay awake wanting her, wanting them. There was no one at the hospital to bring him a soft drink or candy. There was no one there to read to him with silly voices. No one to hold his hand when he hurt. No one to catch him when he fell.

How could being away from him prove to him that she accepted his love? It didn't make any sense. Yet every time she thought about returning to the hospital, she stopped herself. It didn't make much sense to Delany, but to Zach it did. So Delany wouldn't risk it. She wouldn't risk losing Zach forever because she couldn't stay away for a few days. The hardest part was when she had to go to the hospital for one of her continuing sessions with Stan. Knowing there were only a few floors between them drove her to distraction, which only prolonged the session because her concentration was off. Stan, bless him, was as patient as ever. He worked her muscles, and at the end of her session, she was actually able to run for a few minutes on the treadmill.

"It'll be a while before you're running miles again," Stan informed her. "But you should be ready to go back to work in a few more days. Try to sit down as much as possible, though. You don't want to overdo it."

Delany had hugged him for all his help, but as happy as she was about returning to work, emotionally she didn't know if she was capable. Each day dragged by, and it seemed that all she had the energy to do was get up, do the exercises that Stan had taught her to strengthen her legs, eat only enough to live and then fall back into bed. Videos she rented were left unwatched. Focusing on a book became an impossible task. To unwrap her favorite candy bar was beyond her capabilities. Delany couldn't imagine where she would get the energy to teach. No, teaching was not an option for her at this point. When Zach was with her once more, she would be ready to teach again. Not until then.

It was only going to be a few more days, Delany needed to repeatedly remind herself. No, they hadn't put any time limit on how long this separation had to last, but she was convinced that it would only take a few days, and then Zach would be satisfied. As soon as he was released from the hospital, he would come straight to her apartment.

Thank goodness Debbie kept her informed as to when that release would be. Delany would've hated the uncertainty. Every day she would have wondered if today was the day he was coming home. The crushing disappointment at the end of each day when he didn't show would have been too much for her to bear.

Debbie eased Delany's mind about a lot of her concerns. The older woman, diligent in her attempts to keep the couple together, gave Delany daily updates on Zach's progress. He seemed moody, but other than that, he was recovering nicely. That was usually the summation of each of Debbie's reports. As long as Delany knew there were no complications, it was enough to keep her away.

Finally, four days after he'd been admitted to the hospital, Delany got the message that he was being released.

"Get the blush out and put on the lipstick. Dr. Manuela just signed the papers. Zach should be coming for you sometime this afternoon."

There wasn't a word that could describe the size of Delany's smile. "Are you sure, Deb? No mistake?"

"No mistake. Don't forget about my wedding invitation," Debbie reminded the younger woman.

The last time the nurse had made such a suggestion,

Delany had been shocked and pretended ignorance. This time she only replied, "It will be the first one I mail."

Delany spent all afternoon cleaning her apartment. Everything had to be perfect for his arrival. She was even bold enough to make room for his clothes in her closet. Of course, they wouldn't live in her tiny studio indefinitely, but it would do until they could find a place of their own. Delany didn't forget that Zach had rented an apartment nearby, but she assumed he would enjoy the comforts of Delany's furnished and lived-in apartment rather than the sparse rooms he'd been staying in temporarily. In case he did want to move, however, Delany pulled out her suitcases and dusted them off. It never hurt to be prepared.

Before she realized it, the afternoon was gone. Dusk was setting in and Delany began to fret. Surely he remembered where she lived. What if Doc Manny had changed his mind? What if there had been some sort of setback? What if he decided that he didn't really love her?

Delany shoved that last thought from her mind. It wasn't true. He was coming. Only he didn't come that night, and he didn't come the next day. After three days, all her excuses seemed pitiful. Zach wasn't ready yet. It was the only real answer.

At that point, Delany realized she couldn't put her life on hold any longer. Waiting for Zach was getting her nowhere. She knew she wasn't totally fit to return to class, but she also knew that she no longer had the patience to sit and wait. Delany thought about Zach every moment of the day and it didn't bring him any closer to her. It only made her despondent. Besides, her students were waiting for her. She called Dan to let him know that her substitute would no longer be needed. Delany was back.

The waiting hadn't been any easier on Zach. He was the one who had to lie in a hospital bed with nothing to do other than think about Delany. It nearly drove him mad. Four days were four years of tedium, impatience and aggravation. He had made the right decision when he'd told her to leave, of that he was sure. Because it was the right thing didn't mean that it was the easy thing.

Zach recalled the first time he'd been parted from Delany. She had told him that she needed space because she was becoming too dependent on him. So he'd sat at home and missed her company. He remembered feeling miserable.

The feelings of loneliness, the thought of life without her then, was a single drop of rain compared with the hurricane of emotions he felt now. The solitude, like a vise, gripped his soul and squeezed tight. Zach didn't simply miss Delany. He craved her with every intake of breath. His body would harden at the memory of her kisses. His eyes would cloud at the idea of never seeing her again.

When the release papers came, his first instinct had been to claim her. Immediately. His second more rational thought had been to wait until he was on his feet again, and not in the literal sense. If he was going to offer Delany a life, he was going to have to offer her more than an unemployed ex-DEA operative. While he was in the hospital, he had talked to the real-estate agent he had been in contact with before. She'd told him she'd located the perfect spot for his restaurant.

Zach stared up at the brick warehouse on the corner

of 18th Street and Jefferson. It wasn't much to look at, and the buildings surrounding it were even less so. The agent pointed out to Zach where the university planned to put their campus. If she was right, then he would be right in the center of it. Zach imagined all the young, eager college students flocking in to meet their class-mates and moaning over their academic woes.

"I'll take it," Zach declared while he held out his hand for the lease. His only regret was that Delany wasn't here to share this with him. All he needed to do was make one last phone call and then he would feel free to pursue Delany.

"So you're really going to do it," Mort commented, holding the cordless phone to his ear while he tried once more to scrub the bloodstains from the rug.

"More cold water, Morty," his wife called from the kitchen. Not knowing anything about the technicalities of cleaning, Mort obeyed his wife's instructions.

On the other end of the line, Zach could hear Mort's wife in the background. "Will you stop with the rug already? I told you I would replace it."

"Where are you going to get that kind of money? Don't you realize how much it's going to cost you to get that restaurant up and running? Most businesses fail within the first year, you know. I read that someplace." It hadn't been easy for Mort to accept the idea that he was about to lose one of his best agents, but Zach hadn't given him any choice.

"So I have your blessing?" It was important to Zach to know that Mort was okay with his decision. The man had been a good friend and a good soldier to fight with in the war against drugs. "I don't want to disappoint you. There were people counting on me, I know."

"The world is going to have to find another hero,

Zach. Don't worry, there will always be someone who thinks he can save the world.'' Mort didn't know anyone who had done it as well as Zach, but he kept that to himself.

"I appreciate your support, Mort. Any time you come into my place, drinks are on the house.''

"Speaking of that place,'' Mort asked, "are you looking for any investors? I've got some money stashed away in my sock drawer. I've been looking to spend it somewhere. I'd trust you to make a dog pound profitable if you put your mind to it. It's in the genes, you know.''

Zach laughed at the idea. He didn't know if he'd be able to make a restaurant work or not, but it was something for him to focus his attention on for the time being.

"I'll keep you in mind, Mort. Thanks for everything. And send me the bill for the rug. Oh, yeah and the window, too.'' That said, Zach realized that he had pretty much trashed the place.

"Yeah, right.'' Mort hung up the phone before Zach had a chance to tell him that he was serious about that bill. Only he knew it was pointless. Mort was the type to think that blood added character to the decor.

Everything behind him now, Zach was able to look ahead. As far as he could see, it was going to be a glorious future.

"Hey, Ms. Sheridan,'' Cici called from the stands. She sat in the front row, next to the Browns.

Delany looked up and waved. Walking toward the crowded stands, she motioned for Cici to meet her at the rail. Above the noise of the crowd, she shouted, "How come you're not down here running?''

The teasing quality evident in her teacher's voice, Cici returned, "I may have done a lot of stupid things in my time, but I'm not crazy! Only a fool would run against you."

Delany chuckled in response. "I'm not much of a threat. Doc Manny has restricted me to only two laps. Any more than that and I'll collapse."

Although Delany's participation was only for show, the size of the race hadn't diminished at all. Everyone from the school had come out in support of their favorite teacher. The sponsors all sat in the stand excited about the race, but also dreading it, too. For every lap a student ran, the sponsors donated that much more money. Their motto: At least it all went to a good cause. If they doubted that, the speech Cici Delores gave the night before at the annual scholarship fund-raising dinner convinced them otherwise. The Browns had made a difference in her life. Everyone there last night had seen the results of the mentor program. Delany hadn't been able to keep track of all the checks they'd given her.

As Delany headed back toward the competitors, she adjusted her Walkman. It was Orff's *Carmina Burana* today. That particular selection always gave her an extra charge in the last mile. Delany spotted the crowd of high school students, parents and other eager participants all lined up on the track and prepared to start. Doc Manny was toward the rear of the pack of runners, but Delany could feel the weight of his stare on her back, silently warning her to take it easy.

Just a few laps, Delany had promised him, for show. Finally, the race was about to begin. The gun sounded and Delany began to set the pace. Her legs felt good, as if they were happy to be back in their old routine.

School was another routine she was glad to be returning to. Although teaching did drain her, the students were a welcome distraction. Now, after three weeks, Zach only occupied every other minute of her thoughts instead of every minute. It was a small but necessary relief.

As the soprano sang her melody, Delany tuned out the crowd and focused on the path ahead. She didn't hear the screaming or the chanting. She paid no notice to the other runners around her. When she ran, Delany was able to isolate herself from everyone. It was what she loved most about the sport.

A quick glance down assured her that her running shoes were securely tied. The last thing Delany needed was to trip and have her legs crumble beneath her. The spandex tights she wore hugged her legs and seemed to give her support. On top of the outfit she wore the T-shirt that had been designed for the competition.

The race continued on. Around the corner she turned, keeping her pace steady but slow. Her legs still cooperated with her, although she knew they wouldn't much longer.

Delany glanced up and was surprised to see that she had already run her two laps. She thought about slowing down, but convinced herself that one more lap wouldn't kill her. Yes, she was pushing herself, but her legs continued to work and her feet accepted that. Concentrating on her breathing and the track ahead of her, Delany was able to focus on her pace and block out the pain. Realization dawned that she was in pain. After three laps had passed, she could feel her legs cramp slightly. Her muscles weren't ready for the workout she was giving them. In the stands, she spotted Cici cheering her on. For Cici she could run one more lap.

In the middle of the fourth lap, Delany knew she needed to stop or fall. A cramp seized her back, and she stopped immediately to massage the pain away. She tried to keep walking to get off the track before someone crashed into her. After a few steps, though, she could feel her knees wobble. Damn, she didn't want to fall in front of a stadium full of people. Not while everyone was watching her. The next step she took, she realized that falling was no longer an option; it was inevitable.

Delany felt her balance shift. She reached out with her right arm, prepared to brace herself for impact, when she felt two strong arms reach around her waist. In an instant, the arms shifted beneath her until one arm supported her back and the other lifted her under the knees.

Delany looked into the eyes of the man holding her across his chest like a baby, and she wasn't at all surprised to see dark chocolate brown eyes staring back at her. "You're supposed to let me fall. It's good for my motivation." Delany repeated the words she had said to him so long ago. Her hope was that this time his reply would mean so much more.

Zach didn't miss a beat. "I could never let you fall. Not as long as I was there to catch you."

"And will you always be there to catch me, Zach?" Delany asked as her hands stroked his face and her eyes searched for the truth in his.

"I'll always be there to catch you." It was his vow to her. Then, in front of the sponsors, the faculty, her students and even her boss, Delany kissed Zach with all the love she had inside her. The race ended before the kiss did.

Epilogue

"More, Zach," Delany whispered breathlessly, arching her hips as she urged him to give more of himself. "Please, harder."

"The baby," Zach murmured. He wanted to explode with his desire, but he feared what the consequences would be if he lost control. Delany's thighs were clasped around his waist, and her arms pressed his head down so their lips could join. Zach felt himself touching her womb already. He didn't know how much deeper he could go.

"The baby doesn't need you right now, but I do," Delany breathed into his ear while her teeth played havoc with his lobe.

Zach was helpless against the sensual command. Urgently, his hips began to rock against her as he felt his sex slide deep into her wet heat. Making love with Delany was like having an eruption of fire sear his senses. He knew he would never be deep enough; they could never be close enough for Zach. He was enjoying the attempt.

"My child is going to know me intimately if we keep this up," Zach grunted.

"I've always thought a child should be close to its father," Delany returned, her voice spiking into high notes as she spoke. Then the ecstasy washed over her.

As the colors began to fade and the world ceased to spin, Delany released her breath in a delicious sigh. Yes, Zach had definitely formed the bonds of fatherhood right from the start. Delany would never forget his expression when she had first told him.

His junior league baseball team that he coached had just won the championship. Well, the Tacoma Athletic Youth Association championship anyway. Zach had gotten together with other entrepreneurs in the area to work together to stop the gang problem in Tacoma. All the businesses had been affected by gangs in some way. Either they had been robbed or the fear of gangsters had kept customers at home. All the owners were willing to work in concert toward a solution.

Zach had suggested organizing an inner-city sports program that would provide teens with an alternative to gangs. Football, soccer, baseball. For every season, there was a sport for the kids to participate in. Each business provided the boys and girls with uniforms, equipment and a safe place to practice and play at night. The league now consisted of twelve teams. Out of these twelve, Zach had won the baseball championship. He had purchased a trophy for every kid on his team.

"Hey, Zach, you're going to have to get another trophy," Delany had told him. The team was seated in the center of Zach's restaurant. It was a private party for all the participants in the league and their parents—if they wanted to come. There weren't as many parents there as Zach would've liked, but some had come. It was a start. Never did Zach delude himself into believing that his sports teams were the answer to all of Tacoma's problems. There were times when he felt helpless in the face of all that was wrong around him. And every once in a while he would yearn to return to the agency. But all he had to do was look into the face of one of his players. They made him realize that sometimes you had to sacrifice the needs of the many for the needs of the one. Delany had taught him that.

Zach made a quick count of all the trophies. Each member of his team had one. "Hon, I think you need to count again. Remember, history is your field, not math. All my kids have got a trophy."

Delany then placed a protective hand over her belly. "Not all your kids."

First Zach shouted. Then he danced. Then he cried. He hated to cry. He was a happy man that day.

"Umm," Delany groaned, completely contented.

"I'm too heavy. I'm going to squish the baby. It'll have one of those mashed heads." Zach rolled to his side, but he brought Delany with him.

"Yeah, I know. He'll look just like you," Delany teased.

"You're funny, Mrs. Montgomery, very funny." Zach retaliated with a tickle to her ribs.

"No. I'm happy, Mr. Montgomery, very happy." And she was.

* * * * *

This summer, the legend
continues in Jacobsville

Diana Palmer

A LONG, TALL TEXAN SUMMER

Three **BRAND-NEW** short stories

This summer, Silhouette brings readers a special
collection for Diana Palmer's LONG, TALL TEXANS
fans. Diana has rounded up three **BRAND-NEW**
stories of love Texas-style, all set in Jacobsville,
Texas. Featuring the men you've grown to love from
this wonderful town, this collection is a must-have
for all fans!

*They grow 'em tall in the saddle in Texas—and
they've got love and marriage on their minds!*

Don't miss this collection of original Long, Tall Texans
stories...available in June at your favorite retail outlet.

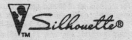

And the Winner Is...
You!

...when you pick up these great titles
from our new promotion at your
favorite retail outlet this June!

Diana Palmer
The Case of the Mesmerizing Boss

Betty Neels
The Convenient Wife

Annette Broadrick
Irresistible

Emma Darcy
A Wedding to Remember

Rachel Lee
Lost Warriors

Marie Ferrarella
Father Goose

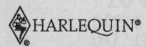 

Look us up on-line at: http://www.romance.net   ATWI397-R

COMING NEXT MONTH